DARK RIVER INN

A TROUBLED SPIRITS NOVEL

J.R. ERICKSON

DEDICATION

For my dad, Jack Jones. Thank you for the gift of words. I'll see you on the other side.

AUTHOR'S NOTE

Dark River Inn is inspired by a true story. To avoid spoilers, that story is briefly retold at the end of this book.

*D*an let off the gas as the road narrowed around a craggy outcropping of rock. His picture of Mel slid off the dash and floated to the passenger floor of his car.

He glanced toward it and then at the clock. Quarter after four pm. The wedding ceremony had started at three. The bride and groom would be in the in-between hours, that golden space of picture-taking, cocktail-drinking, toasting their good fortune and future love.

On Dan and Mel's wedding day, twelve years before, Mel's best friend Bridgette had supplied the wedding party with monogrammed beer glasses. They'd held them as they trekked in their formal clothes up a steep dune that overlooked Lake Michigan. Their pictures showed them red-cheeked with windblown hair, blissfully in love, unaware that the wind had the bridesmaids' dresses blowing up around their heads.

He chuckled at the memory of the photos. Bridgette with her yellow skirt around her head, blue-and-white polka-dot panties on display for the world.

But that had been then, a memory suspended in another life—another Dan, another Mel.

Today, Mel would become one half of Jared and Mel. Jared the accountant with an eye for numbers, Jared with his cycling club and his condo investments and his big group of buddies he met every year for the Michigan Notre Dame game just like they'd done in grad school.

Dan hated Jared, though he never said it out loud. He shrugged and played indifferent on the rare occasion that anyone asked him his opinion of Melanie's fiancé. His opinion no longer meant shit.

It was a strange sensation, watching the woman he'd loved, married and meant to spend forever with move on. Of course, there'd been a hundred moments before the ultimate moment, the final severing of Dan and Mel, as she walked down the aisle with another man, allowed him to slip a ring over her finger, murmured the 'I do's' when the officiant asked for the second time in her life if she promised to stay until death did them part.

Mel had left, but Dan had broken their vows long before the morning she walked out for good.

Mel was only one in a string of failures Dan thought of as he drove the winding road to Drake, Ohio. He tried to make sense of the crash course his life had taken. His best friend Louie had implied there'd been a million clues, that Dan himself had sown the seeds of his destruction. The affair, the obsession with an unsolvable, the eventual crumbling of his profession, the one thing he'd always had, his job as a cop.

Now he was a leaf, adrift, broken off from the tree, sailing on an icy wind—soon to decay and die alone.

Not true, Louie would tell him. *It's 2010, a new decade, and you're barely forty, Dan, you've got plenty of life left in that sack of skin.* But Dan didn't feel forty. He felt eighty, ancient and hard as if a thousand years of bitter wind had turned him to stone.

He'd already put more than three hundred miles between himself and Novi, Michigan, where his life lay in scattered ruins that no one could see but him.

As he turned onto the forest road that led to Bennie's cabin, he rolled the windows down. He could smell the pine trees and the Ohio River. The scent of freedom, their father used to call it when they made the long trek as children to the cabin that had been passed through his own family, father to son, three times. The vice around Dan's chest loosened, and he sucked in a clear breath.

For the first time in weeks, he felt better—not good, only slightly less rotten—and he knew it hadn't been a mistake coming to the cabin, despite the niggling voice in his head telling him otherwise.

He bent forward, stretching his fingers to reach for Mel's picture.

They brushed against it, but he couldn't get hold of the photo. He dropped further just for a second out of the view of the windshield.

When he straightened back up, something hovered in the road.

He bellowed and slammed on the brakes, bracing both hands against the wheel as the tires shrieked against the pavement. The car skidded to a stop, but nothing stood in the road. No *one*. Because that was what he'd thought he'd seen—a figure, a person standing there. But no. The road stretched long and empty, shaded by the tall trees huddling on either side of the grassy embankment.

He'd crumpled Mel's photo as he clutched the wheel. One of her wide brown eyes watched him, but the other had been lost in the fold. He took a deep breath, smoothed the photo out, though white cracks marred the glossy image.

She'd been sitting on a swing, both legs extended, brown hair flying back as she pushed forward. Her smile made his heart ache, and he set the photo on the passenger seat and pushed the gas. Less than a mile to the cabin.

Worse, he hadn't a clue about what came after he unpacked his duffel bag in the isolated little cabin. How many old movies could he watch? How many crosswords could he screw up? How many breakfasts could he eat alone? How many leaves could he rake? He'd brought three books—two Dan Brown paperbacks and some self-help garbage about cops and coping skills Mel had bought him before she left.

He turned down the weed-choked driveway that led to the cabin and parked. Popping the trunk, he stepped out and stretched his arms before twisting from side to side. His low back released an audible pop.

Dan's cell phone rang as he lifted his bag from the trunk. Bennie's name appeared on the screen.

"What's happening?" Dan asked, wedging the phone between his shoulder and ear as he shut the trunk.

"What's happenin' with you? Make it to the cabin?"

"Just now. Looking as ratty as ever."

"She doesn't put on airs, that's for sure."

Dan walked to the cabin and dropped the bag inside the door, inhaling the musty but familiar scent. "No, she does not."

"I meant to tell you the last time I went the chimney wasn't venting that well. Probably needs a quick scrape with the chimney sweep."

"Oh, great. I better not find a fat decayed raccoon in there, Bennie."

Bennie laughed. "I shoot those raccoons on sight. They know better than to get too close."

Dan grimaced at the flash of a memory. Bennie with his shotgun trained on the raccoon who'd climbed up on their metal trashcan at the cabin. He'd shot it at close range and exploded the animal's head all over a birch tree. Blood and gore had clung to the white bark for days until their dad demanded Bennie fill a bucket of water and wash it off. Shooting animals had never been Dan's thing. He'd hunted for deer with his dad and Bennie every couple of years, but he'd never been excited about it. Bennie loved it, loved the hunting, the shooting, the cleaning. He'd strip the animal's hide and tan it in the sun. He'd mount the head or the horns on the wall. The cabin had no fewer than six deer heads, black glassy eyes silently appraising whoever stepped inside.

"There's some venison in the freezer and a couple of trout."

"I stopped at a burger place on the way. It'll be leftovers for me for the next day or so."

"I figured as much. Shoot over to Xander's Kitchen in Black Pine. Best bacon jalapeño burger I've ever had. The waitresses are cute too."

Dan forced a laugh. "Cute waitresses are just a distraction from the food."

"Ha, you need some distractions, Dan—can't be saving the world all the time. Either way, hit up Xander's. And take care of yourself down there. Don't go crackers on me."

Dan stiffened at the comment, almost gave a defensive response, but bit it back. Nothing gave away someone's true feelings like an over-reaction. Of course he wasn't going crackers. He was fine.

"Xander's," Dan repeated. "I'll check it out. And I'm good, Bennie, right as rain, just need some fresh air and a change of scenery. Give Moose a rub for me."

"Will do. He fell in a hole last week on our walk and has been milking it for days, limping around and casting me those 'verge of death' eyes until I give him a sausage. Damn dog is going to eat me out of house and home."

Dan chuckled. "Still cheaper than a wife."

"Roger that, Dan the Man. I'll talk to you later."

Dan stuck his phone in his pocket, then took it back out and turned the ringer off. He didn't want to talk to anyone else. Not that there'd be many people calling, but maybe one of the guys from the station, a break in an old case.

Mia's face floated into his mind. Brace-covered smile and the slightly defiant way she lifted her chin. He'd never known her in life and yet in his mind's eye she was as real to him as the wild grass that brushed his shins as he returned to the cabin.

Except she wasn't real, not anymore. She was dead.

2

*D*an surveyed the simple cabin with its knotty pine walls and sagging jumble of couches and chairs. He hadn't visited Bennie's cabin in years. The last time had been with Mel and their friends—three couples, fishing, a little hunting, a few bonfires. It had been a good time, a long weekend with Mel draped over him in her tight jeans and a range of fuzzy sweaters that tickled his neck when she hugged him.

He hadn't expected the memory of that weekend to still be so poignant, and yet it was the first thing that flooded back upon walking through the door.

Bennie had been married then too, to Jeraldine, Jerry for short, but that marriage went up in smoke when Bennie started spending more time at the bar than at home. Mel's sister and her boyfriend had joined them as well. Dan had never cared for Patsy. She had shrewd, unkind eyes and found it perfectly acceptable to value everything from the worth of his pickup truck to the watch his father had left him before he died.

Dan opened and closed cupboards, getting his bearings for the place. He found an old can of coffee, stale, but good enough for the morning. He paused at the refrigerator, decorated with the bird magnets Mel had bought for Bennie one Christmas. A small plastic cardinal, bluebird, robin and goldfinch completed the set.

The cabin didn't have a washer and dryer or dishwasher, but it had a working television, the old-school kind with a built-in DVD player. Streaming, or Internet for that matter, was out of the question in that neck of the woods. Even his cell phone would only function half the time.

A bookshelf of DVDs occupied one wall; another bookshelf of paperback books stood opposite. If all those failed to keep him busy, a shed of fishing poles would do the trick. There was even a telescope mounted on a tripod in front of the large window that faced the river.

Bennie had bought the telescope years earlier for bird-watching, a hobby that Dan hassled him for at every opportunity. On a wooden stool, beside the telescope, sat a worn copy of *The Audubon Society Guide to Birding*. Bennie had dog-eared any pages he'd spotted a matching bird from.

Dan sat on the stool and put his eye to the telescope. The blurred forest across the river met his gaze and he fiddled with the knobs until the lens cleared and he could see the startling detail of the trees. A wedge of beach ran along the bank of the river, backed by a weedy dune. The water rushed by, leaving a white foamy residue on the sand.

As he angled the telescope to the right, a splotch of color caught his eye and he shifted it back slightly. A young woman reclined on a green and white folding chair, a purple beach towel beneath her feet. She wore a peach-colored high-waist bikini. Long dark curls fell over her tanned shoulders, and she'd tilted her face up to catch the sun, which oddly wasn't there. It was an unusual day for sunbathing, not quite sixty-five degrees, and a muted gray sky obscured the sun above her.

She appeared to be in her early twenties. Her mouth was heart-shaped beneath her small perky nose. As he stared, she inclined her head forward and her deep-set blue eyes seemed to lock on his.

Dan jerked his head back from the telescope, heat rushing into his face. He felt caught, but then his better sense reminded him the Ohio River stretched a quarter mile across to the opposite bank. She couldn't possibly see him sitting in the cabin.

He stared at the long black tube, and after a moment's hesitation, leaned back into the eyepiece.

She no longer looked in his direction, but had tilted her face upwards, revealing her slender neck. Behind her, Dan spotted movement in the trees. He angled the telescope and glimpsed something large—no, some*one* large—ambling through the forest behind her. A bearded man wearing a mosquito-net hat crept through the dense woods.

The man rushed from the forest and onto the beach. As Dan watched, the stranger reached down, grabbed a handful of the woman's hair, and yanked her from the chair. Her face twisted in pain and her mouth opened. Dan released his own shout of surprise as the woman's silent scream appeared through the lens. The man dragged her backward, her bare feet kicking up sand as he pulled her into the woods.

Dan pressed his face so hard against the eyepiece the plastic dug into the soft concave around his eye. He tried to follow their passage, but within seconds the trees had swallowed them.

3

*D*an lurched away from the telescope and fumbled his cell phone from his pocket.

He dialed 911, then realized the woman on the opposite bank had not only been abducted in a different county, she'd been abducted in Black Pine, West Virginia, rather than Drake, Ohio. Worse, not a single bar appeared on the tiny grid of cell phone service.

"Shit," he muttered, running to his car and jumping behind the wheel. No keys.

"Goddamn it," he shouted.

Dan wrenched the door back open and ran into the cabin, flung his bags aside and finally spotted the keys on the kitchen table. He snatched them up and sprinted back to the car. As he sped down the dirt drive, his mind shifted into investigator mode.

"Peach bikini, tan, dark curly hair, blue eyes, full mouth, wearing earrings. They were, um..." He twirled a finger by his ear and tried to remember what Mel called those things with the hoops and webbing in the middle. "Dreamcatchers," he said triumphantly, slapping a hand against the wheel. "Dreamcatcher earrings. And, um... a beach chair, metal, folding, green and white striped fabric. Beach towel."

He spoke aloud everything he could remember about the woman and then he shifted to the man who'd abducted her. "Bearded, six feet at least, mosquito-net hat, maybe sunglasses." The bearded man hadn't been his focus, and the adduction happened so quickly, Dan hadn't gotten a solid look at him. He'd be able to offer investigators little in the way of details about the perp.

He waited until he'd crossed the bridge into Black Pine, West Virginia, to dial 911.

He rattled off what he'd seen, aware that his call was being recorded, that every word he spoke would be scrutinized later. That precise detail mattered most in this moment.

"I'm going to drive the road along the river," he told the operator, but he discovered there was no road along the river. As it was on the Ohio side, dense forests bordered the river and not a single road ran the length of the hidden shoreline. Instead, a crisscross of rural roads zigzagged along the forest.

Dan had no idea where to search, where the woman had gone into the woods. He'd expected a park or a sign with a beach access, but saw none of those things.

A police car turned onto the road, and Dan pulled over and jumped out, waved his arms.

The cruiser came to a stop and two deputies climbed out.

"I called it in," Dan said, striding to the men. "She had to have been taken right around here, but—"

"Here's the sheriff," one of them said. A second cruiser pulled up behind the first and a burly man, bald, likely in his early sixties, stepped from the driver's seat.

"I just saw a young woman get abducted from the beach on the other side of these trees," Dan announced, stepping into the sheriff's path.

"Okay, slow down, partner. Start with your name," the sheriff said.

Dan gaped at him. "My name is Dan Webb. I can fill you in on the rest later, but this woman was literally kidnapped"—Dan lifted his wrist and looked at his watch—"nineteen minutes ago. If there's any chance of getting this guy while she's still alive, we don't have time for introductions. Is there a park along here? A trail people follow into the woods?"

"Paradise Park is about two miles down yonder," one deputy said, gesturing at the road beyond them.

Dan shook his head. "No, it has to be around here. My brother's cabin is across the river, almost directly across from where she was taken. I watched it with my own eyes. We've got to search here."

The sheriff pursed his lips, but followed Dan into the dense brush.

"There's no trail here, nothing," Dan murmured, surprised. He found it hard to believe a young woman would have carried a beach chair and towel through such a wild part of the forest to sunbathe on a stretch of isolated beach. He'd assumed she'd followed a trail, a path formed by young people, fishermen or conservationists.

"Used to be," the deputy said behind him. "Back in my school days there was a trampled path further on." He pointed a few yards to the south. "We'd all come down here for a beach bonfire, some guys rode dirt bikes. There was a farmer back by the road who let the kids use his field to park, but when he passed, his kid took over the house and ran everybody out of there. Course, that was during my high school days, twenty years ago."

"She must have known about the trail," Dan said, though twenty years ago, the girl might not even have been born. That didn't mean she didn't have an older brother or sister or even a parent who'd showed her the secret trail.

"Does seem mighty odd for a young woman to choose this place to sunbathe, especially considering Paradise Park is just down the road. That's where most of the youngsters go. Not to mention"—the sheriff glanced at the sky—"this isn't exactly a fine day for tanning."

"And where's her car?" the second deputy asked.

"Maybe she got dropped off," Dan suggested, "or... I don't know, okay? But I know what I saw. Let's get closer to the original trail. Yeah? I'd rather not walk right on it. There might be evidence, but I'm sure that's the way she would have walked down and likely the man who grabbed her would have."

The two men looked at him skeptically, but the deputy who'd described the trail nodded and walked south. He stopped a few times, propped his hands on his hips and squinted at the ground.

"Seems about here, or..." He walked a few more paces. "Maybe here."

"No, no. I remember now," the second deputy cut in. "There were all them shoes marking the entrance to the trail. Remember, we called it the skeleton tree? It started as a dare and then next thing you know all the kids were doing it."

The first deputy nodded. "Oh, yeah." He slapped his forehead. "The skeleton tree. Should we backtrack and start again?" He directed his look at the sheriff, who looked irritated but waved the deputy to go ahead.

Dan followed the men back out of the woods. They walked through a weedy field until the second deputy pointed. "There it is."

Dan looked up to see a gnarled tree, bare of leaves, strung with at least two dozen shoes. They were mostly tennis shoes, but he spotted two flip-flops and a single high heel that might once have been red but was now a pale pink.

"My daddy would have tanned my hide if I'd have ever wasted a perfectly good pair of shoes like that," the sheriff announced, shaking his head distastefully at the tree. "And if Gary or Bo had ever come home wearing only one shoe, you can bet your ass they'd be getting right back in their truck and going out to find the one they'd lost. Kids today."

The two deputies exchanged a smirk, but Dan felt a chill as he looked at the tree, bleached white from the sun, teenagers' shoes hanging from its bony branches.

"We should walk beside the trail, not right on it. We don't want to disturb the evidence," Dan reminded the men.

The sheriff looked annoyed at the comment, but said nothing.

One deputy stepped into the woods, paused, and again squinted at the forest floor. "Seems it musta been right in here, but not so much as a squished piece of grass."

The second deputy stood shoulder to shoulder with him. They both surveyed the woods. Dan too searched for any evidence of the trail, a bent weed, some tamped-down grass, but the area looked as over-grown as the one they'd been walking in minutes before. "Are you sure this is the spot?"

"Without a doubt," the first deputy said. "We always walked in right at the shoe tree."

The second deputy looked equally confused, but he nodded. "Definitely."

"Well, come on, get on with it," the sheriff said, waving them ahead.

They walked through the trees. Again, Dan scanned for any evidence—a scrap of fabric, a depression of weeds. Nothing.

When they came out on the dune that sloped down to the beach, he knew they were in the right spot. Across the river stood Bennie's cabin.

"That your place there?" the sheriff asked.

"My brother's. Yeah," Dan told him.

As they started down the slope, Dan searched the sand for the foot-prints that had to be there. There were none. More startling was the stretch of smooth sand that ran along the river. There was no purple towel, no green-and-white striped beach chair, no sign that a person had been there at all, let alone been abducted from the place.

4

*D*an felt the men's eyes on him.

"She was right there." Dan gestured limply at the beach.

"You said she left behind some stuff?" the sheriff asked. "A lounge chair?"

"She... yeah, I mean, I guess the guy came back and got it. It's been nearly a half hour. Maybe..."

"You think he abducted this girl, carried her all the way out of these woods, and then trekked back down here to get her beach chair?"

Again, the two deputies exchanged a smirk, and Dan felt warmth rising into his face.

"I don't know. Maybe he knocked her unconscious and then he threw it all in the river."

The sheriff frowned. He fanned a hand at the beach. "I'd expect to see a disturbance there in the sand."

"Yeah," Dan murmured. He walked further down the beach. No footprints, no sharp divots where a chair would have sat. He back-tracked and went the other way. Nothing but smooth sand met his gaze. "I don't understand," he muttered.

The sheriff didn't scan the beach. Instead, he watched Dan, thumbs hooked through his belt loops. The first deputy at least feigned searching the beach. The second deputy snuck glances at the sheriff and then Dan.

"Somehow he covered his tracks," Dan said at last.

The sheriff lifted both eyebrows. "Now you're telling me this guy crept down here and abducted a woman, who oddly enough was sunbathing on a cool cloudy day, subdued her, threw her chair and towel in the river, and then somehow magically wiped away all evidence?"

"I can't find any other explanation. I saw it."

"Been drinking at all today?"

Dan's mouth fell open. "No, of course not."

"Doing anything else? Not two months ago we busted a meth lab barely five miles from here."

Dan tilted his head back and swallowed the rush of furious words he wanted to launch at the man before him. He glared at the sheriff. "No. I'm not a meth user. In fact, I'm a detective on leave from Novi, Michigan."

The sheriff gazed at him steadily, unmoved by Dan's admission. "On leave, you say? For what reason?"

"I don't think that's any of your business."

The two deputies no longer pretended to search the beach. They both watched Dan and the sheriff.

"Generally, it's not. But this little debacle has made it my business, hasn't it?"

"I don't see how it's relevant."

"Neither do I. Not yet anyway. Tim, Perry, come on. We've got real police business to attend to."

The two deputies followed the sheriff up the dune and into the woods.

Dan balled his fists at his side as they walked away. What did they think they were doing? Critical minutes were passing them by. The man could have crossed the bridge into Ohio, taken her out of state. He was getting away. In all likelihood she'd be dead within an hour.

But even as the thoughts swirled through Dan's head, his eyes returned to that flat stretch of sand. No one could have kidnapped a woman, carried her out of the woods, returned to dispose of her things, and made the sand appear as if no one had stepped on it in days. It was impossible.

Dan sat on the bank and propped his elbows on his knees, resting his chin in his hands and gnawing the insides of his cheeks.

For the first time in his life, Dan felt a tremor of what it was like on the other side—the knowledge that something terrible had happened but with no help from law enforcement, no help from anyone. He looked across the river to Bennie's cabin. It was a miniature box tucked into the woods.

As he scanned the opposite shore, his gaze came to rest on another structure, this one slightly upstream from where he sat. It was a hulking beast of a house with gray wood and a square cupola propped on top. He studied it, surprised. He hadn't realized such a house stood so close to Bennie's cabin, a few yards away at most. But they'd always driven in from the east, then took the winding dirt drive back to the cabin. He'd never gone the other way to see what lay further on. Dan had never even crossed the bridge into Black Pine until this very trip.

The house looked dark and quiet, the surrounding woods overgrown. He doubted anyone occupied it, but he wondered. If someone were there, might they have witnessed something? Perhaps through a pair of binoculars. It was a long shot, a Hail Mary kind of thing, but as he rested his hands on the dune he felt as if the whole incident was disappearing like sand through his fingers. There wasn't a shred of evidence the woman had been there, not a footprint, nothing. What he needed was another witness, someone who could corroborate his story.

He walked slowly back through the woods, eyeing the weeds, the branches of every tree, searching for the proof that had vanished as completely as the girl.

He drove to the edge of town and crossed the bridge that returned him to the Ohio side of the river. He turned onto Burns Road and passed the long dirt drive that led to Bennie's cabin.

Dan found the entrance to the house he'd seen across the river blocked by a metal gate. A chain and rusted padlock secured the opening against trespassers.

Dan parked on the road edge. To the right of the entrance, mostly buried by foliage, stood a wooden sign that read 'Dark River Inn' in peeling blue letters.

Dan stepped around the gate and started up the overgrown driveway toward the house. Gravel crunched beneath his boots. He passed a little wooden structure with a sliding glass window, likely for checking in guests. The window looked grimy and, like the sign, the paint on this building had flaked off. Fuzzy green moss coated the roof.

In the surrounding woods, birds chattered, mostly crows with their high shrill shrieks letting the others know of his arrival.

As he approached the back of the house, he noted the faded and chipped gray paint and the grimy windows. A gravel space that had once served as a parking lot for ten to fifteen cars was poked through with weeds and a few saplings. Grand red double doors, paint faded, served as the entrance to the inn. Above the door a lopsided sign hung from a single rusted chain: 'Welcome to the Dark River Inn.'

He circled the house to the river side, where a wide back porch was arranged with battered lounge chairs, their legs bent, their fabric worn and scattered with dead leaves.

The house was neglected but not in ruins. The wood held sturdy beneath his feet as he ascended the porch stairs. The broad glass windows that faced the river were unbroken save several on the upper floors of the house. He leaned into the smudged glass, likely dirtied by years of river water carried on the wind.

He cupped his hands on either side of his face and squinted into the gloomy interior. The room before him had been a dining area. Tables sheathed in white linen stood at angles throughout the room. Tall wood chairs surrounded them. He could not see further into the room, but a long table along a side wall made him think of a buffet set-up, perhaps for Sunday brunches.

He walked back around the exterior to the main double doors that opened into the entrance. He pounded on the doors, though no car sat in the driveway and he felt sure no one had been in the house in a very long time. So much for his additional witness.

The place was locked and appeared undisturbed by vandals. Then again, what vandals would trek so far into the forest to break into an old inn?

He paused in the driveway a final time, considering the large house. In the cupola a flicker of movement caught his eye through the window that faced him. He squinted, studying the dark window, but nothing shifted.

As Dan returned to his car, something blue stuck up from a tangle of weeds on the side of the road. He stepped closer and grabbed the edge of a sign, prising it up from the undergrowth. 'Beaumont Realty,' it read with a number below. He opened his phone and punched the number into his note screen, saving it.

5

*D*an filled a plastic cup with Scotch and sat at the pocked kitchen table in Bennie's cabin that wobbled if he bumped it. The amber liquid sparkled in the lamplight. Dan sipped it and grimaced. He'd never cared for Scotch or any hard liquor really, though for a while there, five months or so, he'd been downing two glasses of vodka every night after work.

He searched for an explanation that did not exist. Had he lost his mind? Imagined the whole thing? Could the girl have been a hallucination? Perhaps the long drive combined with thoughts of Mel marrying another man had pushed him over the edge.

"No fucking way," he muttered. But the words did little to soothe his racing mind and the manic sense of losing control hovered so close he could feel it trying to burst in and grab hold of him once more.

What if they'd all been right—Mel, Chief Evans, his former partner Arnold?

Maybe Dan had gotten in too deep on Mia's case, lost touch with reality, shaken some integral brain function loose after all those sleepless nights. His friend Louie said he'd burned out, singed the wiring in there, needed to get professional help. Dan had told him where he could shove his unwanted advice and that had been the last time they'd spoken, over two months earlier. Now he wished he could give Louie a call, tell him about the girl with dark curly hair and the bearded man in the woods. He wished he had a friend who might believe him, and Louie was about the only guy who would. Then again, maybe not.

Louie had believed Dan's theories about Mia. But then he too had pulled away, unwilling to jump into that dark hole and root around for the perp everyone believed didn't exist, everyone except Dan.

Mia's case had been the beginning of the end. Dan saw that now, though only barely. He still felt a deep current of bitterness at the thought of his own precinct and the men who he'd once shared drinks with, once considered like brothers. They'd become strangers, in much the same way his wife had, in the months after he'd gone too far in the case. By then he'd been sleeping with Mia's mother and talking about the case incessantly. For a while there, he'd stopped sleeping, snatching an hour or two a night, but mostly he paced around the townhouse or up and down the street.

Dan felt a similar urge now. He wanted to drive back to the opposite shore and comb the beach again, but night had fallen and he hadn't completely killed the part of himself that knew better. He couldn't go there this time. Literally. There was nowhere to go. No trail to follow.

He'd called the sheriff's office in Black Pine an hour earlier to inquire about missing persons. Had anyone reported a daughter missing? A sister?

No. No missing person. Nothing. And he thought he'd heard a tinge of incredulity in the dispatcher's voice. Maybe it was in his head, but more than likely word had already gotten around at the station in Black Pine. Some nutter claiming to be a detective called in a phony abduction. Be on the lookout for more crank calls.

"Fuck," he muttered, standing and walking the Scotch to the sink. He dumped it in.

Dan hadn't repaired much in the previous months, but kicking the liquor had been one of his few victories. He'd also hired a woman to clean the townhouse. He'd wondered absently if she'd noted the empty vodka bottles piled in the garage or the grime so thick in the toilet, it no longer looked white at all. After Mel had left, Dan had spiraled. He'd gone deeper into the case, gotten more lost with Mia's mother. Sometimes he'd crash at her place for weeks or just pass out in his car in a park after he'd spent hours retracing Mia's final path from the day she'd vanished.

It had taken another five months after Mel had left for Dan to lift his head from the fog and even then, he'd been forced to. Chief Evans had taken him off the case. Dan had made a half-assed attempt at pulling himself together. He'd ended the affair with Erin Knox. But Mia stayed with him. He still couldn't sleep. He'd lost weight, developed an ulcer, and started sprouting grays in his once thick, dark hair.

Dan paused at the window in the cabin and studied his reflection. He was no longer a young man. He'd officially moved into his fortieth year, and time had drawn ruts and grooves in his formerly smooth skin. His eyes were still bright and blue, but they'd taken on a feverish quality in the previous year and sometimes when people looked at him, he saw fear in their eyes as if they'd just stumbled upon a wild animal who might be vicious. He broke the gaze and walked to a shelf stuffed with books, DVDs and a collection of crap that Bennie accumulated from feathers to loose change.

Dan grabbed a DVD of *Fatal Attraction* from the shelf and popped it in the player before flipping off the lights. He stretched out on the couch and watched as Glenn Close transformed from sexy mystery woman to bunny-boiling stalker. He'd seen the movie before and despite his whirring mind, his eyes grew heavy and he drifted into sleep.

DAN WOKE TO MUSIC. The tendrils of his dream slipped away, but the sound lingered. Notes from a piano played in the dark cottage. He lay, eyes wide, as the haunting melody continued.

Dan turned his head, expecting to see the DVD playing, the song emitting from the box, but the DVD had ended and returned to the home screen. No sound emerged from the television.

He stood, breath rapid from his abrupt awakening, and listened as the piano song faded and stopped.

It took him a moment to propel his stiff legs forward. He walked into one of the cabin's small bedrooms. This was Bennie's room and though it would later seem like an illogical conclusion, Dan assumed the piano had come from an alarm clock, a sleep machine, a gadget of some sort. But there were no gadgets in Bennie's room. Next to the brass bed, the side table revealed only a paperback book, spine broken, and a lamp made from deer antlers.

No dresser occupied the room, no shelf. Dan peeked under the bed but found only a pile of musty quilts. In the opposite bedroom, he found even less—a bed and an empty side table. Moving through the cabin, only half awake, he found no evidence of any item that could have played the song.

As he came up empty, his mind kicked on and he felt uneasy. Not afraid per se. The girl had come back into his head, the girl who'd been abducted. The vision of her mouth stretching into a scream of terror streaked through his mind and he shuddered as the image that replaced her was a long stretch of undisturbed beach.

He couldn't resist the words that accompanied the image—'crazy,' 'losing it,' 'insane.' Which he could justify away, sure. But didn't all people who were going insane believe it wasn't true? Wasn't that one of the hallmarks of insanity? The belief that they were perfectly fine and the world around them had gone mad?

6

*T*he following morning, Dan downed a cup of stale coffee and left the cabin for Black Pine. He'd decided to put the previous day's events behind him. Each time they swam to the forefront of his mind, he drove them back by thinking instead about all the things he'd told himself he'd do at Bennie's cabin in order to get his head on right: fish, hike, read books, target-practice, start jogging again.

Dan pushed open the door to All Your Needs Hardware. A tall slender woman, sixty-ish, with limp blonde hair and black spectacles smiled at him. "Welcome to All Your Needs Hardware. I'm Sadie. Can I help ya find something?"

Dan smiled. "Bait?"

"Oh, sure. I hear the catfish are bitin' right now. Head to the counter straight on back and Herbie can fix you up."

Dan passed the usual hardware stuff—tools, paint, an aisle of bird feeders and seed. He saw one shelf dedicated to 'As Seen on TV' items like Miracle Socks and instant pop-up tents.

At the back of the store, a portly man with a crown of fluffy white hair sat on a bar stool examining a tiny hook with feathers attached. "Help ya?" he asked, not looking up at Dan.

"Yeah. I wanted to get some nightcrawlers."

The man continued to study the hook for another moment and sighed, set it on the table, and took off the blue plastic-framed glasses that had slid to the end of his nose. "These readers are making me cross-eyed. I swear it. Sadie insists I wear 'em but damn if the whole world isn't blurry when I take 'em off. Twenty-twenty for sixty-five years and then boom, sixty-six rolls around and I can't read a page to save my life." He stood from the stool, made a face, and rubbed at his lower back. "Nightcrawlers, you say? Trying to get some catfish?"

Dan chuckled. "In all likelihood the catfish are safe from me. I'm just looking for a way to pass the hours. Fishing seemed as good as anything else."

The man eyed him and opened the door on a mini-refrigerator tucked into a back corner on the counter. He pulled out a small white Styrofoam container. "Crawlers in here, but if you're lookin' to pass some time, why not try fly fishin'?"

"Fly fishing?"

"Sure, we've got all the gear you need. My buddy Vince turned me onto it about ten years ago and, let me tell you, I've never looked back. There's something special about standing in the water watching that line swivel out in the sky. It beats sittin' in a tin boat hunched over like a hunchback—makes ya as crooked as a dog's hind leg. I'm tellin' ya first-hand." He slapped his own lower back. "Did it for fifty years before I wised up."

"I wouldn't even know where to begin."

"At the beginning of course." He laughed and slapped a hand on the counter, winced and lifted his palm. The feathery hook stuck from the flesh just below his thumb. He grimaced and plucked it out. "Hazard of the job, I'm afraid." He shrugged. "But don't tell Sadie. Docs got me on the Lasix, blood-thinner. If I so much as get a papercut she runs for the first-aid kit like her ass is on fire."

Dan followed Herb through the store, allowing the older man to fill his arms with waders, a fly-fishing rod and reel, and a spool of line.

"Hold on, I've got some brand-new flies in the back." Herb headed back down the aisle.

Dan paused at a corkboard overflowing with flyers, business cards, ads for puppies, tractors, and roommate requests. On the top right corner of the board, he saw the block letters 'MISS,' but a tower of other ads covered the rest of the poster. He shifted the fly-fishing stuff into his left arm and with his right hand pried off the tacks to reveal a poster with the big black words 'MISSING' printed across the top. As his eyes fell on the girl beneath the word, he stiffened.

The girl he'd seen abducted from the beach stared out from the flyer.

He read the details beneath the image.

NAME: Ivy Grace Trent
Last seen: August 19, 2000

HIS EYES MOVED past the date and then swung back again. He blinked at the year: 2000. The woman in the poster had vanished a decade before.

7

"*H*ere you go."

Herb's voice startled him, and Dan gasped, dropping the handful of fishing gear. It landed with a clatter on the floor.

Herb guffawed and slapped both hands on his thighs. "Holy crap on a cracker. Scared you so bad I scared my own self. Here." He crouched down and started picking up the items.

"Here, let me," Dan said, not sure if Herb's back could handle the deep squat he'd crouched into. Dan offered a hand to help him stand back up and then bent down, scooping the waders and pole into his arms. He nodded toward the missing poster. "Did they ever find that girl?"

Herb looked at the board, squinted and leaned closer. "This is what I'm talkin' about. Those damn readers are makin' me go blind."

"Ivy Trent," Dan offered.

Herb's eyes went wide, and he rocked back on his heels. "A crying shame, that right there," he said, shaking his head. "Never found her, not a hair. Course most everyone thinks she took off. Everyone except her mama, that is, and these days that woman's a few cards short of a deck."

"Herb Dwiggins! That is a terrible thing to say." Sadie stood at the end of the aisle, hands planted on her hips.

Herb paled and offered her a conciliatory smile. "Sadie, my love, if I'd have known you were listening, I wouldn't have said it."

She glared at him. "That is hardly the point. Annabelle Trent is a lovely, God-fearing woman who has lived through the worst kind of misfortune. First Johnny dies and then Ivy vanishes. It's downright cruel for you to speak of her that way, not to mention it is not very Christian-like."

Herb's face fell.

She stomped over and held out her arms. "I can take those things up to the counter for you," she told Dan, pointedly ignoring Herb.

"I'm sorry, sugar pie," Herb told her, trying to lean in and kiss her cheek. She turned and stomped away before he could get close enough.

"That woman has a radar for any time I'm speaking ill of her friends," Herb whispered from the corner of his mouth. "Or her mother. Mind you, if she were talking about my mother, God rest her soul, she'd be spewing venom like a cobra and ain't no mention of 'Christian-like.'" He rolled his eyes. "Women."

Dan followed Herb toward the front of the store. "They never found her? Ivy Trent?"

"Nope, never did. Sadie can tell you more than me. Her and Annabelle were school chums. They stayed friends for a long time after, but when Johnny died, Annabelle went off the rails a bit." He dropped his voice to just above a whisper. "And then when Ivy disappeared..." He shrugged, lifted a hand to his ear and twirled his finger in the universal signal for 'crazy.'

Dan grabbed a bottle of root beer and added it to the counter where Sadie had already rung up the rest of his gear. "Ma'am, do you mind if I ask you a few questions about the young lady who disappeared?"

Sadie fixed him with her overly made-up eyes, lifting one penciled-on eyebrow. "I don't mind at all, so long as you tell me why you're asking."

Dan thought of the badge he'd left on Chief Evans's desk. It opened doors and put people at ease, but claiming he was a detective in that moment was not true. And yet it was—in his bones, it was. "I'm a detective in Novi, Michigan, on leave currently, but... the job follows you."

"A detective? Oh, goodness." Sadie put her hand to her chest, eyes widening. His revelation had the desired effect. "We sure could use fresh eyes on Ivy's case, Detective—?"

"Webb. But call me Dan."

"Well, Dan, I don't make it a point of criticizing law enforcement, but when it comes to Ivy Trent, our boys really fudged it. Six months passed before they even started looking for her. By then whoever took her had probably skipped town, changed his look. You know, all the things these criminals have learned from watching shows like *Cops* and whatnot."

"Six months?"

She nodded, lips pursed as she neatly tucked his purchases into a large plastic bag. "Annabelle went plumb out of her mind trying to get them to take Ivy's disappearance seriously. She begged the sheriff, Dan. I saw it with my own eyes, down on her knees at the township barbecue clinging to Sheriff Dowker's leg like a little girl who'd lost her doll. That memory haunts my dreams—haunts them. Herb and I helped raise a reward, we paid for flyers. I organized a ladies' group, and we did all sorts of things to bring awareness to Ivy, but we didn't have any clout. Our local news station ran a couple of stories, and that's when the police finally organized a search party for Paradise Park."

"That's the last place she was seen?"

Sadie shook her head, tucking a fluorescent green coupon for ten percent off his next purchase into his bag. "Not seen, no. That's where her mama suspected she got off to that day. Annabelle wasn't home. After Johnny died, she took on a second job working at the Quick Mart. All the kids hung around Paradise to swim, ride their ATVs on the dunes, bonfires on the beach. The usual in these parts. The park covers about a hundred acres, part of it right on the river with a nice sandy beach. Ivy went there regular on the weekends. Later when she didn't come home, Annabelle figured out what was missing—a metal folding chair from the garage and Ivy's bathing suit—so she headed down to Paradise Park, but she never tracked down a single friend who saw Ivy that day."

The comment about the missing beach chair and swimsuit caused Dan's pulse to quicken. Any doubts that the woman from the missing poster was the same he'd seen abducted rapidly faded except for that one minor issue—she'd disappeared ten years earlier. "Is Annabelle still in the area?"

"Oh, yes, little trailer out on Tuttle Road. Ivy's room looks the same as it did the day she disappeared ten years ago. My ladies' group went over once after Annabelle had decided it was time to donate some of her things, begin moving on. Poor dear just broke down on the front lawn when we pulled up in the van. I sent the ladies home and whiled away the day with Annabelle reminiscing about Ivy. In the end, she made the choice not to touch a thing, to close the door and leave it just as it was."

Dan frowned, imagining another mother of a missing child. Erin Knox had done the opposite of Annabelle Trent. She'd gutted Mia's room in the weeks after the child had vanished. She'd put everything Mia had owned into black trash bags and set them up at the curb for the garbage man. Too hard to look at it all each day, Erin had told him. "You're a good friend," he told Sadie.

She smiled sadly and pushed the plastic bags across the counter. "Detective, you go home and consider Ivy. Here." She bent down and pulled a flyer from beneath the counter. It was the same one that hung in the back of the store. "I want you to look at her picture and think real hard about Ivy Trent. She needs you, Detective Webb. I don't believe in happenstance. Something brought you into this store today and drew you to that poster buried on that corkboard." She folded the paper in half and added it to his bag. "Annabelle's number is right there on the flyer."

"Do you think she'd be open to speaking with me?"

Sadie bobbed her head up and down. "Oh, yes, definitely." She grabbed a sheet of note paper and wrote an address. "892 Tuttle Road. Follow Main out here about two miles, you'll come to Tuttle. Take a right another two and a half miles down and you'll see her trailer."

Dan thanked her and walked to his car, slid into the driver's seat and planted both hands on the wheel. He stared at the store, his mind running.

Ivy Trent had been the woman on the riverbank. If he hadn't seen the date on the missing poster, he'd have staked his life on it.

---

8

*D*an intended to drive back to Bennie's cabin. Between the store and his car, he'd talked himself out of visiting Annabelle Trent. If he had any chance of getting his head right, he couldn't be chasing after phantom missing girls.

He gave himself this lecture as he headed out of downtown Black Pine, but instead of turning north toward the bridge that would take him back to Drake, Ohio, he turned east on Tuttle Road.

Annabelle Trent lived in a double-wide trailer on the outskirts of town. Her mailbox was reinforced with a steel pipe wrapped in thick silver tape. A brown minivan, the back bumper rusted through, sat near a sagging porch. Two crab apple trees punctuated the yard, their fruit dangling inedible from scrawny branches.

Dan parked behind the van and studied the trailer. Dark draperies obscured the windows, and he thought he spotted the twitch of a curtain, but couldn't be sure.

When he knocked on the door, the blare of the television quieted, but no one appeared. He knocked a second time, and when still no one answered, he started back down the porch steps.

The door creaked open behind him. "How can I help you?" a breathy voice asked.

He turned to see a small woman with black curly hair streaked silver staring out from behind the screen door. She was diminutive, under five feet tall, and a faded replica of her missing daughter. Her face was lined from her wide mouth to her chin and deeper seams marred her forehead.

"Hi," Dan told her. "I'm Detective Dan Webb."

She stared at him blankly.

"I'm in town on a vacation of sorts and came across your daughter's missing person's poster."

"A vacation in September? In Black Pine?"

He chuckled. "Yeah. More of a sabbatical, I guess. And technically I'm across the river in Drake, Ohio."

She stared at him for another moment and then pushed the door open. "Come in then."

He followed her into the murky interior of her trailer. The only light came from the muted television. A smoky haze hovered in the air, and a scattering of threadbare furniture occupied the small living room.

She sat heavily in a floral-patterned chair, reaching for the half-smoked cigarette in the crystal ashtray on her side table. She lit it with an orange Bic lighter. "Make yourself comfortable," she told him, gesturing the lit cigarette toward a chair that matched her own, but was slightly less worn.

Dan sat down and crossed one ankle over his knee. His eyes started to wander the room, scan the shabby drapes and smoke-dirtied photographs, but he forced his gaze back to Annabelle. Her listless demeanor hid something, a simmering fury, and he wasn't sure that taking stock of her home's interior wouldn't provoke her temper. "Have there been any developments on Ivy's case, Mrs. Trent?"

She closed her eyes and leaned her head back, lifting the cigarette to her lips and taking a drag. She opened her mouth and released the smoke with a sigh. "What case, Detective? According to Black Pine police, Ivy ran away. An adult woman with a crazy mom and a dead dad. What kid wouldn't want to escape this?" With her eyes still closed, her lips tightened into an angry line when she closed her mouth.

"But they opened a missing person's investigation? They added her to NamUs?"

"To what?"

"It's the National Missing and Unidentified Persons System. It wasn't around when Ivy disappeared, but it is now. If they opened a case in 2000, they've likely added her to that system."

"Don't give them too much credit," she muttered.

"They did search for her at some point?"

She opened her eyes and studied him. She had dark eyes, brown, not the blue of the girl on the bank of the river. Those must have come from Ivy's father. But many of Ivy's other features—her petite frame, her full wide mouth, her dark thick curls—had come from the woman before him.

She'd been beautiful once, Annabelle Trent. The remnants of the beauty still lingered, but the in-between years had clearly demanded a heavy toll.

"Six months after Ivy never came home, they finally organized a search. It was winter by then, and any evidence was long gone."

"Did they suspect foul play at that point?"

Annabelle finished the cigarette and stubbed it out. She smoothed two fingers, nails bitten down to stubs, along the purple hollows beneath her eyes. "Some of 'em did, some of 'em didn't. The one who counted, Sheriff Dowker, he didn't. Poisoned by his wife and her ratface daughter, Elizabeth. Elizabeth hated my Ivy because she was the prettiest girl in school. Smart, too. Lived up to her name. She'd gotten a scholarship at a big school, but first she had to take two years of community college 'cause we sure couldn't afford Yale or Harvard on my pay. Now if Johnny had lived, she would have gone anywhere she wanted, grown up in a big nice house, got a car on her sixteenth birthday like he did as a boy. But God had other plans for us, I guess."

"I'm sure it's hard to talk about. But if you're up for it, I'm here to listen to anything you want to tell me."

Annabelle glanced at the TV. "I haven't heard a voice except the one that comes out of that box in weeks. I'm up for it."

"Do you mind if I ask what happened to your husband, Mrs. Trent?"

"Call me Annabelle. I haven't been Mrs. Trent in a long time. Maybe I never really was." She grabbed a packet of gum and fished out a stick, peeled the wrapper off and dropped it in the plastic trash can beside her chair. "I met Johnny in 1979, my junior year in high school. He was a senior. He lived here in Black Pine. I lived across the river in the little town of Hamilton, Ohio. Only a river separates the two sides, but it might well be a galaxy for how different life is from one to the next. Hamilton is a town that peaked in the 50s, relied on timber, then fell into neglect. Nowadays hardly anyone lives there at all. The kids have to get buses to bigger towns. But in my day, there was a little school. All twelve grades went there. That's how few kids we had in town. Everybody lived in trailers or old farmhouses and worked at the mill, Humphrey's Grocery and Liquor, or Mo's Bar."

HE LISTENED, sensing Annabelle had to ease into the dark parts slowly, remember the good stuff first.

"My mom and I lived in a farmhouse divided into four units. Two up, two down. Shared bathroom and kitchen in each. It wasn't exactly paradise." A laugh, this one not bitter, but sad erupted from her. "It's funny, I hated it there. I couldn't wait to get out. Now I look back on those days and miss that place. I miss sitting at the scarred kitchen table while Otis Peterson scrambled us eggs and told my ma stories of Vietnam and living in Thailand and India. He was a retired vet, had traveled all over the world. He only had one leg, but was quick as the devil if he spotted a squirrel eating from one of his bird feeders on the porch." She chuckled. "Good ole Otis. He'd get my ma to laughing so hard she'd wet her pants."

Dan smiled. Annabelle had the first expression of peace he'd seen since he walked in the door.

"I met Johnny on Halloween in 1979. A few of my friends wanted to cross the bridge for a big haunted house the students put on over at Black Pine High. They charged two bucks a head. We piled into my friend Tricia's station wagon. It was her mom's, not hers. I'd never been a big one for paying to be scared, but I went along until some guy jumped out of a closet with one of those—" She made a face and hooked her finger. "Those corn things."

"A scythe?"

She shuddered and nodded. "Yeah, one of those. I walked right back out the way I'd come in and sat on the half-brick wall outside the school. A few minutes later, I turned around to find a guy in a wolf mask. He startled me and I screamed. He pulled it down real quick, and that was my first glimpse of Johnny. The change kind of shook me, him as a wolf to him as himself. He had the palest blond hair, almost silver-looking, tucked behind his ears and dark blue eyes. Baby-faced, that's what people called him. He handed me a cup of warm cider and said he'd made it his personal duty to assist anyone who ran out of the haunted house scared.

"I thought he was trying to be fresh, but later I knew better. Johnny really was that guy. The one who helped people who were scared or hurt or... anything, really. He told me I'd missed the best part and led me back into the school where the haunted house ended at the gym. There was music, tables set up with cider and donuts. A bunch of other stuff too. Dunking for apples, pin the brain on the zombie. We sat down at a table and talked half the night away." Annabelle smiled again and slid one of her dark curls behind her ear. It was a girlish gesture, as if recalling the memory had taken her back to seventeen. "I never did figure out what he saw in me."

"We can rarely see the best parts of ourselves."

She lifted an eyebrow and took out her gum, discarding it in the paper wrapper. She slid another cigarette from the pack and clutched it between her thumb and forefinger. "Ivy got me to quit these. I hadn't touched one in five years when she disappeared. When I bring her home, I'll throw 'em away for good. If God will bring her home to me, I'll never touch another as long as I live."

"Do you think Ivy is still alive, Annabelle?"

She lit the cigarette and took a long pull, letting her eyes drift closed. When she opened them, they were filled with tears. "No. She's not alive, Detective."

"You feel sure about that?" Dan asked.

"A mother knows."

He nodded, believing her. He'd met enough mothers of dead children to know that many sensed, sometimes within minutes, when their child had left the world.

9

"Johnny and me started going steady right away," Annabelle continued. "He wasn't like most boys. He didn't play games and take out other girls behind my back. He only had eyes for me." That girlish smile returned, and she stared into her lap, remembering. "He loved my ma, and she thought he hung the moon. He wasn't turned off by our place either. He'd come over and sit in the community kitchen with Otis chatting about everything— politics, world history, the best fishing spots. He could hold a conversation with anyone and he didn't pretend. He was interested in people, in their stories, in how they saw the world. He'd applied and gotten into some of the best colleges. His parents wanted him to go to Harvard, study medicine or law, but he didn't feel ready to commit to a degree.

"He wanted time in the actual world first, to figure out his purpose. We talked about traveling, maybe taking a road trip around the country, going up to Alaska. We started planning it out on a map. We'd go the summer after I finished my junior year. We used a highlighter to plot our route. Johnny bought us a tent and sleeping bags, camping supplies, even a shotgun to hunt. Two weeks before we were set to leave, I got sick on my way to work. I was riding my bike and didn't even have time to go home and change. I walked into Humphrey's grocery with puke all down the front of my uniform." She inhaled on her cigarette, the orange end glowing red. "That was Ivy making herself known." Annabelle smiled again, but the sadness had crept back into her face.

"You were pregnant?"

"Sure was. It came as a shock, let me tell you. I was so naïve back then. I'd never been with anyone before Johnny. He didn't bat an eye, not to me anyway, but one of his friends told me later that he barely spoke that following week. He walked around in a daze. He didn't show that to me, though. He wanted to be strong, my rock. His parents were furious. My mom was overjoyed—'a grandbaby,' she'd announce again and again.

"Johnny's mom was so mad, he couldn't take it. He moved in with us. He proposed when I was five months pregnant and we went to the courthouse and got married. We'd do a big wedding later on, we decided. Johnny's uncle helped us buy this trailer and the ten acres it sits on. We planned to put a second trailer on the property for my mom, but Ivy wasn't even a year old when my mom had her first stroke. She had to move into a home and over the next three months she had four more strokes, ending with the one that killed her."

Annabelle's cigarette had burned down to a nub in her fingers. She stared at the opposite wall, and Dan followed her gaze.

A large photograph in a silver frame hung on the wall. It showed a woman who resembled Annabelle Trent, though her hair was lighter and her face was animated and joyful. She held a dark-haired child in her lap.

"That's your mother?" he asked.

"Yep. Pamela Lynn Gibson. And my little Ivy. My God, she loved her. That gives me some peace, knowing that they're together now."

"Johnny had passed before Ivy disappeared?"

Annabelle's face darkened. "Hit-and-run accident in 1985. They never caught the person who did it."

Dan frowned. "Here in Black Pine?"

"Two miles from here. He was on his way home from the glass factory. He worked the afternoon shift in those days. It was eleven or so. I still don't know why he pulled off the road. He had a full tank of gas. I hate to think it, but Johnny was liable to be hurrying a turtle along or something. He did that kind of thing."

"Did you find him?"

She looked into her lap. Gravity seemed to draw her face toward her knees. "A beer distributor passing through town found him. He spotted the car with the lights on and slowed. That's when he saw Johnny on the side of the road. Johnny didn't die instantly. Had an ambulance been called, he might have lived, possibly with brain damage, but... he bled to death.

"I didn't get the call until the next day. I was his wife, but do you think the sheriff called me? Oh, no, no way. He called Johnny's mother. She identified the body. She insisted he go to the funeral home that all the Trents had gone to. The battle between us turned into an all-out war over Johnny's body. It's stupid now. He would have been so mad to know I squandered what little money came from the life insurance fighting his ma over cremating his body. That's what he wanted. He'd written it all out. We both had after Ivy was born. But 'Oh, no,' said Mrs. Trent, 'not my Johnny. He'll have a proper funeral at the Holy Trinity Catholic Church and be laid to rest at Black Pine Memorial.'"

"Did you win? Was he cremated?"

Annabelle bit her lip, a tear sliding slowly down one sunken cheek. "Win? No, I didn't win. We cremated him, but I most definitely didn't win."

"Any contact with the Trent family after that? Did they have a relationship with Ivy?"

"No. Ivy was an extension of me after all. Mrs. Trent went so far as to see about forcing us to legally change our name back to Gibson. Nothing ever came of that, just more threats. I should probably be thankful that she wanted nothing to do with Ivy. It could have gone the other way. She might have sued me for custody, found some way to paint me as a negligent parent and taken my girl away."

"She never tried any of those things?"

Annabelle shook her head. "Lucille Trent was not fond of girls. That's what Johnny's cousin Vivian told me once. She loved the boy children, but was cruel to the girls. There was even a rumor that she'd discovered in her earlier years that she was pregnant with a daughter and threw herself down a set of stairs to lose the baby."

Dan grimaced. "Was it true?"

Annabelle shrugged. "I wouldn't put it past her. I guess it runs in the family to seek men who are above our station—I think those are the words Johnny's mama used the first time he took me home to dinner. I'd 'sought out a man who was above my station.' That's where the rift in the family started, on that very day. I should have known they'd never come around. Johnny was sure they would. Especially after Ivy was born. Maybe they would have. Johnny's dad started to stop by once in a while and hold Ivy in his lap, but then Johnny's dad died and after that his mama froze us out.

"When Johnny died, they believed it was my fault. My fault because I'd tricked him into this life. If it hadn't been for me, he would have gone away to Harvard or Yale. Instead, he stayed in Black Pine to eke out an existence at the glass factory. Had everyone lived long enough, we might have come back into the family's good graces." Annabelle released a bitter laugh. "If enough years had passed, my social beginnings might have faded. As it was, God didn't have that plan for us.

"Hardship, hardship, hardship—that's my life. That was my mother's life. She was so impressed with Johnny, so happy because I was getting out. I'd be escaping the life she had. Until of course I got pregnant and then all of our dreams seemed to turn to ash. Maybe that's why Ivy started dating a married man. Maybe it was because her dad died when she was young. I read that once in a magazine that young women without fathers often date fathers, older men, married men with children."

"Ivy was dating a married man?"

Annabelle glanced at her cigarettes, a yearning in her expression, but she shook her head sharply. He imagined she'd just told herself no, she couldn't have another.

"Ivy was happy that summer. She'd finished her second year at the community college and gotten into the University of Pennsylvania. She wanted to be a doctor, the kind who works with kids. She adored kids. She did good in school too, all A's. In the fall, she'd be going away. I was preparing for that. I'd been saving money, and she'd gotten a scholarship. I had a friend who lived in Fairmount, Pennsylvania, and she had a little studio apartment above her garage she'd offered to Ivy. We had it all figured out."

"Tell me about the man she was dating."

"I should have known more. I should have pushed to know more. I was working two jobs that summer, and I wasn't really paying attention. She'd been dating a couple of someones that summer. Kurt Gardner was her high school boyfriend, her first love. They went to junior and senior prom together. Kurt went away to college, but in the summers they'd reconnect. That final summer they'd been on and off. I asked Ivy, and she said she just didn't have those feelings anymore for Kurt, but she hadn't figured out how to let him go. They'd grown so close. She loved his parents and baby sister. She loved Kurt too, just in a different way than she had before. So they still went out once a week or so, to the movies or they'd go to the beach with the other kids from town. But then she..."

Annabelle looked again at the cigarettes and, after a moment of restraint, jerked one from the pack and shoved it between her lips. She lit it and inhaled, a mixture of guilt and relief flooding her face. "In June she changed. Started walking around here like she'd won the lottery. Always smiling and laughing, teasing me. She'd always been a happy girl, that was just Ivy's disposition, but now she was... head-in-the-clouds happy. I suspected it was a new boy, but I tried not to prod her. I asked once or twice and she sort of waved me off, so I could tell she wasn't ready to talk about him."

"Did she eventually tell you who it was?"

Annabelle shook her head. "She never did. In August, she changed. I heard her crying in her room a couple times. One night, I accidentally picked up the phone while she was on the line in her bedroom. I listened to the call. I shouldn't have, but I just couldn't help it. I was worried about her. That's how I found out he was married. She was talking about his wife and kids and how betrayed she felt."

"Did you ask her about him?"

"I thought she'd tell me with time. It wasn't a week after I overheard that call that she disappeared."

"Did you ask her friends if they knew who it was?"

Annabelle nodded. "Everyone. She only had one really close girl-friend, Marnie. Marnie didn't know who it was."

"And the guy never came forward after Ivy went missing?"

"No, which convinced me he had something to do with it. If he didn't, why wouldn't he talk to the police?"

Dan sighed. "To protect his anonymity. That doesn't mean he wasn't involved, but it's possible he stayed quiet to keep from breaking up his marriage."

"Coward," Annabelle hissed.

"True enough, but not totally uncommon. Tell me about the day she disappeared."

"I woke up early that morning. It was a Saturday. The Quick Mart opened at eight, and I liked to be there by seven-thirty. Time to have a cup of coffee, get my register situated and whatnot. Ivy was still asleep."

"You're sure she was in her bed that morning?"

Annabelle nodded. "She always slept with the door open. I peeked in on her right before I left. I got off work around four and stopped for fuel on my drive home. I made it back here around four-fifteen, and her car was gone. I thought nothing of it. She was twenty years old, came and went as she pleased. Around eight, I started to feel"— Annabelle paused, brow wrinkling—"curious. That's it. Not upset or worried. I was just surprised Ivy hadn't been home. I figured she'd gone to the beach. If she were going out that night, she'd usually come home and change her clothes, freshen up. But again, it wasn't crazy for her not to do that. Sometimes beach parties turned into evening bonfires. I fell asleep on the couch about ten pm watching reruns of *Twin Peaks*. I woke kind of startled and I just knew she hadn't come home. I looked at the clock and it was going on three in the morning. That was when I started to worry."

"Had she ever stayed out all night before?"

"Not without calling. Never, not one time. I started looking through the trailer trying to figure out where she might have gone. She'd left a plate in the sink so I knew she'd eaten lunch at home. Her bikini, this pale peach one, had been hanging on the back door of the bathroom and that was gone. So was a beach towel and later I noticed a beach chair missing from the shed. I didn't start making calls until the next morning. I sat up all night hoping the phone would ring or I'd see her headlights coming down the driveway."

"Who did you call?"

"I started with Marnie, then Kurt. Neither of them had spoken to her, so I called her employers, Jeremy at the ice cream shop and Maude at the Dark River Inn. I called the library because she worked there once in a while. I called everyone I could think of and no one had seen or spoken to her. Marnie and Kurt started making calls too and reporting back to me. No one could track her down, so I drove to Paradise Park, but her car wasn't there. I called the police about five o'clock Sunday. I'd been waiting all day, thinking she'd show up."

"You reported her missing on that Sunday then?"

"I tried, but Sheriff Dowker made me feel like a real idiot for calling about a twenty-year-old who'd only been gone for a night. 'Call back tomorrow if she's still gone,' he said. So I did and by then I was half out of my mind, but he still didn't take me serious. Marnie and I started going to businesses and knocking on people's doors. It was about four days after Ivy disappeared that Kurt found her car at the bus station."

10

"Her former boyfriend?" Dan asked.

"Yep, and that sealed things in the sheriff's mind. She took off of her own free will. He made it very clear to me that my daughter was an adult who had every right to leave if she wanted to and I was wasting valuable taxpayers' money by calling up the sheriffs."

"Did she keep a diary? A journal? Anything like that?"

Annabelle nodded. "She sometimes did as a girl, but after high school, I don't know. I searched for one. I've been over every inch of her room and never found one."

"Do you mind if I look through her room?" Dan asked. He'd found more than a few secret stashes in children's bedrooms their parents had previously searched. Cop instincts. Or perhaps unbiased eyes sharpened his powers of perception. A parent looking in their missing child's room was a storm of emotion: grief, anger, fear. All of which blinded them to sometimes even obvious anomalies in the space.

He followed Annabelle down the hall and she paused at a door, drawing in a deep breath as if gathering strength to open it. She turned the knob and pressed a hand against the flimsy wood. The door swung in.

Dan studied the room without stepping in. Thin gray carpet. A twin bed pressed against one wall beneath a single window with a frilly purple curtain. A purple bedspread flecked in white butterflies covered the bed. A worn-looking plush elephant rested against the pile of pillows at the headboard.

Beneath the bed, a row of shoes sat neatly with their heels sticking out. A vanity dresser butted the left wall, the surface scattered with make-up, a CD player and headphones, a pile of CDs not in their containers, two copies of *Cosmopolitan* magazine, and a hardcover copy of *Gray's Anatomy*. Several pictures were stuck to the mirror. He recognized Ivy in two of them. The third was a picture of Annabelle in her younger days with a handsome young man and a small dark-haired child. A family photo of Annabelle, Johnny, and Ivy.

A second dresser occupied the wall to his right. This one too was piled with miscellaneous stuff: balled-up socks, a wooden jewelry box with a tangle of necklaces spilling out. He spotted two packs of spearmint chewing gum, a few bottles of pills turned so he couldn't read the labels. "Was she taking medications?"

Annabelle followed his gaze and shook her head. "No, those are vitamins. She was real healthy. Took a multivitamin and a few others. She was always after me to take my 'supplements,' she called them. She had a protein shake every morning when she woke up."

Beneath the pills, Dan noticed a stack of sheet music. "Did she play an instrument?"

"The piano. Johnny had started teaching her when she was three. I didn't keep up with it, but when Ivy was a teenager, she wanted to take it up again. We couldn't afford a piano, but the school had one and she started taking lessons in town. She played beautifully."

Dan's eyes hovered on the music notes for another moment, his thoughts straying to the night before and the curious music that had arisen from nowhere.

"This is Kurt," Annabelle told him, picking up a framed photograph on Ivy's dresser.

Dan looked at the young man. He was a handsome kid with a dimpled smile and wavy blond hair. He leaned against a dark-colored pick-up truck holding a red springer spaniel whose smile was as wide as his owner's.

"That's Meatball," Annabelle added. "Kurt's dog. Ivy adored that thing."

"Did you ever suspect Kurt at all? Get any weird feelings from him, things like that?"

"No, never." Annabelle set the picture back on the dresser. "Kurt is a great kid. Great man. He's a man now. It's strange. When I run into him around town, I still see that lanky sixteen-year-old who showed up here with a handful of tiger lilies asking Ivy to go out for ice cream. He didn't have a car yet, so his dad was parked in the driveway pretending not to watch the whole thing." Annabelle smiled, but the joy in her face faded as her eyes drifted to Ivy's other photographs.

Dan surveyed Ivy's room. A red and blue triangle flag of the University of Pennsylvania hung on the wall. Over her headboard, a collage of photos filled a poster-sized frame. A large corkboard occupied the wall on one side of the window. More photographs had been pinned, along with notes, concert and movie tickets, fluorescent bracelets likely from nightclubs. He spotted a brochure with a large house with a cupola perched on top. It was the house down the road from Bennie's cabin.

He stepped into the room. "Dark River Inn," he read out loud.

"She worked there the summer she... disappeared. As a lifeguard and helping with the kids. She loved it."

Dan turned, surveying the vanity top, searching out anything that might offer guidance. At the foot of the bed, a suitcase lay open on a luggage rack. Clothes filled the bottom half.

"Was she taking a trip?" He gestured at the suitcase.

"No. She'd started packing for the University of Pennsylvania. She was only a few weeks away from moving."

He stepped closer to the vanity and turned back to Annabelle. "May I?" he asked, pausing with his hand in front of a vanity drawer.

A pained expression crossed Annabelle's face. "I think I'll brew coffee. Would you like a cup?"

"I'd love one. You don't have plastic gloves by any chance?"

"I have a pair of rubber gloves for washing dishes."

"Could you grab those for me, please?"

"Sure." Annabelle left and returned a moment later with a pair of yellow rubber gloves.

"Thank you," he told her, slipping one on.

"Sure. I'll go make the coffee."

Fingerprint evidence had likely been collected a decade ago. Then again, based on Annabelle's description of the investigation, maybe not. Either way, it was an old habit to cover his hands before touching anything that belonged to a vic.

Dan slid the drawer open. It contained Ivy's underthings. He carefully pushed lacy underwear and thongs aside. Underwear drawers were famous hiding spots for women, which had struck him as funny more than a few times over the years. Women believed secret things were safe in a lingerie drawer from prying eyes when just the opposite was true. Certain kinds of men delighted in nothing more than pawing through a woman's panty drawer.

Still, Ivy had tucked nothing into the far corners of her underwear drawer. The next drawer down held balled-up socks, a few packages of nylons, and several bathing suits. As he searched, he kept his eyes open for the peach-colored suit she'd been wearing on the beach. It wasn't there. Again, no secret journal tucked inside. He went carefully through each vanity drawer and then moved on to the tall dresser. Nothing.

He moved to the closet, opening the door. Two rows of hanging clothes occupied the space. A shelf above the top row of clothes contained three shoeboxes, a winter coat, and a pile of stuffed animals not quite as weathered as the elephant on the bed. He lifted the shoeboxes down and lifted the first lid. Photographs filled the space. The one on top was Ivy in a navy-blue cap and gown, Annabelle's arm wrapped tight around her waist. Another young woman stood next to them, wearing a matching cap and gown. Her long red-brown hair lay in a braid over her right shoulder. She and Ivy held hands. Dan flipped the photo over.

'Ivy, Marnie, Annabelle. HS Graduation 1998.'

He wedged the photos up to see if any small book lay deeper in the images, but saw none. He set the shoebox on the bed and opened the second box. This one held a pair of brand-new, jewel-studded silver sandals. Tissue paper was tucked around them. They looked as if they'd never been worn.

He carried the box from Ivy's room to the kitchen, pausing in the hallway at Annabelle's muffled crying. He waited another moment and when he heard the coffee pot releasing its steady dribble of caffeine into the pot, he stepped into the doorway.

"Annabelle, did Ivy purchase these shoes?" He held up the open shoebox.

She turned, not bothering to wipe her tear-streaked cheeks, and frowned at the box. "I don't know. I'd never seen them until after she was gone."

"Did you ever find a receipt?"

She shook her head.

"They look expensive," Dan said.

"I thought so too. Marnie agreed. She said that brand is sold at a boutique in Morgantown, not anywhere around here."

"What were Ivy's spending habits like? Did she splurge once in a while and—?"

"No, oh, no. Not Ivy. She was very conservative. She worked three jobs, after all. Not all the time, but throughout the summer. She bought almost all of her clothes second-hand or on the discount rack. She'd never have bought those unless they were a very good deal."

"And where might she have intended to wear them? I mean, they're not exactly beach sandals."

"I know," Annabelle murmured. "Not anywhere in Black Pine, I can tell you that much."

Dan returned to Ivy's room and opened the third shoebox. It contained a pair of well-worn hiking boots.

He did a final scan of Ivy's room before joining Annabelle in the kitchen for a cup of coffee. "Do you mind if I take the shoebox of photos? I promise I'll return them in a few days."

"Sure, that's fine. I haven't looked through them in ages. It takes a lot for me to open that door these days. I feel like I've failed her."

"Finding a missing child is not a job for a single person, especially not the parent."

Annabelle sighed and turned away from him. "But I'm the only one who cares enough to look."

Dan frowned and searched for comforting words, but words changed nothing. He could help Annabelle Trent. He could help by finding out what happened to Ivy. "Annabelle, can you give me phone numbers for Ivy's friends? Marnie and Kurt in particular?"

Annabelle opened a kitchen drawer and pulled out a pile of junk mail. She drew out something else. Dan saw an old cassette player.

She held it up. "Ivy had a piano recital her senior year at Black Pine. Her best friend Marnie is singing." Annabelle pressed the play button on the recorder.

A haunting melody emerged from the plastic speaker, and a jolt of unease streaked through Dan. It was the piano song he'd woken to the night before.

"*Mad World*," Annabelle explained. "That's what she performed. It was her favorite song to play."

As they stood listening to the song, the hairs on the back of Dan's neck stood on end. The scratchy twang of a young woman's voice floated over the notes from the piano.

And I find it kind of funny
I find it kind of sad
The dreams in which I'm dying
Are the best I've ever had

Dan felt as if someone had crept into the trailer and stood just behind him. He swallowed thickly and turned slowly around.

The living room was empty.

11

On his way back to the cabin, Dan stopped at a sandwich shop and bought a Philly cheesesteak and a bag of potato chips.

He sat at the kitchen table and opened Ivy's box of photos, careful not to get sandwich residue on any of the pictures. He flipped through, gazing at photos of Ivy and Kurt at dances, kissing, sitting on crowded couches with other teenagers, chicken-fighting in the river with friends. In the lower portion of the box, he found photos of Ivy as a baby and toddler, many with her father, Johnny, who looked like a child himself with his pale blond hair and bright blue eyes. He was thin and long, with a lopsided smile and an expressive face. In nearly every photo his eyes were slanted toward his baby daughter as if marveling at the miracle that was her.

Nothing groundbreaking appeared in the box. No images of a secret older lover appeared. After ten pm, Dan put the photos away and lay on the couch, hoping to read himself to sleep.

By midnight, he gave up on the book and the sleep. He slipped on his boots and laced them, thinking of Hoss, the pup they'd had until he'd left home to join the police academy. His dad had named the dog after his favorite character in *Bonanza*, and though it had been a gift for their father from their mother, the dog had always favored her and Dan. For months after their mother's death, Hoss sat in the front hall, gazing expectantly at the door where their mother would burst through at any moment with an armload of groceries and a bit of dried meat in her back pocket for Hoss.

That day never came and each year some of the eagerness in Hoss's gaze faded away. Dan missed the dog suddenly. Missed him, though he hadn't thought of him in years, maybe a decade. It was the images of Kurt's dog, Meatball, that had brought the memories of his own former pet creeping from the past. Hoss had loved the cottage in Drake. He'd burst through the door on summer mornings and scatter ducks or geese on the river, emerging after an hour with his black and white fur matted and his eyes gleaming.

Hoss had been thirteen when Dan left for the academy. His black muzzle had turned gray, and arthritis had withered his hips and caused his back legs to turn in. Still, he'd get a bolt of energy every now and again and take off after a flock of birds or a squirrel. He'd take days to recover, but their dad didn't have the heart to refuse his occasional jaunts. Dan couldn't remember exactly when Hoss had passed, and he felt a tremor of guilt at the knowledge. After he'd left, he'd been living his own life, barely spared a thought for his dad or brother, let alone their aging dog.

One morning, he'd gotten a call from his dad. 'We're taking Hoss in today, putting him down,' he'd said, and Dan had been busy. They were doing a course in defensive tactics. He'd mumbled something—a few consoling words, he hoped—but then hadn't given Hoss another thought. Now the dog loomed in his head, made his chest feel heavy and overfull. He wasn't prone to crying, but he felt the unshed tears for a moment, hovering somewhere down in the dark, behind cellar doors he kept tightly closed. There were people in the world who could open their own cellar doors just a crack, let it out little by little, but Dan wasn't one of them. He feared what might happen to him if he opened those doors.

He stepped outside, the night air cool on his face. The river reflected a pale snake of moonlight on its calm surface. He walked closer to the water and started along the bank, thinking about Ivy Trent and wondering, yet again, if it had all been a hallucination. He'd never had one before, but as a cop he'd met more than a handful of crackpots who claimed Jesus had appeared at their breakfast table or that they'd seen giant chipmunks watching them from the woods. The latter guy had been high on meth and found hiding in a janitor's closet at the local library, convinced those giant chipmunks had stalked him all the way there.

Dan shuddered and glanced toward the woods, wondering what had compelled him to think of that man's story in this moment. His feet sank into the marshy grass in the places where the beach had stripped the slope of sand away.

"Giant chipmunks," he muttered. "What a nut." He released a peal of laughter that sounded overloud as it echoed across the still water.

As he walked, Dan noticed a glimmer of red through the trees. He paused and listened, but no sound broke the night. He'd left his gun at the cabin and he half considered returning to get it, but fought the urge, continuing on, sticking to the sliver of beach to quiet his footfalls. The woods grew dense and pushed closer to the river until he had to walk through them.

As he drew closer to the light, the shape of the hulking Dark River Inn rose into view through the trees. He stepped from the forest into the overgrown yard that surrounded the enormous house. The red light shone from one of the windows in the cupola that sat perched on the top of the house like a figure on a wedding cake.

He studied it, trying to make out if the light could be fire, but he didn't think so. For one, it was too red. It also didn't wave and shift the way fire did, not to mention there was no smoke, no sound of crackling wood, and the house looked as empty as it had when he'd checked it out two days earlier.

Dan moved closer to the house, walking on the back porch and peering into the glass doors. Stillness met his gaze. No one moved inside, and when he circled around to the driveway no car was parked near the entrance. He stood for several long moments puzzling at the red light. It must have been a night light of some sort. Though the explanation didn't quite add up.

He started away from the property, cutting through the woods this time, and then paused. The muted sound of music found him. It seemed to be coming from the house, so quiet he almost couldn't hear it, but if he stood perfectly still, it was there. The eerie notes of that familiar piano song. *Mad World*, Annabelle Trent had called it.

Dan swallowed the thickness gathering in his throat and turned back toward the inn, quickening his pace, but as he emerged from the woods a second time, the light no longer shone in the window and the sound of the music, if it had been there at all, was gone.

12

_T_he next morning Dan woke to a thick fog obscuring the river beyond his window. It was a good day for reading. Instead, he managed to re-read the same page in the paperback book _Into the Wild_ three times before tossing the book aside.

He dug into the box that contained Mia Knox's file and found his voice recorder, tucked it into his pocket, and headed to his car.

He drove slowly through the morning mist and found a restaurant in Black Pine with unlimited coffee refills. He ordered flapjacks with a side of eggs and bacon and flipped through a newspaper discarded by a previous patron.

Despite his strange walk in the woods from the night before, Dan had slept a solid eight hours, and he felt rested and clear. Interest in Ivy's case overwhelmed the niggling doubts of his sanity that had plagued him the previous days. He replayed his conversation with Annabelle from the day before creating a bullet list of things to look into.

He called the number for Marnie, Ivy's best friend, but got a voice-mail machine. He left a message.

Dan didn't call Ivy's ex-boyfriend, Kurt. Annabelle had written the man's address as well as his phone number, and as Dan chewed the last of his bacon, he decided he wanted the element of surprise with Kurt. A phone call would give Kurt time to remember and rehearse.

Dan asked the waitress for directions to the bus station before paying his breakfast tab. He drove to the Greyhound Depot and parked on the street. The bus station occupied a corner brick building. Behind it, buses stood between concrete pillars.

It was moderately busy with people filtering in and out through glass double doors while another group boarded a bus destined for Toledo, Ohio. Ivy's car had been discovered in an area near the station with no surveillance cameras. Possibly a coincidence, but Dan didn't think so. The cameras surrounding the terminal were large and obvious. Anyone hoping to drop her car unseen could easily have noted where the cameras were located.

Dan left the bus station and stopped at a convenience store where he purchased a map of Black Pine, West Virginia. He drove to Paradise Park, where Annabelle Trent assumed Ivy had gone the day she'd disappeared.

Trails crisscrossed the wooded park. At the entrance, he saw a bulletin board with trail maps and other posters. He reached behind the plexiglass, shifting posters aside to reveal a flyer for Ivy Trent. He moved it to the front and pinned it into place.

Behind him, a woman cleared her throat.

He turned to find a fit woman, middle-aged, wearing a green velour track suit. Though she was dressed for exercise, her freshly curled hair and make-up implied a more leisurely outing. A small fluffy white dog stood at the end of her pink leash. It watched Dan from beady black eyes.

"Make a habit of shuffling around the papers in there, sir?" she asked, smiling coolly.

"I figured a missing person's poster takes precedence over a used car auction."

"If she were missing that might be true, but that girl's living the high life up in New York, so the joke's on you."

Dan frowned. "Really? I just spoke with her mother yesterday and heard a very different story. Not only does she believe her daughter is missing, she thinks she's dead."

The woman's eyebrows shot up. "What a terrible thing to say about her own child. Just ghastly, that woman."

"You know Annabelle Trent?"

"We're not friends, if that's what you mean, but yes, I know her."

"Would you mind talking to me about her and Ivy, if you have a few minutes?"

The woman looked at the gold watch on her slender wrist. "We'll have to walk and talk. I'm meeting for a ladies' luncheon in two hours and I need time to go home and get properly attired."

"Five minutes is all I need," he assured her.

"Well, I'll give you ten," she said, appraising him a second time. She cast him a flirty smile and offered her hand. "Celeste Dowker. I didn't catch your name."

"Detective Dan Webb," he said, giving her hand a quick shake and then sliding both hands into his jeans' pockets. "Dowker? Are you—"

"Married to the sheriff. I sure am. I've always had a thing for men in uniform." She released a high laugh and started toward a trail. "This is the only one that's paved. I keep telling my husband we have to do better with this park. The roots on those other paths make a brisk walk impossible." She glanced at him sidelong. "You probably don't walk. You look like a man who lifts weights. Do you lift weights, Detective Webb?"

"I'm out of the habit, but I'd appreciate anything you can tell me about Ivy Trent."

"I'm not one to speak ill of others, but that Ivy Trent was a common tramp just like her mama. My daughter went to school with her, and the way I heard it, she'd had half the boys in this town." The woman made no show of softening her cruel words. "I've not a doubt in my mind she ran off with some out-of-town boy. Not that I blame her. Who wouldn't want to escape the sad little life of Annabelle Trent? An absolute shame that a man like Johnny Trent was wasted on that woman. He had such potential and he could have had any woman in this town, let me tell you. In those days us girls called him a top three— money, family, and looks. He had it all, and he gambled on a skinny little brunette with a nice pair of legs who opened them a bit too easily."

Dan imagined Annabelle's sad smile. "You attended school with Johnny Trent?" he asked, changing the subject before he told the woman beside him where she could shove her opinions about Annabelle and Ivy Trent.

"Sure did. Johnny was the year ahead of me. Annabelle went to school in another town, but even at sixteen she had a reputation. When

Johnny took her to our senior prom, we about fell over dead. I mean come on, think with your head, not your..." She waved dismissively at her lower region. "But he wouldn't listen to reason. His mother threatened to cut him out of the will, all his friends made it very clear what they thought of her. Johnny's mother didn't speak for a week after he brought her home for dinner. Later their housekeeper said Lucille Trent, that's Johnny's mother, had taken one look at Annabelle Gibson at her dinner table and fallen right out of her chair."

"Seems a little dramatic."

The woman held out a hand and examined her fingernails as she walked. "The girls in Black Pine do a terrible manicure. I have to drive over an hour to find a decent nail technician. Anyhow, Lucille Trent ruled with an iron fist. She wore the pants in that family. Rumor has it there'd been inbreeding going on in her family for years to ensure a strong bloodline. The Trents were one of the wealthiest families in town in those days. Senators, judges, attorneys. They all graduated from big schools too." She released a sudden harsh laugh. "That's how Ivy got her name. Ivy League. Annabelle apparently thought it sounded so regal. About as regal as naming your daughter Queen or Princess— names of puppies and prostitutes."

Dan clenched his jaw. No wonder Annabelle Trent looked so beaten down. Annabelle had never had a chance of getting the sheriff's department on her side. "You said your daughter and Ivy attended the same school?"

The woman nodded. "Elizabeth. Now that is the name of a queen, a real one." She blew on her fingernails, though they'd likely been dry for days. "Elizabeth and Ivy graduated together. Class of 1998."

"Did Elizabeth know who Ivy dated? Did they still see one another after graduation?"

The woman jerked the leash as her dog paused for a second too long to sniff the base of a tree. "Matilda, come!" She looked at Dan and rolled her eyes. "Matilda's much fonder of marking her territory than getting exercise. Anyway, they weren't girlfriends by any means. God, no!" The laugh again.

It grated on Dan's nerves, and he looked away to hide the expression of irritation bubbling.

"Elizabeth got into Ohio State. Ivy attended the community college." Her tone when she stated the words 'community college' told

Dan what Celeste thought of Ivy's school choice. "Apparently she wanted to be a nurse or some such thing."

'A doctor,' he almost said. 'A pediatrician.'

"But Elizabeth would see her in the summers. They had a few mutual friends, I guess."

"And Elizabeth was at Paradise Park the day Ivy vanished."

"Oh, sure, all the kids were, but Ivy Trent wasn't there. I mean, you couldn't miss her with that big fluffy hair like some kind of southern pageant girl. She made herself known. If she'd have been at the beach that day, Elizabeth would have remembered. And the boys would have too, especially the boys."

"But no one reported they saw her."

"Not a single one of them."

"Did Elizabeth ever mention that Ivy was dating anyone? Rumors of her seeing anyone?"

"Dating? No. Screwing, pardon my French? Like I said, she had more than a few men lingering around her place. She had that Kurt Gardner all twisted up about her. He'd asked my Elizabeth to the winter formal their sophomore year, but not a month later, that Ivy got a hold of him and he might as well have been neutered."

She paused as Matilda squatted beside a sapling. Celeste rotated the diamond on her finger and crinkled her forehead. A look crossed her face, and she quickly smoothed her fingers across her forehead as if willing the wrinkles away. She fixed her sharp gray eyes on Dan.

"If someone did kill Ivy Trent, I'd take a hard look at Kurt Gardner."

*D*an found Kurt's home address and parked a few houses down. A white pick-up truck stood in the driveway, a man beneath it.

After watching him for several minutes, Dan stepped from his car and approached the house. "Kurt Gardner?" Dan asked the jeans-clad legs poking from beneath the truck.

The man slid out, pulling a bandana off the lower half of his face. A streak of grease split across his forehead and some had smeared in his blond hair. He swiped the bandana at the spot, serving only to spread it further. He stood and nodded. "You've found him."

"I'm Dan Webb. Detective Dan Webb."

Kurt eyed him and held up both palms. "I'd shake your hand, but..."

"No need," Dan told him. "I wondered if you had a few minutes to talk."

"Sure, about the break-in at Mrs. Henley's place?" He gestured to a large Tudor-style house next door.

"No. Actually, I'm here about Ivy Trent."

Kurt's eyes widened, and he brushed his greasy hand on his chin, adding another smear of black. "Did you find her?"

Dan tried to read the man's expression. Did he seem scared by Dan's appearance or merely surprised? "No. But I've been poking into the case, looking to see if there's anything the original detectives missed."

Kurt looked disappointed. "Want a beer? Or a cup of coffee. It's probably cold. My wife made it this morning, but I can turn the pot back on and reheat it."

"Nothing for me. Thanks. Do you mind if I tape-record our conversation?"

"Should I?" Kurt eyed the recorder warily.

"Not if you tell the truth."

"I always have, but that didn't stop the detectives back in 2000 from twisting my words every which way."

"They put some pressure on you?"

Kurt swiped his hands on the bandana and threw it on the hood of the truck. "Yeah, they did. My dad finally hired an attorney. He'd have my ass for talking to you now, but..." Kurt's shoulders slumped forward slightly. "I want to know too. I want to know what happened to Ivy."

Dan held up the recorder.

Kurt nodded. "Go ahead."

Dan hit record. "Were you still dating Ivy when she disappeared?"

"Not really, no. We'd gone out a few times that summer, but after we graduated from high school, I went to Marshall University in Huntington. We grew apart, but when I was home in the summer, I'd take her out."

"And the last summer she was around, you took her out?"

"Maybe three times total. The last time was... kind of weird. I got the feeling she was trying to make someone jealous."

"Why is that?"

"Well, she wanted to go to the Black Pine Country Club. My dad had to pull some strings to get us in. It's one of those yuppie places Ivy would normally have smirked at, but she bought this fancy dress and had her hair done at a salon. Throughout dinner, I felt like she never heard a word I said, and her eyes kept drifting past me as if there were someone else there."

"Did you confront her? Ask her what was up?"

Kurt shook his head. "I had a lot on my mind that night and to tell you the truth, I'd just met someone the week before. Michelle." He gestured back toward his house. "My future wife. We'd met at the bowling alley and just totally hit it off. When Ivy called me and wanted to go out to dinner, I almost said no on account of Michelle, but I really didn't know if Michelle was into me, if it would become anything, so I said yes."

"You weren't in love with Ivy? Or hurt by her being distracted that night?"

Kurt shook his head. "Nah, not really. I mean, Ivy was my first love. A lot of firsts with Ivy. And I still loved her as a friend and wanted her in my life, but... the flame had pretty well burned out for us by the time we graduated from high school. We tried to reignite it a few times, but it just wasn't there."

"What about rumors of promiscuity concerning Ivy? Any truth to that?"

Kurt screwed up his face. "Hell, no. That's all garbage spewed by girls from school. Ivy didn't sleep around. I'd be surprised if she'd ever been with anyone other than me."

"Why would they make those things up?"

Kurt shrugged. "Beats me. I stopped trying to understand the ways of women years ago. Jealousy would be my guess."

"Ivy didn't seem to have a very enviable life."

Kurt smiled. "Not on the outside, no, but Ivy had something. A spark, a light. It's hard to describe, and it's been so long... but she was special. Nothing ever got her down."

"Her mother implied she was dating someone older at the time of her disappearance. Someone possibly married. Did she ever mention anything like that to you?"

"No. Ivy wasn't secretive, but... she didn't put it all out there. You know? Sometimes you meet people and you know their life story in ten minutes. That wasn't Ivy. She kept her feelings pretty close, but not in a sneaky way. Honestly, I think she did it because she never wanted to burden anyone with her problems."

"If she were seeing a married guy, does anyone spring to mind? Any likely candidates?"

Kurt leaned against his truck, crossing his legs at the ankle and staring hard at the ground. "Umm... damn, I don't know. It's been ten years. The biology teacher at Black Pine High, maybe. I only mention him because all the girls had a crush on him in high school. The other guy that pops into my head is Carter Trent, but obviously that's not right because he'd be Ivy's uncle and that's just gross. Not to mention that entire family despised Ivy and her mom."

"What made you think of him?"

"Oh, you know, he's one of the guys always cruising around town in a sports car with a younger woman in the passenger seat. It doesn't seem to matter how old he gets, his girlfriends never pass twenty-five. But Ivy never had anything to do with the Trent family."

"Did you talk to Ivy the day she disappeared?"

"No. I hadn't talked to her since the day after the dinner. She called and apologized for being flaky that night."

"Did she offer an explanation?"

"Just that she'd had a lot on her mind."

"And you helped Annabelle Trent look for her after Ivy disappeared?"

Kurt nodded. "Yeah. Marnie and I both searched Black Pine. There were a bunch of us looking and posting flyers."

"And you found her car?"

Kurt's face fell. "I did. I almost drove right by it, but my buddy Warner was in the truck beside me and he pointed it out. We turned around and drove back. It was in an overflow parking lot by the bus station, tucked in pretty good too."

"Did you notice anything unusual about it?"

Kurt cocked his head. "No, not really. It was weird to find it there, though. Ivy didn't take the bus. She liked to drive, and she had a reliable car. If she were going anywhere, she wouldn't take a bus. It just didn't seem right. We all agreed on that—me, Marnie, and her mom. We told the police as much too."

"The police impounded the car?"

Kurt nodded. "Yeah. Though it sat there for another week first. We drove by it every day to see if they'd taken it. One of my buddies had a dad who worked at the sheriff's office, and he said the sheriff kept saying she'd be coming back and slapping the city with a lawsuit for taking her car. It was wild. He just did not want to do anything when it came to Ivy. I still don't get why he dragged his feet so much."

"Have there been any rumors, Kurt? There usually are in cases like this, especially when years have gone by. Any local gossip about what might have happened to Ivy?"

Kurt drummed his fingers on the side of the truck. "She started over. That's been the prevailing belief. She wanted out of Black Pine, away from Annabelle, and maybe she had some secret inheritance from the Trent family. Mind you, if there'd have been a trust fund or anything, she would have told me about it. There wasn't one."

"So you don't buy that theory?"

"Hell, no. Somebody did something to her. I don't believe for one second that Ivy ever made it out of Black Pine."

*D*an returned to Bennie's cabin and transcribed his conversation with Kurt onto a yellow legal pad. It was a habit he'd picked up in his early days as a detective that had stuck with him. His desk at the precinct in Novi had been stuffed to bursting with yellow legal pads.

He stood and ate handfuls of stale cereal directly from a box of Honey Nut Cheerios he found in the cupboard, too lazy to bother with a bowl and, since he didn't have any milk, not seeing the point. He walked across the room and sat on the stool behind the telescope, leaned down and put his eye to the lens.

He didn't expect to see anything, and yet as he watched, something twitched in the trees behind that little stretch of beach. He dropped the remaining Cheerios on the carpet and grasped the telescope with both hands, focusing on the movement.

He spotted the form of a dark-haired woman in the trees.

"Ivy," he whispered, suddenly wondering if he were about to witness the abduction a second time, as if he'd stumbled into a time portal that kept giving him access to that moment ten years gone by. And then an equally unbelievable idea struck him. What if he interrupted the abduction? What if he reached her before the bearded man did?

He spun away from the telescope, grabbed his keys and sprinted to his car. He pushed the speedometer past ninety as he roared through the forest roads, slowing only when he crossed the bridge into West Virginia. He parked on the grassy shoulder where he'd met the deputies days before and ran through the woods, slapping branches away, ignoring the stitch working its way into his side.

In his early years as a cop, fitness had been a daily must—a two-mile run, weights in the evening—but that had been years ago. The last time he'd run for sport, he'd been twenty pounds lighter. He panted as he covered the last few yards and plunged from the woods onto the beach, losing his balance on a small dropoff and pitching face first into the sand.

"Oh, shit, oh, shit," he mumbled under his breath, forcing himself back to his feet and rubbing the cramp that seized the side of his abdomen.

He swiped the sand from his lips and cheeks and searched for her. The beach stood empty. No bikini-clad Ivy sat in her lounge chair. Above him, sun-pierced clouds hovered beneath an extraordinarily blue sky. The river reflected the vision, a muted version but glorious in its subtlety. The sky felt prophetic, a glimpse into heaven perhaps, and yet no revelation awaited him on the beach.

Disappointment and fatigue flooded through Dan, and he allowed himself to fall onto his butt on the dune edge. As he sat, he spotted a woman several yards down the river. She stood in dark waders, nearly waist deep in the water, casting a pole. She glanced his way, and he knew she'd seen him, watched him tumble onto the beach like a disoriented gorilla. He felt the color rise into his face and held up a hand and waved.

She had long dark hair that flowed down the back of her rolled-up flannel shirt. She was taller than Ivy and older than the girl had been when she'd disappeared.

The pole in her hand undulated in the air, the long silvery thread slicing through the sky as she twitched it back and forth and then cast it into the river.

He considered getting up and slinking back into the woods, avoiding her altogether, but he forced himself back to his feet and walked down the beach. "Hi," he called to her.

She didn't immediately turn, her focus on the line stretching into the dark water. "Get all the sand out of your teeth?" she called, glancing back at him.

He offered her a toothy grin. "I think so, though I might have swallowed some. Are you catching anything?"

"Eventually."

"I'm Dan," he told her. "I just bought a fly-fishing pole from Herb at All Your Needs Hardware."

She nodded. "Herb loves to convert tourists to fly-fishing. He equips them with the gear and they usually show back up at his store three days later with no fish and fly hooks embedded in their fingers."

Dan laughed. "I haven't attempted it yet. Honestly, all the equipment is still sitting in my trunk."

"Did you think you'd walk to the river and see if the fish were jumping this morning?" He heard the smirk in her voice, but she'd turned back to face the river, so he couldn't see her expression.

"Something like that." He considered his mad rush from Bennie's cabin to the beach and felt his embarrassment flaring up a second time.

"If you want to hike back out and get it, I can give you a few pointers."

Dan watched the fluid flick of her arm, the way the fly sailed across the water, and knew it would take a lot more than a few pointers to get him catching fish.

"Yeah, that'd be great." He trudged back through the trees. The adrenaline that had been pumping since he'd looked through the telescope had subsided and fatigue crept in.

He popped open his trunk and stared at the pile of fishing gear. A part of him wanted to get in his Jetta and drive away, not only out of West Virginia, but maybe out of Ohio. He considered what awaited him in Michigan. A married ex-wife? An empty townhouse?

He grabbed the stuff and awkwardly slammed the trunk, returned to the woman on the beach. He struggled into the waders and then stepped into the water beside her. He held out his hand, but she didn't take it, instead holding up her pole in explanation.

"I didn't get your name."

"Cass," she said. "Now release some of that line, about twenty feet. You need enough to draw a curve into the pole. See, like mine. When you cast, you need to cast the line back, look back at your pole, and then bring it back in a straight line."

It took Dan a while to get the hang of casting, but eventually Cass left him to it. An hour passed in contented silence, and Dan understood

Herb's insistence he try the fly-fishing. It had never interested him before, but now, standing in the cool river, the glorious sky above, sparkling water below, he felt the first moments of peace he'd known in months. His internal world seemed to quiet, as if slowly falling into step with the natural world surrounding him. He didn't feel the need to small-talk with Cass or to ponder what had happened to Ivy. His mind, for a short while, grew as placid as the river.

Cass caught three fish, and Dan zero, but he didn't mind. When dark clouds began to mar the blue sky, Cass lumbered out of the river, unsnapped her waders and let them fall to the beach. She wore gray leggings beneath the waders and a black long-sleeved t-shirt.

Dan followed her out, his foot getting caught on a river rock. Before he could right himself, he plunged forward, landing on his hands and knees in the shallow water. Water splashed into his face and soaked the front of his shirt.

He looked up to see Cass's hand outstretched. He took it, their palms both slick with river water. Up close he saw her eyes were more green than blue and she had a collection of three freckles on one cheekbone.

She smiled. "I'm guessing you're not a professional ice skater."

He grinned. "How wrong you are. Put me in skates and I'm as graceful as a swan."

She lifted an eyebrow. "Is that so?"

"No, not even remotely. Listen, do you want to grab a beer? I need to lick my wounds after this day."

"The River Bar's only a couple of miles from here. Good food too, and I could eat," she told him.

"Yeah, me too."

"It's a dive, but they've got fresh fish and good beer on tap."

"Perfect."

They walked back through the woods. Cass easily carried all her gear plus the little cooler she'd put the fish in. Dan struggled to balance the waders, pole, and small tackle box without dropping them.

Shadows had descended over the forest, and Dan peered into the pockets of gloom, a small piece of him expecting to see a bearded man staring back.

When they arrived at the road, Cass walked to a green Subaru parked on the opposite side of the street.

"Follow me," Cass told him, climbed into her car and started the engine. The muffler grumbled loudly as she pulled from the roadside, making a u-turn to head north.

~

THE RIVER BAR stood on stilts with a faded wood porch wrapping around the side of the structure that overlooked the water. White twinkle lights twisted around the bannister of the rickety staircase leading up to the high front door.

As they climbed from their cars a light rain began to fall. By the time they reached the door to the restaurant, the rain pounded against the roof.

Cass took a seat at a booth by the windows, setting her suede purse on the edge. Tassels hung from the purse, many decorated with turquoise and silver beads. Rain lashed at the glass, obscuring the view of the river. Dan sat across from her.

"Cass, how ya doin', girl?" An older woman with a raspy voice and long gray hair plaited down her back stopped at their table.

"I'm just fine, Liberty. How are you and Gene?"

The woman cast a look toward the kitchen and shrugged. "We're doin'. Things have been slow, but that's a blessing some days. What can I get ya?"

"I'll take a Guinness."

"Double that," Dan said. He didn't normally drink dark beer, but felt suddenly that today was a day of firsts and he was going to ride it out. "What's good?" he asked Cass after the woman walked away.

"Everything. Gene Nuckles has owned this place for well on forty years. He and his wife, Liberty"—Cass gestured toward the woman's retreating form—"make everything from scratch."

"That's quite a compliment."

"It's the truth."

"So, if I wanted to try some fresh fish—"

"The gunflint walleye or the grilled trout," she said, tapping a finger on the menu.

"Are you from the area, Cass?"

"Born and raised in Black Pine."

"You've lived here your entire life?"

Liberty put their beers on the table, and Cass lifted hers to her lips, taking a long drink with her eyes closed. "I spent about ten years in Columbus, Ohio. How about you, Dan? I'm assuming you're not local?"

He shook his head. "Novi, Michigan. My brother has a place across the river in Drake, a little hunting cabin. I'm staying there for a few weeks."

"Impromptu vacation?"

"Something like that."

Dan reached for his beer and his elbow hit Cass's purse, knocking it from the edge of the table and spilling the contents on the floor.

"There goes that clumsy swan again." She laughed.

Dan leaned over, helping her gather the spilled contents. A business card had slipped beneath the table. He picked it up and looked at the image on the card. Cass stared back at him from the little photograph. She wore a dark suit and her hair was pulled tightly back from her face. The title of the card said 'Cassidy Osborne, Attorney at Law.' An address in Columbus, Ohio was printed beneath her title as well as two phone numbers and an email address.

"You're a lawyer?" he asked, handing her the card as she stuffed a handful of coins into a side pocket of her purse.

"Was. In my former life."

"You quit? You seem young to have retired."

She took the card and dropped it in her purse without looking at it. "I died."

He waited, but she didn't elaborate.

"And were resurrected from the grave?"

She smiled and feathered her fingers through the suede tassels on her purse. "Resurrected from the surgical table is more like it. I was hit head-on by a drunk driver five years ago. I was rushing to court. He crossed the center line and"—she slapped two hands together—"pow. The car behind me swerved and hit a tree. A mother of four killed instantly. I lay there in the wreck until paramedics arrived.

"My spleen had ruptured, one of my lungs collapsed in the ambulance. My pelvis was shattered, both legs broken in over ten places. I had a traumatic brain injury. A doctor who operated on me told me later that I died on the table. I knew I had. I knew because I remembered watching them operating on me. I was there in the room, sort of"—she hovered her hand in the air—"floating. I could see blood all over my face and arms. Then I felt myself being pulled as if a vacuum were behind me sucking me in. I saw Paw-Paw, that was my granddad, and my mother. They were smiling but also shaking their heads as if to say I couldn't come yet. The next thing I remember is waking up in the ICU."

Dan studied her, but her expression carried no doubt about what she'd experienced.

"I spent a month in the hospital. When I got out, I turned in my resignation at the law firm where I worked. I realized I'd wasted so much of my life chasing money, chasing a title, and abandoning the things I loved most. The mountains, the forests, the rivers. I missed my paw-paw's funeral because I had to be in court. I missed my mother's last birthday. I could fill a room with my regrets as I lay there in the hospital, but I didn't feel pity for myself, no, not at all, because I had been shown all of it and given another chance. Most people never get that.

"So I moved back here into Paw-Paw's log cabin by the river and I started fly-fishing. It helped heal me. Eventually I started offering tours and then I became a river tour guide. I don't drive a fancy car anymore or live in an upscale condo and I've never missed a moment of it, not one single second."

Dan had started to lift his beer to his mouth, but paused as he considered her story. "That's... amazing."

She nodded. "It is that, yes."

Dan thought of his own life left smoldering behind him as he drove away from Novi. He hadn't left to seize the day; he'd run away to hide from his mistakes.

She smiled and pulled the business card from her purse, gazing at it with a bemused expression. "This is a reminder of my paper life, my one-dimensional life. Every time I come across this card, I feel a surge of gratitude for the life I live now. I also feel a terrible sadness for that mother who died, for her children and husband, and even for the drunk driver, Steve, who survived with major brain damage. He lives in an assisted facility now in Columbus. I take a trip up there once a year to visit him and to visit Nikki's grave—that was her name, Nikki."

"You weren't mad at the drunk driver?"

Cass wrinkled her brow and shook her head. "Not mad, no. When I died, even though I described it as this brief thing, it was so much more than that. I had awareness beyond anything I've ever known. I understood things I can't really articulate anymore. I felt Steve's pain—the deep sadness that had driven him to cope with alcohol. I knew his entire life had been one of pain and he was only twenty-five years old. I also knew the most exquisite joy and peace surrounded Nikki. It made facing the aftermath different. Steve and Nikki were not separate from me. They were a part of me."

Dan looked at the window where rain poured down the glass. He thought of the day they'd buried his mother, the icy rain that thrashed against the trees in the cemetery. The way that Bennie wailed, 'We can't leave her in the rain,' as the casket was lowered into the earth. Dan squeezed his hands around his beer glass and swallowed the thickness gathering in his throat.

"It makes death less... terrible," he murmured.

"Death isn't terrible," Cass told him. "Not for the dead. It's those who remain who suffer."

"Yeah."

"Why do you suffer, Dan?"

He looked up to see her studying him, her eyes more blue than green now that no sunlight glittered within them. "What makes you think I suffer?"

She offered him a sad smile. "Call it a side effect from my amazing story."

"Well, I was a cop for twenty years, so I guess it's just collateral damage from the job."

"Was?"

"Am."

She didn't push, but watched him in silence.

"I appreciate your story, truly, but not all of us have a grand awakening. I took a leave. I needed a break. It's gritty and hard and takes a toll after a while."

He expected her to bristle at his comment, but she remained impassive.

Liberty returned to the table. "Ready to order?"

"Fried catfish for me and a side of slaw," Cass told her, handing her the plastic menu.

"I'll try the gunflint walleye."

"Coming right up. Good on drinks?"

"Water for me," Dan told her, downing the last of his Guinness.

"West Virginia is a good place to do that," Cass said. "Take a break, I mean."

"Maybe I'll do one of your fishing tours, try to actually catch a fish next time."

The next morning, Dan received a call from Kit Paulson, the real estate agent who had listed the Dark River Inn. She agreed to meet him at noon.

When he pulled up to the gate at the Dark River Inn, she'd already arrived and stood next to a champagne-colored Cadillac. She wore black slacks with a matching black cardigan. Her dirty blonde hair was rigid, as if sprayed into place. It looked rather like a fluffy helmet.

He rolled his window down.

"I'll open the gate and we can both drive in," she said.

He gave her a thumbs up.

She opened the gate and climbed back into her car. He followed her down the driveway and parked behind her.

"Kit Paulson," she told him, offering her hand, once they both stood beside the inn.

He noticed several pins on her cardigans. Brooches was the proper name. Little jewel-eyed owls and foxes. "Dan Webb. Thanks for meeting me out here. I looked online for this place, but it didn't come up in any of those real-estate websites. Is it on the market?"

"Technically no," Kit admitted, "but James Drake keeps it listed on the chance a billionaire comes along and offers what he thinks it's worth." Kit smiled at him curiously. "Not a billionaire, are you?" Her eyes flicked down to his Detroit Lions sweatshirt and worn jeans.

"Not unless I have a rich, eccentric uncle somewhere who's left me his fortune."

Kit laughed and slapped her hands together. "Wouldn't that be a hoot? I've told James more than once that if somebody had that kind of money, they probably wouldn't be looking in these parts. You can't even get cellular service out here." She held up her phone as proof.

Dan nodded. "My brother has a cabin just down that way. Same problem. I like the disconnect myself, but it seems like an odd place for an inn."

Kit started around the house, waving him to follow. "This is a wood-frame house built originally in the early 1900s by Edward Drake, who started mining in the area in the late 1800s. Richard and Ellen Drake acquired the home around 1950. They updated it, added some flair. It already had elements of the Victorian era, but Ellen just loved windows. Thus, Richard hired contractors to cut larger windows into the river-facing side of the property. Their children grew up here in the summers. They had four: Richard Junior, Allison, Seymour, and James. It was a sprawling estate, quite a posh childhood, but the parents retired, left the inn to the children. James volunteered to manage it, but he wasn't Richard and Ellen Drake. James's wife Regina ran things for a while, but then one summer they shut it down. It had been neglected for some time at that point."

"James Drake wasn't maintaining it?"

"I don't know him well myself, but take one look at this place and it's clear he didn't drop a dime into it during the ten years he managed it. Before that, Richard and Ellen ran this inn like it was the Plaza Hotel. Fresh flowers in the rooms for new guests, a gift basket of whatever fruit was in season along with a bottle of wine and chocolate. My parents stayed here every year on their anniversary, but after James took over, they came back just once. Mildewed towels, hair in the bathtub and the breakfast and dinner every day was scorched black. Supposedly, James got rid of the long-time staff Ellen had hired and put young, pretty girls in their place. Not only girls, but it was enough to raise some eyebrows." She bit her lip. "I probably shouldn't be telling you all this, prospective buyer and all."

"I'm not, not really. More curious than anything else."

"Well, then we better wrap this up." She burst out laughing. "Just kidding. I'm really just a part-time realtor. My husband is the breadwinner in our family. This job gets me out of the house and I can dress up and meet new people. I've lived in Black Pine for thirty years and it's not exactly a thoroughfare for people far and wide. Where are you from, Dan?"

"I'm from Novi, Michigan. Are James Drake and his wife still married?"

"Oh, sure. They've really come up in the years since the inn closed. My impression is that James's wife came down on him hard at some point for the pretty girls running around this place. He put a lid on all that. They started on a good deal of philanthropic ventures, donating money, helping support small businesses. Eventually most people in Black Pine forgot about those early years and James's playboy behavior."

"Was there ever more than looking between Drake and the girls here?"

Kit shrugged. "Nobody ever turned up pregnant or filed any lawsuits or the like. If they had, we would have heard it mighty quick."

"Do you know who Ivy Trent is?" Dan asked, following Kit up the wide back porch.

She glanced back at him and nodded. "Oh, sure. Johnny Trent's little girl who took off back in..." She paused. "I don't even know now. Seven, eight years ago at least."

"Ten years ago. Ten years as of this past July."

"Ten?" She shook her head. "Time sure does fly."

"Did anyone suspect something other than her taking off?"

Kit slid a key into the lock and wiggled it. "This old thing probably hasn't been unlocked in five years." The lock clicked, and she gave him a thumbs up, pushing the door in. "I think her mom was trying to spread the word that Ivy hadn't run away. I remember flyers and a few spotlights on the local news, but no one really believed it. I didn't know Annabelle myself, but people didn't exactly consider her the soundest mind in the land. After her husband got killed, she went a little wonky."

As Kit pushed open the door, a piercing scream tore through the house. Kit jumped back, bumping into Dan, who grabbed her shoulders to steady her. The scream faded and died.

"What was that?" Dan said, stepping past Kit and into the house. He stood perfectly still, listening for footsteps or any other sound that might betray who had made the noise.

"Oh." Kit laughed and walked in behind him. "Old pipes. I remember now. Rob Higgs mentioned that to me once. We work together at Beaumont Realty. He brought a prospective buyer in here, and the pipes let out a shriek that made the man looking at the house drop a whole stainless-steel travel mug of coffee. Scalded himself pretty good."

Dan scanned the room. "It sounded like a woman screaming."

Kit grinned. "That's old houses for you. You can't imagine the odd things I've heard over the years. I listed one a few years back that was always settling and creaking. It sounded like an old woman moaning. Those are hard sells, let me tell you."

"Were there ever any rumors about Ivy Trent and James Drake?"

"Oh, I see where you're going here." She chuckled. "Sounds like a soap opera. None that I heard of, though back then I wasn't exactly involved in the Black Pine social scene. My best friend's a terrible gossip and most of what I heard came from her."

"Ivy Trent worked here the summer she disappeared."

Kit had started forward into the room. "Did she? I never knew that." She eyed him curiously. "What did you say you do, Dan?"

He hadn't told her what he did, and he knew if he said 'detective' in that moment the showing would be over. "I'm a developer up in Michigan. I have some partners looking to branch out into other businesses though, and I came across this place while staying at my brother's cabin. Figured it was worth a look."

She nodded, but didn't smile, fiddling with a gold owl on her lapel.

"What was their season like? Did they operate into September and October?" he asked.

"Oh, sure. Half the time it's still hot after all, and then we start to see the fall colors. Quite a show around here." She walked to the panoramic windows that faced the river and tapped on the glass.

Dan stepped sideways and reached for a smaller side window. He quickly slid the latch to unlock it, but it stuck halfway. He dropped his hand when Kit turned to face him.

"Shall we look at the rest of the inn?"

"That'd be great."

As Kit traipsed out of the room, Dan jammed the side of his fist against the latch. It reluctantly slid sideways.

He followed Kit down a large hall into a foyer with a high teardrop crystal chandelier. The foyer stood three stories high. Ornate high-backed chairs were arranged around a glass coffee table in the center. Benches ran along opposite walls. Near the door, a tall check-in desk stood with a yellowed calendar on its surface. A staircase curved up to the second floor, the bannister thick with gray dust.

Dan searched the details, wondering what if anything could be relevant amidst the old furnishings. Likely nothing considering the inn had continued to operate for months after Ivy vanished.

A grand piano stood in the room's corner, the once-shiny black top muted by the grit it had accumulated in its abandoned years.

"This was the guests' first view when they entered the inn. Mrs. Drake nearly always greeted the guests during her time, but when James took over, Mrs. Ferndale covered the duty. It took away some of the charm of this place, I'm sure. Not that Maude Ferndale isn't great, but I think she was spread pretty thin around here."

"Who's Maude?"

"She helped manage this place for a lot of years."

As Dan followed Kit up the wood stairs, he gazed at watercolor paintings of loons and ducks. At the top of the stairs, he looked back at the chandelier and spotted tendrils of cobwebs hanging from the crystals.

"Why didn't they empty the inn when they shut it down?" Dan asked. "There must be a fortune's worth of furniture and paintings in this place."

Kit shrugged. "I can't say for certain. I believe the intent was to sell it ready for the new owners to open the following summer, but..." She looked back at him. "As I mentioned, there may have been some blowback from the Drake family. In the end, they never really listed it. James put a lockbox on it and gave word to a few realtors in town if they found a buyer willing to pay a high enough price, he'd consider selling it."

They walked the carpeted hallway and Kit pushed open doors to reveal guest suites with beds covered in frilly bedspreads. Solid wood bureaus stood in each room. Some rooms included couches and side tables.

"Can we look at the room on the top?" Dan pointed to the ceiling, remembering the strange red light he'd seen emitting from the house two nights before.

"The cupola? Oh, sure. They're so charming, aren't they? Those special little rooms." She walked to the end of the hall where an unassuming white door stood. Dan would have pegged it for a linen closet. She turned the knob and pulled, but the door didn't budge. "Well, shoot," she said, twisting the knob back and forth.

"Let me try." Dan stepped past her and turned the knob, pulling hard. It didn't move. "Could it be locked from the inside?" he asked, knowing it was a stupid question. If it were locked the knob wouldn't turn.

"Could be. In these old houses"—she pointed at the hole beneath the brass knob—"where they've got those skeleton keys, they lock from both sides. But it's highly unlikely. After all, how could someone have locked it from the inside and gotten back out again?" She laughed, but the sound was shrill and jarring in the muted hall.

"Darn. I really wanted to see that room. You don't have a copy of those keys?"

She shook her head. "Most of the doors on the house were updated. This is the only one with that sort of keyhole."

"Too bad," Dan said. His eyes lingered on the door for another moment as Kit made her way back down the hall to the stairs.

Dan followed her back through the downstairs, stopping briefly to look into the large commercial kitchen still equipped with appliances, cookware and stacks of white porcelain dishes. Dan sniffed the air. "It smells a bit like gas in here."

Kit tilted her own nose to the air. "I'll let Mr. Drake know."

They walked onto the back porch and Kit locked the door behind them.

"Why the name?" Dan asked. "Dark River Inn."

"I'd take you out on the dock and show you, but it looks like it's one splinter away from washing down the river. The water is unusually deep right here in front of the house. It plunges down fifteen feet almost as soon as you slip off the bank. The water is dark because it's so deep."

Dan walked to the edge of the little beach, weedy and thick with river stones. He stared across the river at the stretch of beach where Ivy had been abducted a decade before.

By ten pm, Dan had convinced himself he would not return to the Dark River Inn. So what if he'd unlocked a window? No crime there. He continued to list reasons why he should just go to bed as he laced up his boots and stepped into the cool night air. He flicked on his flashlight and started into the woods.

He stopped when he came to the edge of the Dark River Inn's property and considered the house, not looking for activity, but gauging his own willingness to forge ahead. This was breaking and entering. If he got caught, it would not only end his career, it would be deeply humiliating. Then again, hadn't he already ended his career? Blown his entire world up before packing the Jetta and driving south?

He gritted his teeth and pushed out of the trees, striding across the overgrown lawn.

Dan hadn't realized how high the window stood that he'd unlocked earlier in the day. Even on tiptoes, he found his fingers were a foot short of reaching the frame. If he somehow pushed it up, he sure as hell couldn't hoist himself through it. He walked the perimeter of the house, shining his light along the exterior. After several minutes, he spotted a glint of aluminum buried in vines.

It took some hacking at the brush, but he managed to break the old metal trash can free. He carried it back to the window, eyeing it mistrustfully. He really didn't know if it would hold him. Even if it did, it wasn't exactly sturdy on the sloping weedy lawn that descended from the house.

He slid the window up and braced both hands on the frame, pushing his head and torso through. He was halfway in when the scream shattered the quiet. He jerked up and slammed the back of his head into the window.

"Fuck," he yelped, scrambled the rest of the way in and landed awkwardly on his shoulder. A sharp pain snaked down his left arm. "Damn." He sat up and leaned against the wall, rubbing his sore shoulder. The scream had died in much the same way it had earlier that day, and again it sounded much more like a woman's shriek than air through old pipes.

He sat on the floor for several minutes, listening to the silent house and catching his breath. There was still time to back out, leave the way he came.

He ignored the voice of reason and stood, flicked on his flashlight, and made his way into the back of the house. Halfway up the stairs, a single note rang out from the piano below and Dan froze. He turned slowly, expecting to see a figure in the darkness hovering on the first floor, but no one stood beside the hulking form of the piano. Dan didn't move. He studied the shadows and tried to quell the voice in his head insisting that someone had to be there, lurking just out of sight, crouching behind one of those tall chairs. But he knew there wasn't, and the alternative was almost more disturbing.

He turned and took the last stairs in two long strides, hurried down the hallway and grabbed the knob that opened onto the staircase to the cupola. He yanked it back and forth, but the door didn't budge.

"What made you think it would?" he whispered, feeling stupid for returning to the inn. He'd tried the knob earlier. It was locked or stuck. Short of breaking the door down, he wouldn't be accessing the room upstairs.

He turned and walked into one of the guest rooms. The beam of his flashlight played across the bed, neatly made with a stack of embroidered pillows at the headboard. Nightstands stood on either side of the bed, both containing a small lamp with silk tassels hanging from the shades. This room included a stand with a silver basin for ice next to a round table with crystal glasses turned upside down on coasters. The smell of mold hung in the air.

He stared at the furnishings and shook his head. What an absolute waste. It was one of the things that had always bugged him about rich people, their tendency to let something rot before they'd give it away.

Dan stepped back into the hallway, disappointed, not knowing what he had expected to find but aware he hadn't found it. As he glanced back down the hall, a gaping darkness at the opposite end met his eye. He swiveled around. The door that led into the cupola stood open, as if someone had turned the knob and walked inside. He hadn't heard a sound. No one had forced their way in as he investigated the other room. The quiet had been thick and muted, but now the entrance yawned wide.

Dan crept forward, his hand on the gun at his waist, knowing if he pulled it out, if he discharged it, he'd be officially ending his career forever. His opportunity to walk away from this, to make the choice that smart detectives made, was dwindling with every step he took toward that darkened stairway. Whoever or whatever he encountered up there would see him, would know him, would be able to tell that he'd broken into the house. Maybe something worse would happen, something he wouldn't be able to explain away—as if he could explain any of this. He walked up the stairs on stiff legs, holding his breath for several beats longer than was natural so that every fourth breath he had to gulp extra to make up for the lack. When he reached the top of the cupola, he shined his light into the dark space.

A claw-footed oak poker table sat in the center of the room surrounded by four club chairs. Wall-to-wall windows reflected his own light back to him. He stepped in, swung the light around and froze.

Ivy Trent stood against the opposite wall, her face gaunt and hollowed in the yellow beam. Her eyes were not blue, but a yellowish white. Black tendrils unfurled beneath her pale skin. The ashen flesh of her chest turned black before the darkness swept upward toward those pale sightless eyes. She opened her mouth as if to scream, but no sound emerged. As the black consumed her, Ivy simply faded into the darkness around her.

Dan stood rooted in place. He didn't realize he'd unholstered his gun until the sensation of the hard metal registered in his right hand. He'd lifted it, but only halfway, as if the shock happening in his brain had cut off the automatic response sent to his arm. His opposite hand held the flashlight with equal ferocity. Both his hands ached as he loosened his grip.

He put the gun back in the holster, but did not yet turn from the place he stood. A very real part of him felt sure if he turned his back to the dark corner the thing that had been Ivy Trent would reappear and soundlessly set upon him.

Dan barely registered his strained departure from the Dark River Inn. He crashed back into Bennie's cabin, dead-bolted the door and shoved a wooden chair beneath the knob. He sat on the couch shivering, suddenly icy cold, his teeth chattering in his head. He needed to build a fire, to heap blankets upon himself, to sit in a scalding shower, but he did nothing.

With him moored in place, the vision of her in his head repeated like a car wreck he couldn't jerk his gaze from, unable to wipe it, to delete it, to believe it was a figment of his imagination in the way he'd believed the other oddities were figments. In the way he'd written off even what he'd seen through the telescope, somehow still believing there was some other explanation, that he'd seen Ivy's poster and he'd conjured an image of her, that he'd had a mental break, that he really was losing it. All of that was obliterated by seeing her in the beam of his light.

Mel and Dan had once taken a trip to a haunted hotel. She'd talked about going for years and Dan had shrugged her off. In those final years when Dan had been failing more than he'd been succeeding, he'd surprised her with the trip as a consolation prize for the vacation to California they'd planned for Christmas, but which Dan had canceled at the last minute.

It had been a haunted hotel in Georgia, an old antebellum style with four-poster beds, fireplaces in every room, antique candelabras on the tables. And everyone was involved, gasping if the lights flickered, if rain fell, if the butler suddenly burst into the room with the soup, if a cat meowed or a dog barked from the kennel outside—whatever, it was all good fun. Dan had thought of it all as a funny charade, something he'd only mildly paid attention to for Mel's sake.

Seeing Ivy was nothing like that. Spooking himself in a group at a haunted house was an entirely different experience than being alone in the dark, deep forest in an unfriendly place with a dead woman, her face tortured, a desperate plea forming on her lips as she vanished into the darkness.

In movies and books, there was rarely anything to fear from ghosts. They were friendly, a puff of air, so intangible as to be almost nothing, but Ivy Trent had not been those things. And that realization led to the next, the question that he had no answer for.

What was she then?

Dan didn't want to ask that question. He did not want to open a door into the secret, sacred, uncorrupted place in his head where he could still trust the world around him. If he allowed the vision of Ivy Trent into that realm, he'd never get her out. What could he trust if he could not trust his own mind?

---

*I*n the morning, Dan woke to a loon on the river. Its haunting call echoed across the water. The mournful cry came a second time, and a chill ran down Dan's spine as he remembered the previous night.

He sat up and stamped his feet down hard on the wood floor. Solid, real. He couldn't get caught in the web of mystery first thing in the morning. Not that mystery, anyway.

"Just the facts," he mumbled, stood and jerked his sweatpants off the floor, shoved in one leg and then hopped into the other. He pulled on a hooded sweatshirt.

It had gotten cold the night before. When he walked into the front room, he could see cool fog hovering over the river. He didn't see the bird whose melancholy sound had pulled him from sleep, but the cry came again.

He made coffee and drank it so fast he scalded his tongue. After a shower, he put on clean clothes and stuffed the dirties into a laundry sack, slung it over his shoulder and hurried to his car. The chill morning had left a thin layer of frost on the grass and trees. His windshield too, but the rising sun had already begun to melt it away. He started the car, turned on the defrost and gazed for a few moments at the river, at the mist obscuring the opposite bank where he'd first seen her.

'You're losing it, brother,' Bennie had said to him several months before, when Dan had not left his house in days and he'd scattered papers from one end of the living room to the other. When Mel had already moved out and moved on. When whispers around the precinct were getting louder.

Bennie had been trying to call him, and Dan had been blowing him off. Frustrated, his brother had driven two hours to his house to check on him. Bennie had talked to Mel, who told him she too hadn't spoken to Dan in weeks. She was worried about him, but she couldn't get sucked in anymore. The papers had been filed. She had to put up some boundaries now.

"You're losing it, brother," Bennie had told him when Dan refused to go out for a beer or a drive. Instead, he'd sat in the middle of his living room floor, a notebook in his lap, scribbling like a madman as he wrote and re-wrote those last hours of Mia Knox's life.

But was that what he'd been writing? No body, no crime. He didn't even know if she was dead and yet he did. Even now, even after all the repercussions for his insistence on a truth he couldn't prove, he knew she was dead.

And he knew Ivy Trent was dead too. There was no doubt about that now.

A thought flickered in his head, a question. *What if you're wrong? What if they're all right? What if you really are losing it?*

Was that how people with schizophrenia felt? Or those with Alzheimer's? A terrifying sense that the one thing you most relied on, the organ that literally shaped your sense of the world, might be faulty, might be broken?

"No." He shook his head and put the car in drive, turned away from the river and down the long drive back to the road.

He'd go to the laundromat, wash his clothes, and focus not on the ghost, but on who had killed the woman.

SEVERAL HOURS LATER, Dan pulled back down the dirt driveway to Bennie's cabin. He observed a vehicle parked by the cabin. It was a small SUV, maroon with a bumper sticker that read *96KRM—The Rock Station.* Beneath that, another bumper sticker stated *Arrive Alive—Don't Drink and Drive.*

"Louie," Dan said, and then he spotted him.

His best friend for nearly thirty years stood on the bank of the river. He'd turned at the sound of Dan's car and walked towards him, grinning.

Dan climbed out, their last conversation, the hurt words already fading into nothing at the sight of Louie's face.

"Well, I'll be goddamned," Louie said. "Sherry always said you were the next Unabomber."

Dan laughed and touched his face where the dark stubble had grown from a five-o'clock shadow to an almost-beard. "I forgot my shaving kit," he admitted. On his many trips into Black Pine, he'd never picked up a razor. Now he'd need an electric one to fight through the grizzle.

"It suits you," Louie said. "I myself still get carded with this baby face." He touched his smooth chin.

"You weren't getting carded at sixteen," Dan told him. "You've looked fifty since we were in junior high."

"That's why I got all the pretty girls."

"The easy girls, you mean."

Louie clapped his hands together and covered the space between them in three long strides. He wrapped Dan in a bear hug. Louie was large, nearly six foot seven and weighed at least two hundred and fifty pounds. Dan was tall at six foot three, but Louie was a goliath.

"How'd you find me?" Dan asked, only halfway joking. He hadn't told Louie he was heading to Bennie's cabin. He hadn't spoken to him in a month.

"Bennie called me."

Dan wrinkled his nose. "Still pulling the little snot-nosed brother tricks, I see." Dan opened the back door of his car and pulled out his laundry sack, filled now with clean clothes, and a paper bag of groceries.

"He's wrapped up in that new security gig. Said you sounded a little twitchy the last time you talked."

Dan tried to remember their last conversation, but came up empty. "So you're what, here to set me straight?"

Louie rolled his eyes. "Not a chance. I saw an opportunity to get out of town is all. Sherry's sister and mother are visiting. I would have spent the weekend in a portajohn if it got me out of there."

"Oh, thanks. You always were the flatterer." Dan started back toward the cabin and Louie followed.

"Man, I haven't been here in ages. What a trip. Looks the same."

"Yep, our lives fall apart, but this beast doesn't get so much as a gray hair."

"No gray, but it's got some green up there." Louie gestured at the mossy roof. "Bennie better scrape that off."

"I've got it on my list," Dan lied. He had intended to do some work around the cabin, more to distract himself than anything else, but he'd honestly not noticed the mossy roof. Now that he looked at the cabin, he realized more than a few spaces had been neglected. A screen hung askew from one of the bedroom windows. All the paint had flaked off the shed behind the cabin.

"Is your life falling apart, Dan?"

Dan shrugged, but continued walking. "It's not exactly coming together, that's for sure."

"Have you talked to the chief in Novi?"

Dan laughed. "The last time that man saw me, he looked like he wanted to punch me in the nose. Friendly catch-up calls haven't exactly been a priority."

"But you are going back? At some point?"

Louie opened the cabin door, and Dan walked inside. His eyes darted toward the table where Mia's box sat open on the floor. On the table lay the missing poster for Ivy Trent and a scattering of notes. He dropped the laundry sack on the floor and set the groceries on the counter. "I don't know if they'll be holding a 'welcome back' party for me. I'm not sure what my plans are."

"Well, you sure as shit don't have any other skills. I hope you don't intend to move down here and become a lumberjack. You're a good detective, Dan, one of the best. You can't let this one fuck-up take you out of the game."

Dan sighed. "And here I'd hoped you just popped in for small talk."

Louie opened the refrigerator and pulled out two bottles of beer, not asking Dan if he wanted one, but simply twisting off the top and handing it to him. He walked to the couch with his own beer and sat down, legs wide, staring at Dan with the no-nonsense look he usually unleashed in the interrogation room.

Dan sighed and took a drink, wrinkling his nose. "Ugh, skunky.

This is left over from Bennie." He grabbed Louie's beer and dumped them both in the sink, returned to the paper sack and fished out a six-pack of stout, which he'd bought suddenly thinking of the Guinness he'd drunk with Cass at the River Bar. He handed one to Louie, who frowned but popped the top.

"What's this all about, Dan? Coming down here, hiding out."

Dan sipped the stout and sat in a kitchen chair. "How was Mel's wedding?"

Louie lifted an eyebrow. "Mel? Is that why you've turned tail and slunk off to the ends of the earth?"

"I didn't turn tail. I needed some time to think and some quiet."

"And the neighbors were too loud at your place?"

Dan bit his cheek, irritated at Louie's badgering. A part of him wanted to tell him to fuck off, get lost, but he couldn't. They'd been friends for too long, and he'd already burned too many bridges. Who would be left if he sent Louie away too? "I felt like it was all crashing down on me. I needed to be somewhere that didn't... bring up so much shit."

"What do you mean?"

Dan shifted, took another drink and held the beer in both hands, staring at the condensation gathering on the dark can. "You know how the social workers who meet with victims always talk about triggers? Places that trigger victims. The place they were raped or whatever."

"Yeah."

"I started to feel triggered by everything at home. By the places Mel and I had good times, by the roads Mia Knox walked in the days before she disappeared. It was like every place I passed was a bomb that exploded in my head. It wrecked me, man. I couldn't handle it anymore. I threw my bag in the car and started driving."

"Okay. And has this change of scenery helped?"

Dan considered and then nodded. "Yeah." It had too, because he wasn't thrust into a daily cyclone of painful memories or nagging questions. "How was it really? The wedding?"

Louie glanced at him. "You sure?"

Dan cracked a smile. "It's been over a year since she split. I'm fine."

They both knew that wasn't true, but it had been over a year. He probably should be fine.

"It was your typical thing. Dry chicken and green beans. Mel's maid of honor bawled her eyes out during her speech and the best man slurred so much the only part I caught was 'remember that time we went skinny-dipping in the dean's pool?'"

"Jared Burns went skinny-dipping in the dean of school's pool?" Dan asked sarcastically. "I'd have to see it to believe it. Not that I'd want to."

Louie chuckled. "Apparently, he had a wild streak in his youth, but he sure doesn't have it anymore. Honestly, Dan, I don't know what Mel sees in the guy."

"He's predictable," Dan muttered.

Louie cocked an eyebrow.

"That's what Mel told me once. He's predictable, stable. Everything that I'm not."

"You're all of those things, or you were, and you will be again. Every detective gets a case that throws them. Some guys get thrown a little harder, a little further. This is yours. You pick yourself up, dust off the ass of your pants and keep going."

"Did she seem happy?"

Louie looked away from him and bobbed his head. "Yeah. Mellie's a cheerful kind of girl, though. She always seemed happy with you too."

Dan looked him in the eyes. "You don't have to sugarcoat it for me. I want her to be happy. I do. I wanted it to be with me, but I royally fucked that up. Now I just want her to be happy. Period."

"And she is."

"Were they going on a honeymoon?"

"Yeah. The Bahamas or Jamaica or such."

"Such a cliché. Jared is a walking, talking cliché."

Louie smiled a little, but didn't jump on the hater bandwagon. Dan knew that Jared was actually a pretty nice guy. He'd done some digging when Jared and Mel first started dating. No record, one speeding ticket in the previous five years, clean as a whistle. It had been both a relief and a disappointment. More than a few nights he'd imagined storming Mel's apartment with a rap sheet two inches thick, revealing that her new love was actually a career criminal imitating a stand-up guy. No such luck.

Worse than the clean record had been the opinions of the handful of guys who knew him. 'Jared's great. He'll give ya the shirt off his own back if you're cold.' He organized a yearly fundraiser for kids with cerebral palsy because his own nephew suffered from the disease. He paid his taxes on time, owned a nice ranch house on a golf course, and took his parents on vacation every year. He was so stand-up Dan wanted to gag.

"Mel and I went to New Orleans on our honeymoon. Rented one of those shotgun homes, spent five days gorging ourselves on beignets and sex. Fucking best week of my life."

Louie smiled. "Beats my honeymoon. Sherry insisted on Las Vegas. Might have been fun except her sister and ma came along. Cirque du Soleil, Blue Man Group. I swear if I never see another Elvis impersonator, I'll die a happy man."

Dan laughed. They'd shared their honeymoon stories before. Louie had even called him once from Vegas to tell him how Sherry, her sister and mom had been glued to a row of penny slot machines for three hours and he was ready to drown himself in the resort pool if the waitress didn't bring his rum and Coke.

"Seems like a lifetime ago," Dan said.

Louie nodded. "It was. I've got two kids now. Shit! Look at all this gray." He fluffed up the front of his hair, once a thick dark black. It had faded and a shot of silver poked through.

"I'm with ya," Dan said, gesturing at his own hair. He had considerably less gray than Louie, but a few more strands worked their way in every year.

"And how about that missing poster on your table? What's that about?"

ver the vigilant detective, Dan thought wryly. "Her name is Ivy Trent. She went missing ten years ago."

"And you decided instead of taking a break, you'd jump right into a missing person's case in a county you have no jurisdiction in, while you're on suspension?"

"I didn't have a choice. She..." Dan almost said 'she chose me.' "Something happened. Something unbelievable."

He remembered how he'd wanted to tell Louie that first day, how he'd felt sure that Louie would be the person who would believe him, but now that the man sat before him, he struggled to find the right words.

"What happened?"

Dan gestured at the telescope. "I was looking through Bennie's telescope my first day here. I saw a girl sunbathing across the river."

"And you were spying on her like a perv?"

Dan ignored him. "This guy came out of the forest and grabbed her. He dragged her back into the woods. He abducted her."

"Holy shit. You saw her get kidnapped? Did you find her?"

"Well, that's where it gets bizarre. It happened across the river. That's Black Pine, West Virginia over there, so I rushed out of here and called their sheriff's office. They sent out the sheriff and a couple of deputies. We walked down to that beach and there wasn't a trace of her. No footprints in the sand, no lounge chair, no towel, nothing. And mind you, the guy who grabbed her didn't take that stuff."

"He came back for it and covered his tracks?"

"You'd think so, except that sand was undisturbed. I mean completely smooth, not like someone had brushed away the prints or whatever. There was no proof that anyone had been there that day or for days, maybe even weeks, beforehand. There was also no evidence anyone had walked through the woods. No trail, no broken weeds."

"Could you have gotten the location wrong?"

"I walked that beach a hundred yards in either direction. The sheriff blew me off, and I racked my brain trying to find out what had happened." Dan grabbed the poster from the table and walked it to Louie, handed it to him. "Until I saw this in the hardware store. This is the girl I saw get abducted."

Louie gazed at the page, his lips moving. Dan watched him mouth her name, Ivy Trent, but the crease in his brow deepened as he read on. "Last seen on August nineteen, 2000? I don't get it."

Dan returned to his chair and sat. "She was abducted from the bank of the river ten years ago."

Louie frowned. "I'm still not following you."

"Something happened. I don't know, like a time warp or some crazy shit. I looked through that telescope and witnessed what happened to her a decade ago."

Something flickered in Louie's eyes, and Dan's stomach clenched. It had been fear. Fear for Dan, fear for his sanity, but then it was gone. "What makes you jump to that conclusion?" Louie asked. "I mean, it's not exactly the simplest answer. Or even a remotely logical one."

"I know," Dan admitted. "I didn't at first. But then I talked to Ivy's mom. The only things missing from her room were a light peach bikini —that's what she was wearing on the beach—a lawn chair and a striped towel. Her mother had always suspected she'd gone to a beach, but no one knew for sure."

"You realize this story is completely bonkers?"

Dan nodded. "I do, but it's also true, Louie. I don't know how it's true, but it is."

"Why does it have to be that girl?" Louie pointed at the poster. "Why can't it be someone who looks like her?"

"That telescope takes you in close. It's like looking at someone through their window. I could see every detail on this girl, dream-catcher earrings, peach bikini that came up kind of high. These are details the mother confirmed. It's the same girl and the day I saw her it was cloudy and kind of cool. No woman was out there sunbathing. I saw something that had happened ten years ago this past July."

"I'm going to need another beer to get my brain loose enough to hear this story without wanting to check you into the nuthouse." Louie stood and walked to the counter. He pulled out two more cans from the plastic rings. "Why are you buying this black stuff? It's liable to give me the shits."

"You're welcome to Bennie's three-year-old Budweisers."

Louie rolled his eyes. "Got a bar near here?"

"In Black Pine. Twenty minutes about."

"Forget these." Louie stuck the two cans in the refrigerator. "Let's head that way. I've got a hankering for a big fat cheeseburger. Sherry's got me on a chicken and veggies diet. I've been dreaming about red meat for a month, I kid you not. I had a dream the other night, I woke up to let the dog out to piss and my mailbox was a steak. I walked over and started chewing on it."

Dan laughed. "Bennie told me about some burger joint that's good. We can get some beer there too."

~

"So, what do you think, Louie?"

Louie picked up another fry, swirled it in his ketchup and popped it in his mouth. He chewed thoughtfully, took another swig of beer, and then belched beneath his cupped hand.

"What do I think?" he asked, furrowing his brow. "A lot, not much that's helpful though. I wonder, 'Has Dan officially gone bananas?' Then too, could you have witnessed this ten years ago and suppressed it?"

"I wasn't at the cabin when it happened. I can tell you that much for sure."

"But you don't care to address the bananas part?"

"Would it matter if I did?"

"Probably not. My third and most unreasonable but also preferred explanation is that... you saw something that happened a decade ago.

You saw it because... I guess maybe she wants you to solve her murder."

"You actually believe that?"

Louie took another drink. "This helps." He tapped a finger on his glass. "I grew up Catholic, man. There were all kinds of illogical stories in the Bible. Mind you, modern-day spirits were all demons and if you encountered them you were being lured by the devil, but I've tended away from that belief system. Sherry is firmly Protestant, whatever that means, and I'm an attendee who's open, but not committed to any one thing. I've heard a lot of stories. Remember that case I worked a few years back with the kid abducted from the school playground? It had been six days. We were sure he was dead, nabbed and murdered by some pedophile, but the mother was calling me all hours of the day and night. She kept dreaming her son was in a room with clown wallpaper and toys everywhere. He was crying for her."

Dan nodded. He remembered Louie telling him about the case.

"We ended up getting a call from this guy who was worried about his daughter. She'd been acting strange, wouldn't let him in her house when he stopped by. He thought he saw a little boy looking out from an upstairs window, but she didn't have a kid. We went and knocked on her door and she pitched a fit. Attacked my partner, tried to shoot us both, but couldn't get the safety off the gun she had behind her back. Anyway, we got her down and cuffed. I walked into that house and upstairs. There was a door locked from the outside with one of those little slide bolts. I opened that door to find this creepy kid's room. Clowns on the walls, a zillion stuffed animals piled in the corner. A little boy is sitting on the bed. It's Michael Henry. The kid who'd been abducted." Louie dragged his beer across the table and tilted it up, finishing it.

Dan lifted his own and did the same. "His mother had been dreaming about the room where her kid was being kept and she'd never been there?"

"Never in her life. Never met the woman, nothing. The woman who stole the kid, Lynette, wanted a baby, but didn't have a boyfriend, probably never would either. She was a little off."

"Did you ever tell anyone about it?"

"I told Sherry. Like I said, the mom was calling me constantly. When I told Sherry where we found the kid, her eyes about fell out of her head. We talked about it non-stop for a couple of weeks and then real life works its way back in. I mean, what do you do with a story like that? Call the *National Enquirer*?" He chuckled and shook his head. "But let me also say this, Sherry has had her own funny experiences. Right after her grandfather died when she was a little girl, she woke at night and saw him standing in her doorway. He tipped his hat at her and then he disappeared. She didn't find out he was dead until the next morning."

Dan sighed and leaned back in the booth. "I have to tell you, it's a relief to hear this."

"I bet. Living in an isolated cabin is enough to have you questioning your sanity. Throw in a ghost and you're really in trouble."

"You think it was her ghost?" Dan thought of Ivy the night before, and gooseflesh prickled over his forearms.

"The ghost of something, anyway. The experience, maybe. Shit, I don't know. But there are people who work in this stuff, you know? Haven't you ever watched any of those ghost hunter shows?"

Dan gave his friend a wry look. "Seriously?"

"Well, not the obnoxious ones who constantly scream that somebody just breathed on their neck, but like, the legitimate ones."

"Oh, yeah, of course, the legitimate ones. And how in the hell do I find those?"

"How do I know? The yellow pages? The internet. Maybe you need to summon one with one of those..." Louie gestured with his hand as if he were sliding something across the table.

"A ouija board?"

"Yeah, right. One of those."

Dan rolled his eyes. "Maybe the internet. I haven't been online since I left Novi. My email's probably so full of spam it'll take a month to clean it out."

Louie slapped his hand on the table. "Psycho Sally!"

"Say what?"

"Psycho Sally. That's what we call her in Brighton. Psychic Sally, if you want to be polite about it. She calls us once a year, usually claiming to have psychic information about some case or another. I've got her contact information at the office. Hold on." Louie took out his cell phone and punched in a number.

'Bathroom,' he mouthed at Louie before standing and making his way into the dimly lit restroom.

He peed and washed his hands, but as he started toward the door, he saw the name 'Ivy' scratched into the single, scarred bathroom stall. A thousand other words surrounded it.

Billy was here. Eat my dust. The burrito will give you the squirts—avoid at all costs.

Ivy. A jagged heart surrounded her name and a crude knife had been drawn jabbing into the side of the heart. Small black drops trickled from the heart, likely meant to be blood.

It didn't hold any mystery, but it still unnerved him as he walked back to Louie.

"Sally Mitchell," Louie said, handing Dan a napkin on which he'd written the woman's name and phone number.

"And what? I just call this woman out of the blue and tell her I think I've seen a ghost?"

"Shit if I know. Maybe call her and don't tell her anything. She's psychic, after all. She should be able to tell you herself plus what you ate for breakfast."

Dan laughed. "Sounds likely."

"Ye of little faith."

Dan rolled his eyes. "Has she ever been useful? Ever given you anything that helped with a crime?"

Louie shifted his jaw and bobbed his head slowly. "Kind of. We had a guy go missing a couple years back, and she called to say she was sure he was dead in a silo. Just so happened, the guy had an old silo on his property. We searched it and sure enough, there he was."

"Murdered?"

"Suicide. Thing is, we would have got to the silo eventually. Not to mention anyone who knew the family knew there's a silo on that property."

"That's it?"

"Well, my old partner Roy, remember him?"

"Yeah. The guy with the screecher laugh."

"That's the one. Made nails on a chalkboard sound like wind chimes. Anyway, he worked a case before we were partners. A little girl who'd been abducted. Psycho Sally called the station a few times. He intercepted a couple of those calls. Sally insisted the girl was dead and had been buried beneath water. Not like a pond, but more like a pool. Roy did some digging and found out the girl's neighbor had been putting in a pool when she disappeared. He kept digging, and the guy had a record for exposing himself to children. They got a warrant and sure enough, little girl was buried beneath that pool. Pretty sad stuff, but it convinced Roy. He'd never admit it, but I'm pretty sure he consulted Sally on quite a few cases over the years. He's a P.I. now down in Florida, and I wouldn't doubt he still calls her up when he's got a doozy he's working on."

Dan took out his cell phone.

"Calling her now?"

"Why not? Might make it less awkward if I can say I'm with Roy's former partner."

Sally didn't answer. Dan listened to her voicemail recording. She sounded a little wary.

'Hi, this is Sally Mitchell. Leave me a message or find me online at SallysReadings.com.'

"Hi, Sally, this is Detective Dan Webb. I got your number from a detective in Brighton, Michigan, and wondered if we could talk about a case." Dan left his number and ended the call. "Maybe she can also offer some insight into the future because I sure as shit don't know what's coming."

Louie grinned. "Another round, my friend, and we don't need a psychic to tell us that."

19

The following day, Louie made egg sandwiches with the fixings he'd bought from the store the evening before. After they finished eating, Louie threw his clothes in his duffel bag.

"You gonna be okay, Dan? Down here on your own?"

"Sure, why not?" Dan asked, following Louie out to his SUV.

Louie didn't answer but raised an eyebrow before opening his passenger door and tossing his bag on the seat.

"What comes next?" Louie asked, leaning against his SUV, his jumbo travel mug filled with coffee resting on the roof of his car.

"Drive down the road and check my voicemail. Zero service at this place, so I have to hoof it out of here to get anything done." Dan rolled his eyes. "Hopefully, I'll have heard from Ivy's friend, maybe even Psycho Sally."

Louie chuckled. "You're sure it's not the ex-boyfriend? You already interviewed him."

"Not unless I left my instincts at the border when I crossed out of Michigan. The guy had an honest face. He and Ivy were pretty well done that summer. I'm leaning towards the secret lover."

Louie opened his driver's door. "Those secret lovers are a pain in the ass. I worked a case last year on a guy whose wife"—Louie did air quotes—"'fell down the stairs.' Everybody thought he was having an affair, but we could not find a trace of this chick. Turned out to be a dude and not just any dude, the vic's own brother. We couldn't find him because he was sittin' right in front of us."

Dan sighed. "Don't plant that seed in my head. I've been looking at guys. I don't want to add the entire female population of Black Pine to my suspect list."

"Suspect list." Louie laughed and shook his head. "Don't go putting in to get transferred down here, old man. Golf season is a short six months from now and I'll be scheduling a tee time the first day the snow melts."

"They wouldn't take me down here if I crawled into the sheriff's office and licked the sheriff's boots."

Louie grinned. "Now that I'd like to see."

"Yeah, yeah. Give Sherry and the kids my love."

Louie grabbed his coffee, climbed into his SUV, but Dan caught the door before he pulled it closed. "Louie, I'm sorry about—"

Louie held up a hand. "Ancient history, man. Remember that time in eighth grade when I blasted you in the face with the kickball to impress Jessica Fuentes?"

"How could I forget? I thought you broke my nose."

Louie laughed. "Well, you reaming me out was kind of like an emotional kickball to the face, so we're even." As he pulled away from the cabin, the brake lights lit up and he rolled down his window. "Don't go too far into the weeds on this one, Dan. Easy to get lost in a place like this."

Dan saluted him and watched Louie drive away.

As he returned to the cabin, his cell phone rang. "This is Dan," he said.

"Hi, Dan. This is Ivy's friend, Marnie returning your call."

"Marnie, hi. Thanks for getting back to me. I'd hope to chat with you about Ivy Trent. Would that be possible?"

"It definitely is. I spoke with Annabelle yesterday. I can't tell you how relieved I am to hear you're looking into Ivy's disappearance."

"Do you have some time to meet today? I'd like to ask you some questions."

"Absolutely. I'm at Black Pine Middle School on Price Road. No school today. I'm catching up on grading."

"I can be there in twenty minutes," he told her, grabbing his car keys and heading for the Jetta.

"Okay, I'll meet you out by the playground."

~

As he approached the school, he saw a woman sitting on a bench watching the empty playground. She wore an oversized green and black checked sweater—a man's sweater, he thought—paired with torn jeans and faded tennis shoes. Stones crunched beneath his feet and she turned, holding her hand up in a wave.

"Dan?" she asked, standing and taking a few steps toward him.

"That's me. And I take it you're Marnie Lutz?"

"Marnie Fitzpatrick these days." She wiggled her left fingers, where Dan spotted a small diamond encircling her ring finger. "It's pretty depressing to think about. My best friend in the world wasn't standing up there with me. Ivy had this great schtick where she'd pretend to be drunkenly giving a maid of honor toast at my wedding. She'd teeter around, ticking off on her fingers all the times we got into trouble."

Dan arched an eyebrow. "Did you guys get into a lot of trouble?"

Marnie laughed and pushed her wavy auburn hair over her shoulders and away from her face. "Not the kind you're curious about. But we fancied ourselves troublemakers when we were little. My mom had a spinning door of boyfriends. We used to put frogs in their trucks, tie their shoelaces together, hide their cologne—nothing to get us arrested... or killed," she breathed.

"Do you believe Ivy is dead?"

Marnie looked away from him, eyes returning to the playground where a row of swings sat listlessly. "I don't see how it could be anything else. Regardless of what the sheriff's office said, Ivy would never have taken off without telling her mom. Never in a million years."

"Shall we sit?" Dan asked, gesturing to the bench.

"Mind if we walk instead? I've been in there catching up on grading all day. My back needs a break."

"Sure, of course." They started toward the playground where a narrow dirt track wound along the outside of the soccer field. "What grade do you teach?"

"Sixth. That strange time when they haven't quite plunged into the petulant teenage years."

"Sixth…" Dan tried to remember sixth grade. "What age range?"

"Depends—eleven to thirteen usually."

"Thirteen," he repeated. He'd been twelve when his mother had died and the spark that would drive him to become a cop and eventually a detective had begun to shape his life.

"Yeah, they're good kids. Still curious and hopeful about the world. High school goes a long way towards dulling that twinkle, unfortunately."

"I believe it. I've never understood why people referred to high school as the glory days. The only glorious thing I remember was the bell ringing at the end of the day."

She grinned. "I wish someone had told me the teachers felt the same way."

Dan reached in his coat pocket and pulled out his little voice recorder. "Marnie, do you mind if I record our conversation? It helps me to replay things later on, find connections."

"Go for it. I'll do just about anything to help find Ivy. For years, Annabelle and I organized a big search on the day of her disappearance. We'd pick a new section of Black Pine to search. Usually, a couple news stations would come out. For a few weeks there'd be renewed interest in the case, but"—she shrugged—"nothing ever came out of it."

"Where did you search?"

"Paradise Park, the property on Tuttle Road, the wooded area near the ice cream parlor where Ivy worked, isolated spots we used to party as kids."

"How about the property by the Dark River Inn?"

Marnie frowned and shook her head. "I remember we talked about it once, but the Drakes made a stink. They claimed an investor was considering purchase and it would foil their sale."

"Did that seem strange to you?"

Marnie took a breath and glanced up at the cloudy sky before shaking her head. "Nah. People like the Drakes always force you through all kinds of red tape. I searched it, though. Me and a couple friends. We went out there a few years after the inn had closed and picked through the woods and along the river."

"Find anything there?"

"No, nothing. The big problem is we had no clue where she went that day."

"She never told you about plans for that Saturday?"

Marnie shook her head and reached back for a handful of her hair, weaving her fingers through it as she walked. "I hate to admit it now, but we were a little strained that summer. Ivy had gotten into the University of Pennsylvania. They offered her a scholarship. We'd always planned to go to West Virginia University together. I was pretty upset and did the shitty thing young women do, which is not tell her why I was mad and act like a passive aggressive A-hole.

"Eventually we would have gotten over it. I would have thrown a little tantrum and told her why I was hurt and she would have hugged me and told me to stop acting like a jackass, but we never got the chance. I'm at fault for that. For more than that too, because I was chumming around with some other girls we'd graduated with that summer to punish her." Marnie released a frustrated sigh and flung her hand back behind her again. "I'm still mad at myself when I think about it. If I hadn't pushed her away that summer, I'd know who she was going out with. I'd know where she was going to be that day. I probably would have been there with her."

"Regret won't change anything, Marnie," he told her, hearing how flimsy his words sounded, so flimsy he'd never been able to take the advice himself.

She tugged on her sweater. "Yeah, I know. But tell that to my brain at two am when I'm lying there thinking about how it could have been instead of how it is."

"Did you know about her seeing an older man? Annabelle Trent mentioned—"

"I knew she was seeing someone new, and that she was keeping him a secret. A week before she disappeared, I stopped by her house to borrow jumper cables. I was driving an old Ford Escort, and the battery died every other day. She'd gotten all dressed up, and I asked her why. She said she had a date, but when I asked her with who, she said she'd tell me soon. I had no clue about the 'married with kids' thing until Annabelle told me after Ivy disappeared."

Dan frowned, disappointed. He'd hoped the best friend would have inside information the mother hadn't been privy to.

Marnie caught the look. "I know," she said. "I should have known. What kind of person has no idea that her best friend is dating a married man? I failed her."

Dan looked at her sidelong. "Who do you think it was? Or could have been?"

Marnie bit her lip. "I've gone over it a thousand times. I have a list, but…" She shrugged. "Are any more likely than any others? I can't say."

"Did anyone ever question the men on your list?"

"Some of them, I think."

"Was there a particular person who you suspected, though?"

Marnie sighed. "One guy. Not for the affair, mind you. No way, but… he spooked Ivy."

"Go on."

"Right across the street from the ice cream shop where Ivy worked is this bar called Ringo's Watering Hole."

"I passed it in town."

"Yeah, it's a real dump, but it's always had a happening night life of a certain kind. Bikers, local drunks, townies and usually a few guys who came from out of town to hunt or fish. There was a guy who used to go in there pretty regular. He didn't live in Black Pine. He had a place across the river."

"Okay."

"He'd walked over to the ice cream place a few times and asked Ivy out. He'd be pretty inebriated and leaning all over the counter. She turned him down and then one night he followed her home."

"In a car?"

"In a truck. And Ivy was on a bike because her mom's car was in the shop and Annabelle had borrowed hers. Ivy didn't mind biking into town. It was July, warm nights, and Black Pine had always been safe. She shut down the ice cream shop at around eleven at night and got on her bike. She saw him watching her from his truck across the street. He started following her. He didn't even try to hide it. Just stayed right behind her back wheel, brights shining on her. It terrified her. She called me that night. It was the first time she'd just picked up the phone and called me in the middle of the night in months."

"Did he ever make contact with her? Try to grab her?"

"No. He just followed her all the way to her driveway and when she turned in, he stopped his truck for a minute and then did that thing where you peel out. I told her to call the cops. Her mom was at work. She was all alone in that trailer."

"But she didn't?"

"No. After talking for about twenty minutes and watching for him out the window, she calmed down. She didn't want to make a big deal out of it."

"That's a pretty concerning story. Did you tell that to the police?"

"Yeah, I did, and when Annabelle sounded the alarm about it, they told her he had an alibi."

"What was his name?"

"I don't remember his last name, but his first name was Bennie."

20

*D*an didn't immediately call Bennie. He couldn't say why, only that he wasn't ready to confront his brother about the disturbing story shared by Ivy's best friend.

He parked beside the cabin, but flicked his gaze back to the river and more importantly to the opposite bank. The only way someone could have known about Ivy Trent sunning on that beach was if she'd told them or if they spied her there. And coming upon her in a wooded stretch of isolated beach seemed unlikely. But what if you were sitting in a cabin across the river looking through a telescope?

It was a risky move. It took twenty minutes to make the drive from the isolated cabin to the stretch of woods that backed the beach. Another five to ten minutes to walk down there. In that space of time her friends could have shown up; she might have left altogether and gone home. But then again, how often did predators look at those logical flaws in their plan?

The word 'predator' made him cringe. Bennie wasn't a predator. He was a birdwatcher, a guy who cut the Dilbert strip out of the funnies every week and hung it on the refrigerator. Yeah, he'd had his issues over the years and they mostly sprang from the bottle, but he'd never been violent, never hit his girlfriend or ex-wife.

That you know of, a voice whispered in his head. The detective voice, the voice that didn't take his feelings about Bennie into consideration when he contemplated the likelihood of the man's guilt.

Dan pushed into the cabin and stared around the room. He didn't know what he sought, but he felt compelled to begin in this place on the chance some bit of evidence might offer an exoneration of his brother or, worse, a condemnation.

A trunk sat at the end of a ratty couch. Round watermarks from glasses and coffee mugs marred the surface. He flipped the latch and lifted the lid. A pile of musty blankets lay in the trunk. He hauled them out and stacked them on the couch. Beneath those lay board games, old faded ones they'd played as kids—Risk, Life, and the bottommost game was Séance. That had been his cousin Rowan's favorite game during the weekends when she accompanied the brothers and their dad to the cabin. Rowan had loved the creepy voice of the dead Uncle Everett that emitted from the table.

Rowan had become a newspaper reporter in Michigan. They'd caught up a few times a year, but not this year. This year Dan's life had been unraveling, and he'd left the half-dozen calls that came in from Rowan unanswered.

In the bottom of the chest, he found a few decks of playing cards and a worn photo album, but nothing else. He pulled out the album, the detective voice urgently whispering in his ear to set it aside, to not get distracted. Instead, he walked to the chair by the window and slumped down, flipping it open to the first image. His own face stared back at him, though nothing in the face resembled the man in the chair. This was Dan as a toddler, gap-toothed and grinning, a harmonica clutched in one pudgy hand. Tucked in the pocket of his denim overalls was a scruffy stuffed frog that he'd dragged with him everywhere.

The next page showed another child version of Dan, this time sitting on his mother's knee on the porch steps at their home in Battle Creek. She tilted her head, her eyes on Dan's leg as she tried to maneuver a single red tennis shoe on his round foot. Dan himself was thrown backward on her lap, arms outstretched as he reached for a black and white cat standing just out of reach on the porch. He couldn't remember the cat's name now. There'd been a rotating barn door of cats in those days.

Bennie had been the cat-lover, the one who named all the litters and kept track of them, but in this photo, Bennie had not yet been born and his mother had not yet started having her episodes. He flipped a few pages on to where Bennie first appeared, a blue blanketed bundle resting awkwardly on Dan's lap, their mother's hand supporting Bennie's flaky little head. They sat on the long sofa that had been in their living room.

The pictures lasted until Dan was around twelve and Bennie nine. Fishing in the Ohio River, climbing trees at the cabin, and then the last one, the four of them at home in the backyard. Their mother sat in a lawn chair, her form gaunt beneath the quilt their dad had rested in her lap. She smiled, but her eyes glowed with the knowledge of death. She'd gotten so thin that summer, skeleton-like, and their father had taken to bringing home boxes of donuts at night, most of them the sticky jelly kind that Dan and Bennie despised, but their mother loved. Except she hadn't eaten them. Their dad hadn't known that. Instead, she and Dan and Bennie walked to the pond at the end of their road and tossed them into the water for the fish and ducks. The other donuts, the chocolate-covered and powdered ones, Dan and Bennie gobbled up themselves.

To look at their mother's final images, most would think cancer or some other wasting illness had ravaged her, but it had been her own mind consuming her from the inside out.

Dan tossed the album aside and leaned his head back on the chair. The death of their mother had been hard on all of them. Maybe Bennie most of all, though Dan hadn't known it at the time. He'd been too absorbed by his own feelings, his own grief to consider how the loss of their mother at nine years old might have shaped Bennie's life. Only later when their dad had reminded Dan to take it easy on Bennie had Dan considered how it all might have affected his baby brother.

DAN LEFT the cabin and drove into Black Pine to ensure he had decent cell service. This was one call he didn't want to drop.

He parked in a grocery store parking lot and dialed Bennie's number. His brother answered on the second ring.

"Hey, man, what's up?"

"Not much," Dan lied. "How are things in Kalamazoo? New job going good?"

"Oh, yeah, it's the bees' knees. I spend eight hours sitting in a metal folding chair shining my light on squirrels that set off the motion detectors."

"Louie said you liked it."

Bennie sighed. "I do. I just didn't realize I'd be patrolling the back forty. I rather hoped to bust some thieves, see some action."

"Action is never as exciting as it sounds."

"For you, maybe."

"Listen, do you know a woman named Ivy Trent?"

Bennie said nothing, and Dan wished he could sit face to face with his brother. "Doesn't ring a bell."

"Really? Young woman who went missing in Black Pine about ten years back."

"I didn't spend much time in Black Pine."

"You sure, Bennie? I have it on a pretty good authority that you asked Ivy Trent out a few times."

"Okay, all right. I knew her," Bennie said.

"You lied to me?"

"Yeah." He let out a strange laugh that Dan hadn't heard before.

"Why? Why lie?"

"Well, I used to see her. I took a liking to her. I asked her out a few times, and she turned me down. I guess it embarrassed me. I don't know. You mentioned her name. I didn't want to relive the humiliation."

"Of a twenty-year-old turning you down for a couple of dates?"

"Sure, yeah."

"Care to explain to me why her best friend said you were stalking her?"

Silence, followed by that strange laugh. "Stalking her? I wasn't stalking her. You remember Billy Blane? He loved Ringo's Watering Hole across the bridge. That's where the trouble started. We'd go over there on Friday and Saturday nights and tip a few back. A handful of times I walked across the street. Ivy Trent worked at that little ice cream shop there. I'd get an ice cream and flirt with her. She seemed to like it just fine, but then I asked her out and she turned me down flat."

"Okay…"

"I let it get under my skin a bit, that's all. Honestly, I felt like I dodged a bullet with Ivy Trent."

"What does that mean?"

"It's embarrassing, to tell you the truth. One of those nights I was sitting in my truck outside of Ringo's. I'd had a few too many. It was Missy Connor's birthday, and she'd been buying rounds for the bar. The bartender cut me off after I went to hit a ball on the pool table and fell flat on my face. He gave me a Styrofoam cup of coffee and I went to my truck to sober up. I was angry. Angry at the bartender, at my ex-wife, at Ivy for all the times she turned me down. I was angry at my former business partner for screwing me out of my half of the moving business.

"I saw Ivy shut the ice cream parlor down alone. She walked out and got on a bicycle. I followed her home in my truck. She lived a few miles out of town on Tuttle Road, in a double-wide with her ma. I followed her all the way, and she was scared, pedaling like the devil rode behind her.

"The next day I felt like a total shit. I couldn't believe I'd done that. I went to the ice cream shop to apologize. She took one look at me through the window and tore ass into the back, sent her manager out a few minutes later to get rid of me. When she went missing, I was just waiting for the cops to come pounding on my door. They could have caught me in the crosshairs of whatever had gone on with Ivy Trent. I'd brought it on myself, but they never did. I'm surprised to hear that her best friend said that about me. I don't understand why the police never came calling."

"The police never came calling because they believed she ran away because her mother was losing her shit and her father was dead."

"Yeah. I'd heard her dad died when she was young. Too bad."

"Bennie, is there anything you're not telling me about Ivy Trent?"

The strange laugh again. This time it tickled the hairs in Dan's ears in such a way that he wanted to fling the phone out his driver's-side window.

"No, God, no. I never saw her after that day at the ice cream shop. I stopped going to Ringo's after that. I didn't want to risk running into her. I had half a thought if I showed up, her boyfriend or some brawny lad she was chumming around with might come out and pound my head into the pavement."

"That was it, then? Never spoke to her after the day you tried to talk to her at the ice cream shop?"

"Nope, never did. Listen, I gotta jet. Moose is whining at the door. Last thing I need is him pissing on the carpet in here. Place is shitty enough without reeking of dog piss. Before I go, what's got you asking about Ivy Trent, anyway?"

The question was loaded. He could almost see the bead of sweat trickling down Bennie's forehead.

"Came across her poster and started asking around. Thought I'd make myself useful down here."

"Moose, chill, I'm coming. All right, good luck with that, Dan." Bennie ended the call before Dan could respond.

Dan sat and stared through the windshield. He wanted to believe Bennie, but the sound of his brother's voice troubled him. It had a tone he'd heard in interrogation rooms. Fear, desperation, maybe even guilt.

A car pulled into a parking spot near the grocery store, and Dan watched Cass step from her battered Subaru. She disappeared into the store. He climbed from his car and followed her inside.

He walked along the front of the aisles, spotting her by the laundry detergent. She held a bottle in her hand, reading the label.

"Hi," he called, holding up a hand.

She glanced up, studied him for a moment and then smiled. "Dan. How are you?"

He took a few paces down the aisle toward her. "I'm good. I was in the parking lot and saw you come in."

She nodded and held up the detergent. "I'm out and have two hampers full of clothes eyeballing me every night when I go to bed."

He smiled. "I just hit the laundromat myself. Least favorite place on Earth."

"I can relate to that," she agreed, dropping the detergent into her cart.

"Want to put your laundry off for another day and come over for a burger?" He hadn't intended to ask the question. When he'd followed her inside, he'd done it rather stupidly, with barely a thought beyond saying hi.

"At your place?"

"Sure. I've got a grill. I thought I'd get burger fixings and some beer."

"I've got a couple bottles of wine in my car."

"Then wine it is," he said.

She glanced at her cart and then back at him. "No time like the present for putting off laundry. I'll follow you?"

"Perfect," he told her.

21

*D*an and Cass finished the bottle of wine, sitting on a blanket at the end of the little dock that jutted out from Bennie's property. The night had grown cooler, and Dan had brought out an extra blanket, wrapping it around Cass's shoulders.

"My mom died from breast cancer," Cass said. "It hurt. It hurt to see her fade away. She'd always been so shining. She smiled and laughed and twirled. Even as a grown woman you'd see her twirling around the yard when it rained. It was something she and Paw-Paw, my grandpa, did when she was young. It never got old."

"She sounds great."

"She was. What was your mother like?"

Dan eyed the empty bottle of wine. "Another bottle?" he asked.

Cass smiled. "If I have another glass, I'll be in the river when I try to stand up."

Dan nodded. He wanted to get the bottle anyway, avoid the question, but he stayed put. "My mother was… complicated."

"In what way?"

Dan lay back on the dock, stacking his hands beneath his head and gazing at the dark sky. "She suffered from mental illness. I always kept it a secret. We told people she died of a brain aneurism, but she killed herself."

He couldn't see Cass's face from his angle, but he felt her watching him. Deeper, he felt guilt at the revelation. He'd loosed the family secret to a stranger.

"I'm sorry," she told him.

"It happened a long time ago. I was twelve. I came home from school one day and found her in the garage. She'd shot herself in the head in her driver's seat."

"Oh, my God. That's terrible."

"Yeah. It was worse for Bennie, my little brother. He'd stayed home from school sick that day. My mom told him she was running to the store for groceries and he needed to stay in bed until she got home. He didn't, of course. Bennie wanted to go outside and play. He went into the garage to get his skateboard and saw the windows of the car splattered in blood."

"He didn't call the police?"

"He went back in the house, crawled into my parents' closet and hid."

Cass's hand rested softly on his leg. "I'm so sorry, Dan."

He'd told almost no one about his mother's suicide. There'd been an understanding in the family. It would tarnish her memory, their father said. And then they'd moved to a new house in a new town and gone forward with their new story. 'Mom had an aneurism in the garage.' They'd said it so many times it had started to seem like the truth. Dan had never even told Mel. She still believed their mother had simply fallen dead in the garage one day as she left for the store.

His mother's parents had already been dead and her only sibling, a brother who lived in Mexico, rarely called or visited. He too had been told the aneurism story. Only their father's brother and his mother had known the truth. But they too agreed that a small lie was worth it to cover up such a painful truth. Dan had told Louie, his first friend at his new school in Holt. He'd blurted it out one day while they were riding bikes. Louie had kept the secret as closely as his own family had.

"I felt so guilty afterward. She'd asked me to take out the trash that morning, and I'd been in a big rush because it was field day at school. I should have done it. I should have done more to make sure she had a good day."

"That's not how it works." Cass lay down beside him, taking his hand in hers.

"I know that. But I didn't understand it then. I really thought it was all that simple. I should have protected her."

"Protected her from herself?"

"Yeah. She'd tried it before. More than once, I'd bet, but I only remember the one time. My dad busted down the bathroom door. She'd cut her wrists. They went to the hospital and our neighbor came over and sat with me and Bennie. We went to visit her a couple days later and she looked so defeated, as if she'd failed."

"How did Bennie handle her death?"

"Not well. He was angry at her. Maybe he still is. He felt betrayed. How could she abandon us? That kind of thing. But I knew she'd been sad for years. She'd go through these phases where she'd be good for a while, happy and normal, making us lunches and cleaning the house. Then she'd kind of slip into a funk and it would just get darker and darker until some days she didn't get out of bed."

"How about your dad? What did he do?"

"He did his best to pick up the slack during those times. Maybe that's why I felt so much responsibility because he'd kind of put it on me. 'Take tea to your mom,' 'go cheer up your mom,' 'check on your mom.' To his credit, he was busy. He worked full time at the cereal plant, he had to take care of the house, run us kids everywhere. It was a lot, more than most people can handle, and he did it without complaining. He never got mad at her either. I rarely saw him yell."

"I can't imagine," Cass murmured.

"Me either," Dan said. "The life, I mean, his life. Two sons, a depressed wife."

"Is he still alive?"

"No. He passed a few years ago from a heart attack. He was mowing his lawn and just... went down on his knees."

Cass sat up and gazed at him.

Dan tilted his face to look at her. He hadn't expected her to kiss him, but when she did, he felt something break free, as if he'd been carrying a backpack full of sand and the straps had snapped. She tasted like the wine. Her hair was long and silky, falling across his cheek, and just that sensation alone, the cool sheet of her hair, filled him with deep and utter peace. Not desire, though that was there too. It was the absolute calm that he noticed, the wave of okayness he hadn't felt in so long he almost wanted to cry at the sensation.

"Take me to bed, Dan," she murmured into his ear.

$\sim$

IN THE MORNING, Dan walked out to Cass, who was wearing one of Bennie's old sweatshirts. She sat, pantless, her bare legs tucked beneath her on the ratty plaid chair. His file for Mia Knox lay open on her lap.

He froze, breath catching, both hands braced against the door frame.

She heard him and looked up, her frown tilting into a smile. "Good morning," she said, though the words faded as she gazed at him. She glanced at the papers in her lap and then quickly shut the folder and returned it to the cardboard box. "I'm sorry. It was sitting out. I didn't mean to…"

Dan found his breath and strode into the room. He almost snatched the box from the floor, almost shouted, but some niggling voice that sounded a lot like his ex-wife was reminding him why she left—the brooding, the outbursts.

"It's okay," he said stiffly. "Want some coffee?" He made an abrupt turn and headed for the kitchen. She'd already made a pot.

"I could use a warm-up," she said, coming to stand beside him at the counter.

Dan stared hard at the mugs. He was struggling to choose one, to see their shapes in the tumult of images and facts rolling through his head.

LEFT SCHOOL AT THREE-FIFTEEN, *witnessed petting Mr. Vilmore's dog on Parsnips Road, purple Velcro wallet missing from her bedroom, never picked up her last check at Leona's Diner where she bussed tables on Saturday afternoons, no proof of life after May seventeen, 2008.*

"DAN?" Cass touched his elbow, and he jumped, knocking her coffee mug against the edge of the counter. It splattered the remains of her lukewarm coffee on Bennie's sweatshirt.

"Fuck," he bellowed and his words had an edge, an accusation.

Cass stepped back. She set the mug on the counter and turned, walked back toward the living room. He watched her pull on her jeans, yank off Bennie's sweatshirt. She reached for her own.

Dan stayed rooted in place, watching, waiting as she picked up her purse and made for the door.

He'd stop her, grab her hand, and pull her back.

He didn't.

She didn't look back at him, but instead walked out into the half-light of morning. He heard the rumble of her car engine and then that too faded, and he was left with his breath, quick and loud, and the barely discernible hum of the coffeepot.

"Way to go, Dan," he muttered.

Dan didn't bother with coffee. Unable to help himself, he walked to the box and sat down, pulled the file off the top, peeled it open.

A picture of Mia was paper-clipped to the left side. She sat on a boulder, knees pulled to her chest. Her jeans had holes in both knees and she wore a red t-shirt, the logo blocked by her legs. Her dirty blonde hair was long over each shoulder. She smiled, revealing teeth covered in braces. Her gray-blue eyes looked bright.

She'd been fourteen when she'd disappeared less than two years before.

Her face haunted him. He'd stared at the picture a thousand times, more. He'd read the words in the file until they'd become seared in his memory.

May seventeenth, 2009. She'd gotten up that morning and gone to school. She walked, as she did every morning, with her best friend Kimberly, who lived one block over. Mia wore white jeans and a pale blue v-neck t-shirt that was short enough to reveal a sliver of skin above her waistline. Her hair had been loose, the way she always wore it. She'd talked about getting her braces off that Friday, about the winter dance two weeks away. She'd been invited by Freddie LaSalle, another eighth grader who she'd had a crush on for months.

Mia and her mother were going dress-shopping that weekend. Kimberly hadn't been asked to the dance, so she was going stag with several other girlfriends. She was disappointed and a little jealous, but mostly happy for Mia, who had a harder life than Kimberly. Kim's parents were still married, and they made sure she had a new backpack and school clothes every year.

Mia didn't get those things. Her single mother, Erin, worked at a grocery store and barely made ends meet. Sometimes she babysat other people's kids or cleaned houses on weekends. Mia wore hand-me-down clothes and got free lunch at school.

That day Mia had her normal classes. She attended all of them. She aced her pop quiz in history. She got her best time in the mile during gym class. No one reported that Mia seemed sad, that she spoke of running away. It was a perfectly ordinary day, a good day. At lunch she sat with Kimberly and a few of their other friends. Mia got the taco salad and a chocolate-chip cookie. After school she walked home alone because Kimberly had choir practice.

That was where the timeline skewed. She'd normally take Main Street to Gilmore Drive, turn right, follow that two blocks, left on Sycamore and reach her house, the third on the block, left side of the road. But this day, she'd taken Main to Parsnips and turned right. She'd stopped to pet Mr. Vilmore's dog, a five-year-old Dalmatian who jumped at the fence when Mia walked by. She petted the dog and waved hello to Bernadette Crisp, who was across the street washing her car in the driveway.

And then nothing. No other sightings. Mia continued down the street and vanished into thin air.

Had she ever made it home? Had someone abducted her in the three blocks between the Dalmatian and her own home? Had one of the residents lured her inside? Had she made it home and left again? Had she called someone for a ride and been picked up?

Those were the unanswered questions, the questions that had plagued Dan. The questions he'd gone over again and again while sitting at Erin's pockmarked kitchen table until one night she'd offered him a drink. He'd said no a hundred times. Mel was waiting for him at home. He'd already been coming home too late for weeks. But that night he'd said yes, and the drink had ended with a kiss.

Dan barely remembered sleeping with Erin that first night. He only remembered the desperation in that kiss, the way she'd sobbed against him, and then the affair that would end his marriage and likely his career had begun. The lust and the fervor to find Mia had all become tangled, warped.

In the end, he'd failed. Failed at finding Mia, at helping Erin, at healing his marriage, at keeping his job. He'd failed on every possible level and the sight of Mia's picture brought the same knot to his stomach. He pulled it from the paperclip and started to tear it in half, but stopped halfway down the photograph. Mia's bright eyes weakened him. He let go and watched the picture drift to the floor.

Beside him sat Ivy Trent's picture. She smiled from the missing person's poster. Two young women, unrelated, gone without a trace.

*D*an almost took a shower and then noticed he still smelled of Cass, so he skipped it, sliding on jeans and a long t-shirt. He walked outside to the wood pile and picked up Bennie's axe, swung and chopped wood until sweat poured down his face and his shoulders ached. His phone beeped from the stump where he'd set it, a rare moment of cell service. He walked over and picked it up to see two new voicemail messages.

He listened to his messages. The first was from his dental office in Novi, reminding him he was due for a cleaning. The woman's voice cut in and out as he played. He deleted the message and listened to the next.

"Hi, this is Sally Mitchell returning your call."

Sally the psychic. He went to his car and climbed behind the wheel, not wanting to risk losing service while they spoke. As he drove the road toward Black Pine, he called her back.

The woman answered after the first ring. "Hello," she said.

"Hi, is this Sally Mitchell? This is Dan Webb."

"Dan Webb? Ah, yes, the detective."

"Yeah. I got your number from Louie McDougall. He's a detective in—"

"Farmington Hills. Yes, I'm familiar with Louie. How can I help you, Dan?"

The question in his mind was, 'Don't you already know?' And he had a glimmer of how irritating it must be for psychics, the expectation they knew everything coupled with a constant badgering to prove their knowledge.

"I'm looking into a case informally, a missing woman in Black Pine, West Virginia. I... well, I've had some weird experiences that I'm trying to put into context."

"Such as?"

Dan stared through the windshield, watching trees pass, wondering why it felt hard to even tell a psychic of the things he'd seen. "I think I might have seen her, the missing woman."

"Alive?"

"No."

"You believe her spirit is reaching out to you?"

"Something like that."

"Dan, I'm in Michigan. If you can send me something of the woman's I might be able to help, but I have a friend in your vicinity. Howard Mazur is his name. You can visit him in Huntington, West Virginia. Perhaps he'd be able to help you understand the experiences you're having."

"Sure, yeah. Sally, just out of curiosity, do you get any kind of... like..."

"Impression about your missing girl?"

"Yeah. Is that possible while we're talking on the phone like this or...?"

"It's not impossible. Give me a moment to see what comes up."

He waited in silence, listening to the woman breathe.

After several moments, she cleared her throat and spoke. "I'm getting a vision of leaves and vines—the sort of thing that crawls up the walls and lattice."

"Ivy," he whispered.

"Yes. I don't know if that's relevant. Another image I'm getting is... well, it's a hole in a floor. A crawl space, perhaps. I don't know if that's connected, but there you have it."

"Anything else?"

Sally didn't answer for a moment. "You're very muddled, Dan, conflicted. There's a lot happening within you, I think. So many things, it's hard to be clear on what I might connect to the missing girl. Woman, she's a woman, but... well, oddly I sense a girl too.

Again, I can't quite distinguish her, but if you'd like to send me something..."

"Yeah, let me ask her mom. What's your address, Sally?" He leaned over and popped the glove box open, pulled out a scratch pad and pencil, keeping his eyes on the road.

He wrote down Sally's address as well as the number for Howard Mazur. After he ended the call, he immediately punched in Mazur's number. A man answered breathlessly on the third ring.

"Hello?"

"Hi, is this Howard Mazur?"

"Yes, yes, this is he."

"My name is Dan Webb. I'm a detective looking into a crime in West Virginia. I received your number from Sally Mitchell."

"Sally bade you call me? Well, Sally knows, oh, yes, she surely does. How can I help you, Detective Webb?"

"I wondered if we could talk face to face? I've had some odd experiences—"

"Give me twenty minutes and I'll be ready for you." The man rattled off an address and ended the call before Dan could say more.

Dan drove to Huntington, using the small GPS navigator Bennie had bought him for Christmas two years before, which was stuck to the inner windshield of the car. He rarely used it, concerned that relying on the thing would dull his own powers of memory, but he'd never been to Huntington and didn't care to fiddle with a map.

The address Mazur shared led Dan to a squat cinder block building that had been painted bright blue. There was no sign outside and only a single small truck stood in the parking lot.

The glass door revealed a long, carpeted hallway. Dan knocked on the glass. A man popped his head out from a room and then hurried out, pulled open the door. He was nearly as tall as Dan, but quite thin, with large spectacles magnifying his brown eyes.

"Hello, hello," the man told him distractedly. He waved Dan into the building.

"Howard Mazur?" Dan asked.

"The last time I looked in the mirror anyhow. Follow me. We'll go to my office."

"I tried to call back and let you know it would take longer than twenty minutes for me to drive here, but your line was busy," Dan told him.

Mazur nodded. "Sure, sure. My work always seems to muddle the lines of communication. Not a problem, though. Those who need to get in touch always find a way."

Dan followed him down a long hallway that ended in three doors. Mazur pushed open the door on the right, revealing a square office lined with bookshelves. A huge oak desk stood in the room, buried in loose-leaf papers and folders. An ancient-looking computer sat on a card table. More paperwork lay scattered around the table and on the floor beneath it.

"Have a seat." He pointed at a folding chair stacked with books. "Just pop those onto the floor. Don't mind the state of things."

Dan eyed the title of the book on the top of the stack. *Principles of Astrological Geomancy* by Frantz Hartman. Dan didn't know what geomancy was, let alone the rest of it. He slid the books under the chair and sat down.

"What do you do?" Dan asked. He'd envisioned something more... New Agey, misty fountains and crystals hanging from silver thread.

The man didn't bother clearing his own chair; he sat directly on top of a stack of books, cleaning his glasses on his shirt before gazing at Dan through inquisitive eyes. "I am a scientist of the unusual, the indeterminate, the unreliable."

"Which means what exactly?"

The man chuckled. "Most of us know extraordinary things happen in this world. Impossible things. Things that will never happen twice no matter how many double-blind ultra-controlled research studies we set up. I have devoted my life's work to exploring those things. Forget laboratories. I go into people's homes, into the forest, into abandoned hospitals. I see it with my own two eyes.

"Let me tell you, there is nothing more real than that. No scientific journal will ever convince me more than firsthand experience, and that is why, despite the scientific community's desperation to refute paranormal activity, most people still believe in ghosts. Because most people have had their own otherworldly encounter. They might never tell a soul, but there's been some"—he fluttered his hand—"glitch in the matrix, if you will, shudder between dimensions that allowed them to glimpse that all is not as it seems."

Dan nodded, leaning forward on his chair. He'd been a skeptic his entire life, but the man's words resonated. "What about seeing something that's already happened? Like, let's say a car crash happened twenty years ago and yesterday a kid was walking down the street and saw that crash. But then he blinks and the cars are gone. Is that possible?"

The man smiled. "If it happened, it's possible. Isn't it?"

"Well, yeah. But have you seen things like that or heard of people who have?"

"Yes. Both."

"And what does it mean?"

"I don't presume to ascribe meaning to anything, my dear man. I'm the unbiased recorder of events. However, I think you'd like to know why it happens, and for that, I have a theory. Case studies suggest that people rarely witness mundane past events, such as a woman walking to get her mail or a child riding a bicycle. However, if that woman is shot by her husband while retrieving the mail or a vehicle strikes the child, then we have a situation more likely to leave an energetic impression."

"An energetic impression?"

Mazur nodded. "A tear in the fabric of reality, perhaps. An imprint on the energetic structure of that place, so powerful that time does not rewrite it. I don't know the science behind it. I would love to, of course. What I know is that it has happened before and it will happen again. Traumatic events leave a trace not only in here"—he tapped his head—"but out there as well."

"And anyone might come along and witness this vision from the past?"

The man held out his empty palms. "Again, I don't have an answer, but I don't think so. Everything is connected. You are not merely there while I am here. We are two bodies composed of billions of cells vibrating in harmony. You are affecting the energy of this room, including the desk, the chairs, the curtains and, of course, me. My energy is affecting you.

"I believe when a person witnesses a past event, something in their energy has lined up perfectly with the energy of the place and the energy of the past event to cause their eye to perceive that previous thing. Are some people more capable of this? Yes, I hazard to say they are. Psychics, mediums. Label them however you like, but many of them have a special openness, a resonance that allows them to perceive things that many of us might sweep past oblivious to.

"My own focus on these studies for forty years has created a resonance of sorts in me. Still, that doesn't mean I am psychic. I'm no Sally Mitchell. I cannot predict the future; I can't read your past. Not at all. Instead, if I am in a right place at a right time for some paranormal occurrence, I am more likely to see it than someone who is busy checking their watch as they hurry to work."

Dan considered the explanation, which again resonated, but left him no closer to answers.

"If you would permit me," Mazur said, standing and hurrying to one of his bookshelves. His hands moved in a flurry across the tops of the crammed books. He held up a tape recorder. "Found it! I must have ten of these, but I set one down and"—he waved a hand—"this room just gobbles it up."

"You want to tape-record my story?"

"Yes, please. And I see from your expression this makes you uncomfortable, but let me assure you I work in the strictest confidence. No one will hear this recording except me."

"What will you do with it?"

Mazur returned to his chair, resting the recorder on a stack of books on his desk. "I will study it, search for commonalities between your stories and other such experiences. I will, at some future point, visit the site of the event and take some samples."

"Samples?"

"Oh, yes, soil, vegetation, water if it's available. I will measure EMFs and changes in temperature from one area to the next. I have done this…" He scrunched his brow. "Fifty or sixty times at least. It's not a vast library of samples, but it's growing. I will also bring a psychic or medium to the site at some later date, and they will record their own impressions. They're in the dark, of course, in order to get a pure impression rather than something skewed by prior knowledge. It's quite an undertaking but a worthwhile one."

"And this is work you do for a living?"

"Oh, yes. In the beginning it was a labor of love fueled by my own curiosity and what I could spare from my day job as a professor, but over time, it grew and grew. I never sought donors, they simply appeared. A young lady deals with the finances these days. She's quite good, keen mind." He tapped on his temple. "And much more"—he looked at his cluttered office—"put together than I am. You must always work within your strengths, I say. Which is why I am looking into the science of your encounter and you, a detective, are investigating the abduction. It's truly amazing how all come to this world with a gift."

"Okay," Dan said. "I'll do the recording."

Dan folded his hands in his lap and recounted his story beginning with his drive to Bennie's cabin and how, within an hour of his arrival, he'd sat down on the wooden stool and put his eye to the telescope. He recounted Ivy lying on the beach, the man creeping through the woods behind her, and then the abduction itself.

"I've wondered if it could have been a prank, a practical joke," Dan admitted, "but there's no way. For one thing, they could never have known I was watching. Two, I saw her face. It was real. And three..." His eyes flicked to Mazur. The man watched him with complete absorption. "It's her on the missing person's poster. There's no question about that. The girl I saw abducted is the same girl who disappeared ten years ago."

After Dan finished telling his story, Mazur asked him to draw a detailed map of the location Ivy was abducted.

"How soon will you do your experiments or whatever?" Dan asked, gesturing at Mazur's notes. He suddenly wondered if the man's findings might get him closer to discovering what happened to Ivy.

"Soon, I should think, though I must reach out to a medium I have in mind. She may not be available."

"There's something else," Dan said. He hadn't told Mazur about seeing the apparition of Ivy Trent, nor the haunting piano music. "I think I've seen her ghost."

Mazur scratched his chin and lifted one eyebrow. "This is a separate experience from witnessing the abduction?"

"Yes. I went into an inn that's near the cabin I'm staying at. It's been closed for a decade, but Ivy worked there the summer she disappeared."

Mazur nodded slowly. "She's chosen you."

"But what do I do now? I'm a detective, for Christ's sake. I can't put a ghost on a witness stand. What does she expect me to do with this information?"

The man looked at him, amused. "Well, let's consider for a moment why she chose you. You're a detective. You investigate crimes. If someone sent you an anonymous letter about an abduction and murder, you couldn't put the letter-writer on the stand, but you'd still have to build your case. So build your case. Think of it this way, Detective Webb. You're being handed a gift, insight from a source who knows intimate details of the crime. Maybe she can't communicate in the standard way, but she or something is communicating with you. It's your job now to find the cold hard facts, isn't that what you say in the police business?"

"I've been trying. I'm banging my head against the wall, trying to get information about the last days of Ivy's life."

"Everything leaves a trace, Detective Webb. Find the traces."

It was dark when Dan returned to Bennie's cabin. The glow from the television lit the window and yet he hadn't watched TV that day. He'd never turned the set on and he definitely hadn't left it on.

Dan stepped from his car, drew his Beretta and released the safety. He could hear the television from within the cabin. It was blaring as if someone had cranked it to full volume.

He crept to the door and pressed himself against the cabin exterior, scanning the property, but the dark woods made it impossible to make out if someone crouched nearby. His flashlight was inside the cabin.

Moving along the exterior, Dan peeked in windows, searching for an intruder, but the cabin looked unchanged. He saw no one tucked into a corner. Finally, after he'd walked the entire exterior and returned to the door, Dan twisted the knob and shoved the door open, leading with his gun.

He went straight to the television and flipped it off, but the movement didn't cast the cabin into silence. Instead, more sounds found him. Rushing water. The kitchen faucet was turned on, water pouring into the sink.

He turned slowly, gun raised, searching for movement. Nothing. He went to the sink and turned the handle to the off position.

More rushing water sounded from the bathroom. Dan pushed the door to the bathroom open with his foot and reached in, flicking on the light. It was empty, but both the sink and bathtub faucet were cranked all the way to the left, water surging out and into the drains. He turned off each, skin prickling over his arms and neck.

No other sounds met his ears, but he moved methodically through the cabin, searching the two bedrooms and the closets before returning to the front door and locking it.

"*D*o you know Cassidy Osborne?" Dan asked Herb as he set the batteries on the counter the next day.

Herb grinned and elbowed Sadie, who stood beside him at the register. "What did I tell ya?" he asked his wife.

"Oh, stop it, you meddlesome old goat." She grabbed the batteries and scanned the package.

"We sure do know Cass. I take it you've met her?"

Dan wondered at the gleam in Herb's eye. "Am I missing the joke?"

Herb shook his head dramatically. "Oh, no, not at all. No jokers around here."

Sadie rolled her eyes. "Herb fancies himself a matchmaker, though he's like to put a raccoon and a cow together on account they both have tails."

Dan laughed, but Herb's amused smile didn't waver. "Sadie, my love, you're forgetting about Paula Blossom and Mitchell Redfox, not to mention Howard Shuck and Janice Tippens. And let's not leave out—"

"Sure, sure, we get the point, Herb, you're the guru of love. That will be five ninety-five."

Dan pulled out his wallet and extracted a ten-dollar bill.

"It's Tuesday?" Herb asked, scratching a bit of fluffy hair by his temple. "Cass leads tours at Paradise Park on Tuesday and Thursday. You'll find her there." Herb winked at him.

Sadie handed him his change and jostled Herb aside, moving closer to the counter. "Annabelle told me you stopped by to talk to her about Ivy. I just wanted to say thank you, Detective Webb. I haven't heard that much hope in her voice in years. I knew someone would come along and revive Ivy's case. I just knew it."

"Knew it, did ya? Sadie fancies herself some kind of clairvoyant."

"Herb Dwiggins, I swear—" She spun around.

Herb held up his hands as if Sadie meant to beat him around the head.

"Have you guys ever been out to the Dark River Inn?" Dan asked.

Sadie paused, dropping the hand she'd raised to swat her husband, and turned back to Dan. She pursed her lips. "Hardly. The Inn was not meant for townies, Detective. I'm quite sure the Drakes converted the inn with some high-falutin' visions of presidents and oil moguls."

Herb grinned. "Not true, not true at all. My brother and his wife stayed at the Dark River Inn every year for their big holiday prime rib dinner."

Sadie rolled her eyes. "Your brother's an attorney and happened to be on the board of zoning appeals. The only reason they got an invite was because Richard Drake wanted that building outside of town zoned commercial—"

"Oh, pish-posh," Herb said, fluttering his hand by Sadie's face to silence her. "Richard and Ellen Drake are fine people. Do they have money? They sure do, more than most of the good people of Black Pine will see in a lifetime, but they're also generous. The library, the new high school gymnasium, the addition at the urgent care, all courtesy of the Drakes."

"And don't forget the wetlands that are now a three-story parking structure. We have the Drakes to thank for that as well."

Herb started to argue, but Dan interrupted them. "The Drakes' son took the inn over? A man by the name of James?"

Herb made a face. "Now there is an apple who fell mightily far from the tree. None of his father's modesty or integrity. He ran that place into the ground in record time."

"His wife makes hornets look friendly," Sadie added.

"Finally, something we agree on, my love," Herb said, grabbing Sadie's hand and kissing her fingers.

She shot him an irritated look, but didn't pull her hand away.

"Were they involved in the search for Ivy Trent at all? Did they offer a reward? She worked at the inn the summer she disappeared."

Sadie arched her eyebrows. "The way I heard it, James and Regina Drake wanted nothing more than to distance themselves from Ivy's disappearance. In fact, we had a girl who worked here one summer who said after Ivy went missing, the staff at the Dark River Inn was forbidden to speak her name."

"That seems rather extreme."

"It's also a rumor," Herb chimed in. "Not saying it ain't true," he quickly added when Sadie glared at him.

"Any other rumors about the inn and Ivy?"

"Like what?" Sadie asked.

Dan considered offering the potential connection between Ivy and James, but if he said it now, he'd have to question every person who mentioned it in the future. He couldn't afford to start the rumor himself. He needed to know if it already existed. "Nothing in particular."

Through the window, Dan watched a black Mercedes Benz convertible pull to the curb. A man with slicked-back pale blond hair climbed from the car, pulling off his dark glasses and tucking them into the breast pocket of his dark blazer.

"Who's that?" Dan asked.

"Carter Trent," Sadie said, wrinkling her nose.

"Ivy's uncle?"

She huffed. "I'd hardly call him that. The Trents did their very best to distance themselves from poor Annabelle and Ivy. Cut out their own brother for choosing a small-town woman."

"Any rumors about the Trents and Ivy? Johnny's family?"

"Not that I heard. You'd think they would have put some pressure on the sheriff, put up some reward money or something, but they never uttered a word about Ivy, not a single word."

"Thanks, guys," Dan said, holding up the batteries and walking backwards toward the door.

"Keep us updated on developments," Sadie called as Dan slipped outside.

～

DAN FOUND Cass standing thigh-deep in the river. The group she led had spread out. One man stood close to her, face wrinkled in frustration. Dan saw why. His line was tangled in the lures that decorated his hat.

Cass shot an occasional glance toward the man, but didn't help him. She looked slightly amused.

As Dan walked along the bank, he saw Cass noticed him, though her face remained expressionless.

He waved at her and then found a spot on the ridge of the dune to sit and wait. It was a half hour before she made her way into the shore. Dan didn't mind. Sitting on the river was peaceful, slightly less so thanks to the man who'd tangled his line. He'd finally untangled it only to trip over a rock in the river and go splashing forward face first. Cass had held out a hand to him, and the man had looked stricken and miserable. He'd managed to get his line out, though.

"What do you need, Dan?" Cass asked, pausing on the sand and unclipping the suspenders on her waders. She let them drop and stepped out of the heavy rubber boots. She wore faded jeans and red wool socks. Her sweatshirt stated 'I'm Wild and Wonderful in West Virginia' in yellow block letters.

"I'm sorry about the other day, Cass."

"Water under the bridge."

"If that's true, then you'll join me for lunch?"

She revealed no emotion, just looked back toward the group. They'd begun to wade back up the river in her direction. The clumsy one was struggling with his line again. "A couple of these folks want to take me to lunch, so I'm on the hook for that. Pun intended."

"Meet me after for a drink."

She sighed and reached back to her dark ponytail, adjusting the little elastic band that held it in place. "Is this a social call or something else? I get the sense you have something on your mind."

"I do, but I also just wanted to see you. I've been thinking about you... a lot."

She arched both eyebrows but said nothing. "We're grabbing lunch at the Taco Palace. There's a bar nearby, Ringo's. We can grab a drink in there."

The name 'Ringo's' caused the hairs on Dan's neck to rise, but he nodded. "Great. Ringo's it is."

---

*R*ingo's was a hole. A place Dan was not surprised Bennie had once frequented, but was surprised Cass did.

When she walked in nearly an hour later, he'd devoured a plate of nachos and half a beer. He considered ordering a second brew, but asked for coffee instead. Beer made him sleepy, not to mention forgetful.

"Hi, Beetle," Cass called to the bartender, giving him a wave. "I'll take a tonic water when you get a sec."

The burly man with a full dark beard might have smiled, though it was hard to see his lips beneath the coarse hair. "I'm on it," he told her.

"Beetle?" Dan asked as Cass took the chair across from him.

"Jerome, according to his birth certificate, but you'd be hard pressed to find anyone who calls him that. His daddy was Ringo, the owner of this place, and Beetle grew up here in the bar. His parents had a place out back. He carried a shoebox with beetles in it everywhere. He was constantly adding leaves and grass and bits of French fries when he sat up at the bar. He'd show off his beetles to all the customers. Earned him a nickname that stuck."

"Beetle," Dan mused. "There are worse nicknames."

"Yep, there are."

"You know a lot about the people in this town? Their history?"

Cass shrugged. "It's a small town and I've lived here for most of my life, if you cut out those ten years in law school and working at a firm."

Beetle appeared with Cass's drink and Dan's coffee. He flicked his gaze at Dan, giving him a more appraising look than the one Dan had received when he'd first walked in an hour before. Cass sipped her drink and said nothing.

"I really am sorry for the other morning, Cass. I... Mia Knox is part of the reason I'm here. She disappeared from Novi, Michigan less than two years ago."

"You were the detective assigned to her case?"

He shook his head. "There was no detective assigned to her case. They thought she was a runaway. Her grandmother came to me, insisted the girl wouldn't run. I knew the grandmother. She worked at the bagel shop I stopped at for a coffee and bagel most mornings. I started looking into it and I agreed. Nothing in Mia's life pointed towards a runaway."

"What about her parents?"

Dan shifted in his chair, the weight of regret tugging him down. "No dad, just a single mom. Erin. She was distraught. She didn't know if Mia had run away, but the more we talked about it, the more unlikely it seemed. I guess Erin wanted to believe it, but couldn't. I got in too deep. I chased every lead for a year, most of it on my own time because the department didn't buy a story of foul play."

"Why, though? If you didn't think so and neither did her mother or grandmother?"

"There were a few things. She'd taken off several times after fights with her mom, but she always ended up at her grandmother's house. Her school I.D. card was found at a bus station. She'd stolen fifty dollars from her mom's purse. Little things that pointed to the possibility that she took off, but my gut told me otherwise."

"You never found her?"

Dan shook his head. "I... I couldn't do anything else, think of anything else. My marriage failed. I started neglecting the cases I was assigned to."

"Your marriage failed?"

"I had an affair with Erin Knox." He watched her face as the words registered, but Cass didn't look taken aback or disgusted.

He'd only spoken those words once before to Melanie. He'd never said it out loud to anyone else. It had been after she'd already left. She showed up at their townhouse one night demanding answers.

'Just tell me,' Mel had begged. 'Tell me so I know I wasn't crazy for thinking it.'

He hadn't wanted to tell her, had still been clinging to the notion that once he'd solved Mia's case, he and Mel would get back together, attend couples' counseling, go on a second honeymoon, whatever it took.

But he'd stood there in the dark yard, the moon white overhead. Mel's eyes had been red-rimmed, her face thin. She too had been paying for his obsession. She'd lost weight in the previous months, looked gaunt beneath the moonlight, and he'd understood then the damage his lies were causing. Mel deserved so much more than that.

'Yes,' he'd said finally. 'Only for a couple of months, but yes. It was happening.'

She'd let out a little guttural cry—anguish and relief rolled into one. He thought she whispered 'I knew it,' but he couldn't be sure. Then she'd walked to her car, climbed behind the wheel and driven away.

"Your wife found out?"

Dan nodded. "I came to my brother's cabin in Drake to get my head right, then I stumbled on Ivy Trent's case." He imagined telling Cass that he'd witnessed Ivy's abduction through the telescope, but closed his mouth instead.

"Are you still a detective, Dan?"

He shrugged. "I don't know. I'm on suspension. They're reviewing my conduct in the Mia Knox case. I didn't fight it."

Cass frowned and sipped her drink. "So you came here to get away and now you're digging into the disappearance of Ivy Trent?"

Dan sighed and wrapped his hands around his mug of coffee. "Apparently I'm a glutton for punishment."

"Maybe you don't want to be a detective anymore? Then again, maybe you're so much a detective that you can't let it rest when you see injustice in the world."

He smiled. "That makes me sound much more honorable than I am. I'm tenacious, that's about it."

"But you are seeking the truth. You are fighting for people who can't fight for themselves."

He took a drink. "That was the point in the beginning. When I went into the academy, when I pushed to become a detective, but... I don't know what it's about now. The families are part of it, they are, but there's also this..." He closed his eyes and searched for the elusive word that could describe that sense of drive, that inability to put it away until he'd uncovered every facet of the thing. "Compulsion. I don't know what else to call it."

Cass swirled the little black plastic straw in her glass. "Compulsion," she repeated. "That makes it sound negative."

"It hasn't felt very positive lately."

"And what is my role in all this? A distraction from the compulsion?" Her tone wasn't angry. She watched him again, her expression unreadable.

"You ask me like I know." He chuckled. "I don't know, Cass. I don't have ulterior motives—well, not entirely. I saw you and... you felt good to me. Like someone at ease in the world. I haven't felt that in a long time. This place has been helping me, it really has, but it's also presented this mystery, this horrible mystery, and I can't turn away from it."

"You shouldn't turn away from it. Maybe everything else that happened occurred to bring you to this moment, to uncover what happened to Ivy."

"Fate? An all-powerful orchestrator of the universe?"

Cass studied him. "I'm not sure we can define it. I'm not sure we should even try. I told you my story, Dan. I don't need anyone to convince me there's more to life than this." She waved a hand dismissively at the room.

He looked beyond her to the men slumped at the bar, to the table of couples eating burgers and fries, eyes fixed on a basketball game playing on the TV suspended in the room's corner. It all looked very flimsy—dull and sad beneath the dim orange lights.

"It's sleazy to feel jealous of someone who nearly died in a car crash, but if it could give me some of your faith, maybe it's worth it."

"Then again, maybe you'd have just died or woken up and remembered nothing. We get what we need, I think. I needed that."

"And apparently I need to keep repeating the same mistake again and again until my brain explodes."

She took a drink. "What is it you want, Dan? I don't doubt you wanted to see me, but what else do you want?"

"I want to find out what happened to Ivy. You're local and I'm very much an outsider. I need someone on the inside."

Cass laughed. "I live in a remote cabin outside of town. I fish and go to the grocery store. I'm not the kind of local you need."

"I disagree. You've lived in Black Pine your whole life. Do you remember Ivy's case? Did you know her or her family?"

Cass finished her drink. "Hot tea, Beetle?" she called. "Have any of your lavender chamomile?"

"Just brought in a fresh batch yesterday," he told her, reaching beneath the counter and pulling out a plastic bag filled with tea satchels.

"Lavender chamomile tea? That's an odd beverage choice for this place," Dan commented.

"Beetle makes it himself and sells it at their local farmer's market. He grows the chamomile in his garden."

"I would not have pegged him as a tea maker or a gardener."

"People will surprise you if you let them," Cass said. "To answer your question, I did know Ivy, small town and all, but not well. I gradu- ated a decade ahead of her, but I remember when her dad died, Johnny. My mother knew Johnny and she was pretty heartbroken by the whole deal, for Annabelle too. My mom knew all too well the life of a single mom, so she related to her. She died the year after Ivy went missing, but she called me in Columbus when it happened. Said Annabelle was running all over town screaming that someone had abducted her daughter. Sheriff Dowker was saying she'd gone insane, the usual small-town drama."

"You weren't in the area when she vanished?"

Cass shook her head.

"How about the Drakes? Know them at all?"

Cass smiled at Beetle as he dropped off her cup of tea. "I knew of them. It's impossible to live in this town and not know the name Drake."

"Did you know James and Regina Drake personally?"

"Yeah. Not Regina, but James. Believe it or not, he and I went out a few times when I was in high school. His family lived across the river in the summer, at the place they converted to the inn. He and I met on the beach on the Black Pine side of the Ohio, the same stretch where you and I met. Nobody uses that beach anymore, but we used to go down there all the time in my school days. There was this funky tree we'd throw our shoes into. We called it the skeleton tree." She laughed.

"Stupid, the things we do when we're kids. Anyway, I met James down there at a beach bonfire one night and we ended up dating the rest of the summer."

"What was he like?"

"He was... insecure. That's what I think of when I remember James. His dad and his brothers and sister were such big achievers. He had a very high bar set for his life and he talked about it a lot, how he'd been the runt in the litter, the thick one, the short one, the dull one. Which was strange because all the girls in Black Pine thought he was Mr. Wonderful."

"But not you."

Cass tilted her head. "I did, but more than that, I saw he was human. He wasn't the fantasy people imagined when they looked at the Drakes. He was vulnerable, real. But never in front of anyone. When people were watching, he was all show. That's what did us in. I couldn't handle the public persona. He was two different people. In private he was quiet, introspective, self-deprecating even. In public he was boastful, arrogant. It got old."

"When did it end?"

"Right before I started my junior year. I broke things off, and I heard the next year he'd gotten engaged."

"Did you guys stay in touch?"

"Not really. We've seen each other around town over the years. After my accident, he sent this big bouquet of flowers up to the hospital in Columbus. I thanked him once when I was back in town, but I got this look from his wife like she didn't know about the flowers and she didn't appreciate the sentiment. I steered clear of him after that. What's past is past."

"Did you ever hear anything about James being unfaithful to Regina?"

"Do you think he was involved with Ivy Trent?"

Dan studied her. "That's a big leap."

Cass looked amused. "It's where you were going, though, right? James Drake and Ivy Trent?"

"I've wondered, yeah."

Cass pulled out the tea bag and rested it on the saucer beneath her cup. "It's not a stretch. I can say that. James was the kind of guy who always had something to prove. In my opinion, there are a few ways men like him do that." Cass held up three fingers. "Fast car, trophy girl-friend, and fancy house. He's got the car and house."

"He's also got a wife and children."

"He sure does."

"Did you ever hear any direct rumors that involved Ivy and James?"

Cass sighed. "I told you my paw-paw's place is on the river."

"Yeah."

"Well, the summer that Ivy went missing, I came back for my yearly visit. My mom had moved in with my paw-paw because she'd gotten the diagnosis and needed help. In the morning, Paw-Paw and I would fish, but one morning in June he ran into town to get maple syrup. I was getting my gear on and heard voices. I looked through the binoculars and saw a little rowboat. There were two people in it, kissing, laughing. I could see James, but the girl had her back to me."

"Any chance it was his wife?"

Cass shook her head. "Dark curly hair, long down her back. Regina Drake has dark hair, but it's always been short and stick-straight. It wasn't her."

"Ivy Trent had black curly hair."

"I know."

Dan picked at the remnants of the chip crumbs on his nacho plate. "I wondered if you could look into James's finances for me. You mentioned you were a finance lawyer."

"I'm not an attorney anymore."

"I know. But I thought you might still have some connections." She didn't say anything at first. He was grateful she at least didn't look pissed at the request. "How will this help you find Ivy?"

"I'm not sure it will. I'm following leads, chasing hunches. Some-times you just have to keep tugging strings until the whole thing unravels."

"And you believe her disappearance is connected to James Drake?"

"I've talked to a lot of people and this is the closest thing I've come to a lead in terms of who Ivy might have been seeing. I have to look more closely." He didn't mention the other things, the unexplainable things that put Ivy in the Dark River Inn.

"I'd keep this theory to yourself. James's parents have moved on from Black Pine, but that name still has a lot of pull in this town.

Regina and James are in with the handful of people who make things happen. They'll sue you if they get even a whiff of what you're up to."

"Would they have cause to do that?"

"Just don't step out of line. That's my advice to you."

"If you were me trying to find out about an affair, where would you look, Cass?"

Cass looked away from him, brow creased. "Co-workers. You said Ivy worked at the inn, so in all likelihood their affair started there, right? How else could it? I remember one year at my firm HR did a lunch-and-learn series on appropriate relationships in the office. They cited statistics saying something like fifty percent of people at any company will get romantically involved with a coworker. Long hours together, no spouses around."

"Except Regina worked at the inn too."

Cass bit her cheek. "Maude Ferndale. I'd start with her."

"What did Maude do at the inn?"

"She ran it for years even before James and Regina took over. She was Ellen Drake's right hand, so to speak. She stayed on until the inn closed. My paw-paw was close friends with her husband and they'd come over once in a while. I haven't seen her in years, but she'd pick up on things. If anything was going on at the inn, she's like to know about it."

"Is she still in Black Pine?"

"Sure is. She's a townie, probably wouldn't leave if you tried to drag her out in chains. She works over at Burnside Insurance on Main Street. It's not three blocks from here on the right. You can't miss it."

"Thanks, Cass. And I'm sorry again about the other morning. I—"

Cass held up a hand. "No hard feelings, Dan. How about this? The River Bar has a Friday night fish fry. You can make it up to me."

"It's a date," he told her.

She stood and slung her bag over her shoulder. "I've got to get my poles ready for tomorrow. Good luck with Maude." She headed for the door, waving at the bartender. "Stay cool, Beetle," she told him.

Dan finished his coffee, dropped twenty dollars on the table, and left for Burnside Insurance.

"*M*aude Ferndale?"

The woman had been digging through the recycle bin next to the large counter. She looked up, pushing a wave of silvery hair away from her eyes. "Yes?"

"Hi, Maude. Cassidy Osborne told me you worked here. Have a minute to chat?"

The woman stood up, casting an exasperated look at the bin. "I had an invoice here for office supplies and can't find it for the life of me. I fear I've tossed it into the cardboard box of vanishing things. Once it's in there, it's as good as gone."

"Would you like some help?"

"What do you have in mind?"

Dan lifted the container and tilted it sideways. "May I?"

"We'll be wading through paper for weeks."

"Nah." He used one hand to fan the papers across the counter, managing to lose only one, which flitted across the room and landed by the door. He retrieved it and grinned. "This it?" He held up the invoice from a store called Office Depot.

Her mouth dropped open. "Well, golly gosh darn, if you aren't some kind of miracle worker. How'd you do that?"

"Entirely dumb luck." He handed her the invoice and piled the rest of the papers back into the container.

"I'm obligated to that chat now, I'd say. How can I help you, sir?"

"Call me Dan," he said. "I'm looking into a missing person's case."

"Are you a private eye?"

"No, a detective, off duty. But I heard about Ivy Trent and figured I'd check out a few things."

Maude nodded, sighing. "A conundrum, that one. Half of Black Pine says she skipped town; the other half says somebody threw her in the river."

"People have said she was thrown in the river?"

"It's more a phrase than a fact. Those folks reckon she's dead by somebody's hand."

"What do you think?"

"Oh, Lordy, according to my husband, thinkin' is not one of my finer qualities."

Dan waited, watching Maude as she chewed her lip.

"If I had to say one or another, I'd be with the river folks."

"Why is that?"

"Oh, there's plenty of reasons. She left her car and all her things at her momma's house. Plus, she was a real good girl with big dreams of gettin' her momma out of Black Pine. Some girls are the type to run off. Ivy Trent didn't strike me that way."

"Can you think of any reason that she would run away?"

Maude chuckled. "We all have reasons, don't we? For Ivy, though, life in Black Pine wasn't picture-perfect. Family stuff, no money, that sort of thing."

"Anything else?"

Maude's eyes darted to the side. She set her mouth in a grim little bud, and he could see her weighing the thoughts in her head.

"No one will find out about this conversation, Maude. Okay? I'm off duty here. I'm just trying to find a thread to pull on."

"Dan, why did you come to speak with me about Ivy Trent?"

"Because you worked with her at the Dark River Inn the summer she disappeared."

Maude nodded slowly. "I thought that was why."

"And I'm wondering if you heard or saw anything unusual while you were there."

Her shoulders pulled slightly forward, and she knotted her hands on the counter. "I might have seen something once." Her voice had dropped lower.

Dan stepped closer to the counter.

"I was cleaning one of the rooms on the third floor and looked out the window." She paused, and Dan bit back the urge to ask, 'And then?' "Ivy had just finished her shift. She started around the inn wearing only her suit and a towel wrapped around her waist. Mr. Drake came out of the woods and sort of grabbed at her. I was annoyed at first, thinking he was flirting with the staff and being inappropriate, but then she followed him into the woods. I stood right there and watched, waiting for them to come out. They did after a few minutes and the look on her face... she looked like a love-sick puppy. It broke my heart, to tell you the truth."

"Do you think they were having an affair?"

"I never saw anything like it again and I kept my eyes out for it, but..."

"Did you ever tell anyone about what you saw?"

Maude shook her head. "I didn't think it mattered."

"Is that the only reason?"

Maude's face fell. "The Drakes have a lot of pull in this town, a lot. If I'd have come forward with something like that, I wouldn't have this job. I wouldn't have any job."

"If I wanted to look deeper into this affair theory, who could I talk to? Did Ivy have any friends who also worked at the inn?"

Maude frowned and something flickered across her face, apprehension perhaps. She didn't want to give him names. Not a surprise considering her clear concern about the Drakes. "A girl named Heather," she said after a long moment. "Heather Longfellow. She works at the hospital here in town. My hubbie was in last month for kidney stones. Heather's a good girl. I hadn't seen her in years, not since... well, not since that last summer at the inn."

"She was friends with Ivy?"

Maude nodded. "She might be able to tell you more."

"Thanks, Maude. Can you direct me to the library? I wanted to look up a few things online."

"Sure can. Drive on through town here. You'll get into the neighborhoods. Take a right on Mills Road. Two blocks down, it's on the left. You can't miss it. The Drakes put some money into it quite a few years back, had a new sign built that's about ten feet high."

"Thanks, Maude. Is there anything else you can tell me about Ivy before I go?"

She cast her eyes away from him and he knew she had more to say, but she pursed her lips together and shook her head. "I best get back to this," she said, gesturing absently at a stack of papers. "The filing stacks up quick around here."

Maude didn't look at him as he bade her farewell and walked to the door.

~

AT THE LOCAL Black Pine library, a two-story brick house converted into a library in the previous century, Dan gave up his driver's license in order to use a computer. He typed 'Dark River Inn' into the search engine and waited to see what popped up.

The first result was a web page for the inn; however, when he clicked on it, he received an error message. 'Page no longer available.'

He returned to the search results and found reviews for the inn. He opened the page and scrolled through the reviews. They'd all been posted a decade-plus before. Many of the reviews spoke about how they'd visited the inn during its peak in the 80s, but in the 90s their subsequent visits were quite disappointing.

He found a review from October 2000 by a user named K.Riley.

SPENT one long and disturbing night at the Dark River Inn. If you're looking for a place with literally screaming pipes, creaking floor and lights that turn on at four am when you're sound asleep, this is the place for you. Let's not forget the woman standing over me in the middle of the night. Pretty sure they let their young staff run around doing whatever they want. I was pleasantly surprised to find my wallet and watch not stolen after the girl slipped out. I wouldn't spend another night in this place if they paid me a thousand dollars. Visitor beware.

ANOTHER REVIEWER, posting only as Anonymous, left a similar, though less detailed, review.

. . .

THE BATHTUB TURNED on in the middle of the night and nearly overflowed while I slept. Will not be staying again.

DAN RETURNED to the search bar and typed in 'James Drake, Black Pine, WV.'

The first result was for a web business called Drake Digital Marketing. Dan scrolled through the site. The 'About' section was brief, with a short paragraph about James Drake, who graduated from Ohio State with a marketing degree. Dan clicked on the image beside the bio. James looked young in the photograph, probably early thirties. He had sandy hair, a clean-shaven face, and he wore a dark suit.

Dan returned to the main page and found articles about the Drake family, most of which were published by the small newspaper in Black Pine, highlighting the Drakes' various philanthropic endeavors and donations.

He found a recent article from 2010 titled 'James Drake Carries the Drake Torch.' The article spoke of the large sums donated by James and Regina Drake in the previous years, which included support for a new children's floor at the local hospital. The article included a photo of James and Regina. He'd held his looks, though Dan saw some lines around the man's eyes. He wondered if the Drakes had Botox or plastic surgery. They both looked very good for fifty. James Drake looked younger than Dan himself, despite being ten years his senior. It was easy to see why a young woman would have been attracted to him. Guys like James had no problem catching the eye of younger women.

Dan printed off the most recent photos he found for James Drake. He stuffed them into the folder he'd brought with him, gazing at the top image from a 2000 article published two months before Ivy vanished.

If his theory was right, James would have been having an affair with Ivy when this photo had been taken and the man had the appearance of someone walking on the clouds. His smile was extra bright, his eyes shining, his body loose. He also looked nothing like the bearded man who kidnapped Ivy Trent from the beach.

In that article, James stood alone in front of a three-story brick building. The sign above him read 'Drake Digital Marketing.' The caption beneath his image said 'Drake Digital Marketing Finds a New Home in Former Trent Bank Building.'

"He bought a Trent building," Dan murmured, wondering how, if at all, James's connection to the Trents might have been linked to Ivy.

He typed in 'Johnny Trent, Black Pine, WV.' The search engine returned links to several articles, most published in 1985 in the months after Johnny Trent, son to the notable Lucille and the deceased Charles Trent, of Trent Bank, was hit and killed on Tuttle Road in Black Pine. The first article, published a day after his death, covered half of the front page with a headline 'Prominent Son Killed in Hit-and-Run Accident.' Rather than posting a picture of Johnny with his wife and daughter, the paper had run a shot that featured Johnny standing with his influential family. The two parents and three sons were all blond, the men a shade of light blond like corn silk and the mother a darker blonde. Their faces were chiseled, their teeth white and sparkling, and they wore formal attire as if preparing to attend a ball. When Dan read the quote beneath the photo, he realized that was exactly what they were doing. 'The Trent Family Dressed to the Nines at the Morgantown Bankers' Ball.'

The article also offered the scant details Sheriff Dowker had given regarding Johnny's death. He had been hit sometime after midnight on Tuttle Road. The only clues left by the driver were green paint on Johnny's clothing and body. Police believed the death to be accidental. They had no leads.

Future articles were small snippets buried in the later pages of the newspaper. In 1995, a ten-year anniversary story covered the unsolved hit and run, stating police believed a 1980s olive-green Ford Bronco was responsible for the accident, though police had not been able to locate a vehicle in the area.

Dan paused when he saw Ivy's name in the anniversary article. 'Fifteen-year-old Ivy Trent had this to say about her father's death: "My dad had a heart of gold. I can't believe the person who did this to him can live with themselves. Someday, I'll find out who destroyed my family. Someday I'll know the truth."'

Dan exited the screen and logged out of the computer. He looked at the printed photo of James Drake in the 2000 article. He scribbled a ragged beard on James's face, followed by dark sunglasses. The disguise changed James's image considerably, but did it turn him into the bearded man? Dan bit his cheek and tried to remember the man he'd seen. He shook his head, frustrated. For the first time, he understood the look he'd seen on the faces of so many witnesses, the internal struggle as they tried to force their brain to recreate an image that had only been there for seconds to begin with.

"Fuck all," he muttered.

The woman at the circulation desk looked up sharply, frowning.

"Sorry," Dan said too loud, garnering a second scowl of irritation from her. She glanced down at the sign propped on her desk. 'Quiet, Please,' it stated.

Dan left the library, but he didn't drive straight to the cabin. Instead, he returned to the road on the Black Pine side of the river and walked through the forest to the beach. The river sluiced by, shimmering and silver. He returned to the spot he believed Ivy had been the day she vanished.

"It doesn't make sense," he murmured, sitting heavily on the sand.

He tried to imagine dapper James Drake parked at the road, plastering on a fake beard and hat, creeping through the forest in jeans and a flannel shirt, snatching his own girlfriend by the hair and dragging her like a caveman into the forest. Two thoughts immediately followed the image. The first was that James was not the bearded man and the person who'd abducted Ivy had been a complete stranger who had stolen her from the beach and carried her away to a place Dan would never uncover no matter how hard he searched. The second was that it was some sick role-playing fantasy. Ivy lay on the beach and her Neanderthal lover grabbed her and dragged her off for some rough sex in the forest.

Out of the two scenarios, the first was the most believable, but it was also the theory that would potentially make Ivy's case unsolvable. Stranger abductions were by far the hardest to crack. Every cop knew that. With no links to the victim, the perpetrator could remain completely unknown unless they'd left evidence, but ten years had washed away any evidence on the beach or forest. Which left only Ivy's body for evidence.

"But that doesn't explain the Dark River Inn. It's connected," Dan said, dismissing the stranger theory and standing up.

In the forest behind him, he heard the crunching of twigs. It might have been a deer, but it sounded larger. Dan ducked lower and walked a few yards down the beach, tucking behind a sloping dune.

A man broke from the trees, carrying a heavy-looking hiking bag on his back. He clutched a small black box and walked with it extended before him. Large black headphones covered his ears. After a moment, Dan recognized him: Howard Mazur.

Dan stood and stepped from the dune, putting up a hand. Mazur faced away from him, turning in a slow circle. When he spotted Dan, he gave a little jump. Dan walked toward him and Mazur fiddled with the black box before taking off his headphones.

"If it isn't Detective Dan Webb," Mazur announced. "Out here doing your own sleuthing, eh?"

"Pretty much," Dan admitted. "Getting anything with that thing?" Dan gestured at the little black box.

"This is a tri-axis EMF meter. And yes, I surely am, but whether those are signals from the great beyond or merely a power-line signal, it's hard to say."

"Do you need any help?"

Mazur shook his head and shrugged off his backpack. "Best if I work alone. The more bodies, the more energy, the more information I have to part out later."

"I'll get going then. Will you call me if you come across anything... useful?"

Mazur smiled. "Sure will, my boy, though don't get your hopes up. As I mentioned, my work is on the fringes. You won't be taking anything I find today into a courtroom."

Dan chuckled. If he hadn't already ruined his career, explaining to a prosecutor that his primary evidence included electromagnetic frequencies and changes in in air temperature would seal his fate.

He walked back to his car, scanning the woods yet again for any evidence that Ivy had been there all those years ago. It was futile, but he couldn't help it.

As he pulled his driver's door closed, his phone rang. Louie's name popped on the screen.

"Hey," Dan answered.

"Hey, just got done for the day, thought I'd call and see what kind of progress you're making on the girl's case."

"Avoiding going home to see your wife?"

"Ha, no way. She called me at lunch and said she's making meatballs for dinner. I need something to distract my stomach on the drive."

Dan chuckled. "Well, I talked to Psychic Sally."

"Any profound revelations?"

"Not much, but she directed me to a guy here in West Virginia. He didn't help with the case, but at least convinced me I wasn't totally mental."

"Well, he's worth his weight in gold then. How'd he do that exactly?"

"Just told me other stories, same kind of thing you did, only better."

"Wise-ass."

"You know it. I have had a couple of interesting conversations, though. I'm thinking I might know who Ivy was having an affair with that summer."

"And you reckon that's the guy who offed her."

Dan sighed. "If it's not the guy, then I'll be running into a brick wall. That's the only lead I've got."

"Who do you reckon it was?"

"I'm looking at a guy named Drake. He owns the inn over by Bennie's place. He shut it down the fall after she disappeared."

"Hmm, that's telling."

"I thought so too. I've heard other strange stories too."

"Strange how? Like the ghosty stuff?"

"Yep."

"You're not going to have a midlife crisis and become one of those ghost-trackers, are you? I won't be able to hold my head high in the department anymore if my best friend goes from detective to ghost-hunter."

"Just follow my lead and pretend we don't know each other."

"Very funny. Call me when this one breaks wide open," Louie told him.

"Will do."

As Dan pulled from the roadside, he caught a glimpse of the tree dangling with shoes in the rearview mirror. He frowned and drove away.

$\mathcal{D}$an called the Black Pine Hospital the following morning as he drove into town. "Is Heather Longfellow available? She's a nurse."

A woman at the ICU nurse's station picked up. "Let me direct your call."

He sat on hold for nearly five minutes before another woman's voice came on the line. "This is Heather," she said.

"Hi, Heather. My name is Detective Dan Webb. Maude Ferndale told me how to reach you. Is there any chance you'd have some time to talk with me today?"

"About what exactly?"

"Ivy Trent."

Someone said Heather's name in the background. "I'm coming, give me twenty seconds," she told the person. "Sure, Detective. We're doing shift change right now then I'm off."

"I'm on my way into Black Pine. I could be to the hospital in ten minutes?"

"Meet me at the benches out front."

~

"You wouldn't be Heather Longfellow?" Dan asked, approaching the woman who sat on the bench in scrubs.

"Guilty as charged." She made a face. "That's an inappropriate thing to say to a detective, huh?"

He smiled and sat down. "I'm off duty, so I think you're safe. Maude Ferndale mentioned you quit your job at the Dark River Inn rather abruptly in October 2000?"

The woman, Heather, had the harried look of someone just coming off a twelve-hour shift. She sipped her coffee, closing her eyes as if savoring the watery-looking beverage. She nodded. "I'm almost there. Give me another two sips and I can talk."

They sat in silence while she finished half the cup. The set of her shoulders softened and the grooves in her forehead smoothed out.

"This place stresses me out," she said, nodding toward the hospital. "My husband wants me to transition to a general practice, but..." She shook her head. "I'm afraid I'd get bored."

"Makes sense. Cops who move from the street to the desk struggle with that as well."

"Exactly," she murmured. "Dark River Inn. That seems like a lifetime ago."

"Ten years," he said.

"Ten years, two marriages, three kids, five years working the emergency room, now two in ICU. The death of my mom, my brother, my waistline." She laughed and despite the life events she'd just tallied off there was a genuine smile. "Life is unpredictable, that's for sure. We never know what's coming, no matter how well we plan for it. Ivy should work in there. She wanted to be a doctor, had the brains for it too. I hadn't ever even considered medicine. I was going to get a business degree, go work in some big city doing PR or marketing." She laughed again, but now her smile looked sad.

"Did you know Ivy well?"

"I got to know her well that summer. I was a year below her at Black Pine High, so we hadn't been friends. I always thought she was... I don't know, stuck-up. She was beautiful, had a boyfriend on the football team, the usual drama. But once I actually met her and spent time with her, I realized she was none of the things I'd believed. She'd do little things for people. I turned nineteen that summer and she made me earrings, little dreamcatchers. I'd commented on a pair of hers earlier in the summer and when my birthday rolled around, she showed up to the inn with a little silver box with those earrings inside. I still have them."

Dan remembered the woman on the beach, the memory already becoming grainy with the passage of time. She had worn dreamcatcher earrings. "Can I ask if you witnessed anything out of the ordinary regarding Ivy that summer?"

"That's a hard question because like I said, I didn't really know her before that summer. I noticed some ups and downs, though. I saw her crying in her car once after her shift. That was maybe a week before she went missing. I started over to check on her, but then Mrs. Drake called out that she needed me to pull the kayaks into the shed, so I never had the chance. I guess what I noticed is that some days she seemed sort of blissed out and other days she'd have these sad looks on her face."

"Did you guys ever talk about guys? Relationships?"

"A little here and there. Regina Drake didn't leave much room for chitchat, but during the first part of the summer, Regina was up north staying with her mother in Ohio. James Drake ran things while she was gone, and he was way more lax."

"Regina was gone early in the summer? When did she come back?"

Heather waved at two women who exited the hospital in scrubs. "Regina came back in… August, I'd say. It's hard to remember exactly now, you know? That must make your work hard, talking to people about things that happened ten years ago."

"Ideally, it doesn't happen that way. Part of the reason you hear so much about the first forty-eight hours and all that. Let's get back to the topic of guys and any you remember talking about."

"I had a boyfriend that summer who was always blowing off our dates, so I did most of the talking. Ivy told me to kick him to the curb, but of course I didn't. Ended up marrying him two years later and divorcing a year after that." She shook her head, exasperated. "Ivy had dated a guy named Kurt in school, a real hunk, but things had cooled off between them. I did get the feeling she had someone, but she never said anything specific about him, not his name, not that they had plans."

"What made you think that?"

"The blissed-out thing was part of it, but I spotted gifts in her car a couple times. The boxes looked like they might have lingerie in them.

She asked me once to cover a weekend shift because she was going out of town and she had that twinkly 'running off with a lover' look. I had planned to pester her about it when she got back, but then we didn't have overlapping shifts for a week and I forgot."

"If I said a few people in Ivy's life suspected she was seeing an older man, perhaps a married man, would that surprise you?"

She tilted her head to the side, considering, and then shook her head no. "Honestly, that would explain her staying so quiet about it all the time. Not to mention the lingerie."

"Why the lingerie?"

"It's just not a usual gift for a twenty-year-old boy to give. You know? These were the boxes you might get from a Victoria's Secret. Shiny and expensive-looking. My boyfriend in those days thought a romantic gift was a dime-store teddy bear or a CD he'd burned."

"Yeah. That makes sense. I don't recall being much of a Casanova at twenty. Not at forty either, I'm afraid. Do you have any idea who the man would have been? Anyone in town you'd consider a prospect?"

She scrunched her face. "Hmm... gosh, I don't know. No one who springs to mind, but I'll think about it the next couple of days."

"And why did you quit? Maude said you left abruptly?"

Heather played with a bracelet on her left wrist. "Maude's right. I did quit out of the blue, but she knew why. Everyone knew."

"Why is that?"

"Because the Dark River Inn was haunted."

"Haunted?"

"Yeah, I know it sounds crazy, and what's crazier is that nothing weird had happened all summer. Then in late August weird shit started going on. Sometimes you'd open a door and hear this terrible scream. You'd set something down and turn around to find it moved to the other side of the room. I was putting away lifejackets at the end of the season and the shed door locked on me. I was screaming and crying, pounding on the door. I was terrified. This guy Dewey who did some odd jobs around the place opened the door and looked at me like I'd lost my shit. He said the door wasn't locked."

"Is that when you quit?"

"No, I quit when I saw..." Heather lifted her cup to her mouth, a slight tremble in her hand.

"Go ahead. This won't get back to anyone."

"I saw a person who looked like…" Heather chewed her lip. "It didn't just look like her. I swear it was her. I saw Ivy."

27

*D*an studied Heather. "You saw Ivy alive? After she'd been reported missing?"

Heather shook her head. "Not alive. There's a big mirror in the entryway at the inn. It's on the wall behind the piano and it's huge, eight feet high, five feet wide. I stopped in front of it one day. My hair was back in barrettes and I was fixing them. Suddenly Ivy was there, right behind me. Her eyes looked... dead. I don't know how else to describe them.

"I screamed. Maude and Regina Drake came running from the dining area. They'd been putting out lunch for the guests. We only had about eight that weekend. I started crying, saying Ivy had been there, I'd seen her. Maude put an arm around me, but Mrs. Drake stared at me like I'd puked on the floor. She was so disgusted. She snarled at Maude to get me out of there. Maude walked me to my car and told me to take the day off, but I never went back."

"Did you quit?"

"Not formally. But I had no intention of ever setting foot in that place again."

"Did you tell anyone what happened?"

Heather looked pained as she gazed across the parking lot. An ambulance, lights flashing, but no siren on, pulled up at the emergency room entrance. "No, I never did. Maude called me. She was really sweet, said she'd deliver my check herself and asked me not to say anything about what had gone on. There'd be a little bonus on there from the Drakes for my loyalty, something like that. They didn't want the inn to get a bad name. I don't know if I would have talked about it, anyway. I've told my husband. He's the only one before you. It's a relief talking about it now. I regret not doing it then. I should have gone to Ivy's mom. Maybe it wouldn't have mattered, but…"

"What do you think it means, Heather?"

"I've asked myself that question a thousand times. If she died, why would I see her at the Dark River Inn? I guess that's the place I get stuck. If she's haunting the inn, does that mean she died there?"

"Is there anyone else who saw things? Experienced things?"

Heather nodded. "I'd say most of the staff did, but good luck finding them. A lot of college kids worked there for a summer and then moved on. Dewey's still in town. He's got a place in the woods outside of town. Pretty rustic and don't sneak up on him or you're liable to get a bullet in the back."

Dan frowned. "Sounds like a great guy."

Heather laughed. "He's good people, just a little rough around the edges."

"You've stayed in contact with him since working at the inn?"

"Not on purpose. My husband is his nephew. We go visit him once a year. He keeps to himself, maybe comes into town once a month to stock up on essentials, though he hunts and fishes for most of his needs."

"Would I be crazy to swing by his place?"

Heather cocked her head. "Hard to say, but only one way to find out."

AFTER HEATHER GAVE HIM DIRECTIONS, Dan drove out of town into the hilly wooded area that Dewey Longfellow called home.

Dan turned at the mailbox that had been fashioned from a log and drove down the overgrown rutted driveway that led deep into the trees. He couldn't see a destination and after several yards the pathway became so rutted, Dan stopped his car and climbed out. He walked the rest of the way, spotting the tendril of smoke rising from the cabin's chimney before he saw the structure itself. Rustic was putting it kindly.

Five feet from the door, Dan heard the click of a shotgun pumping behind him. He froze and lifted his hands slowly.

"This is private property," a man growled.

"I'm here to see Dewey Longfellow," Dan announced, holding still.

"What fer?"

"Your niece sent me. Heather."

"Then put yer mitts down, you fool."

Dan bit back his retort and lowered his arms, turning to face the man.

Dewey Longfellow looked as rustic as his cottage with a tan, weathered face and a thin, spindly body sheathed in tattered corduroy pants and a deer skin vest layered over a pilled flannel shirt. "Heather ain't got no business sending strangers up here," Dewey grumbled as he ambled past Dan to the cabin door. "You comin'?" he snapped, not turning to look back at Dan as he disappeared inside.

Dan followed him, though he wondered if he'd made a mistake leaving his gun in his car. If Dewey acted as unhinged as he looked, Dan would be at a sore disadvantage inside the man's home.

The interior of the cottage was warm. A fire blazed in a wood-burning stove. A black pot on top of the woodburner released a spicy, rather delicious aroma. The inside of Dewey's cabin was at least better than the outside, with a hodgepodge of worn furniture draped in wool blankets. A mangy dog that had likely once been yellow snoozed on a rug in front of the woodburner.

Dewey stirred whatever was in the pot before settling into a rocking chair. He didn't offer Dan a seat, but Dan opted for a worn plaid chair whose springs groaned when he sat down.

"Smells good," Dan said, nodding at the pot.

"Stewed rabbit."

"I've never had it."

"Well, I hope you're not looking for an invite because I didn't make enough for two."

"Nope, just stopped by to ask you a few questions."

"Then get to askin'. The cold season is comin' and I've got wood waitin' to be cut."

"I'm looking into the disappearance of Ivy Trent. Heather told me you worked at the Dark River Inn the summer she disappeared."

A mild curiosity flitted across the man's face. "That I did."

"I wondered if anything strange happened that summer, either before Ivy vanished or after. Anything that might be relevant to her case."

The man plucked a toothpick from his shirt pocket and poked it between his teeth. "Strange, huh? Pulled a six-foot eastern kingsnake out of a kayak. Watched some teenager bottom out a speed boat on the riverbank."

Dan tried to hide his annoyance. "Anything relevant to Ivy, I meant."

"Well, then you might have said so."

"I did."

Dewey took the toothpick out, looked at it, and pushed it back into his mouth. "Took a funny picture Labor Day weekend. Might be that's pertainin' to the girl."

"How so?"

"Bunch of those college kids crowded up by the river. They wanted me to take their photo before they all headed off to their big schools and jobs. I snapped a few pictures. The first two looked normal enough, but the third..." He removed the toothpick and tapped it on the arm of his rocker. "The dark-haired girl was in the photo—the one who'd gone missing."

"Ivy was in the picture?"

"Seemed so. Standing in the group a little off to the side, not looking at the camera, but beyond it, gazing up at the inn. Chilled me to the bone."

"Did anyone else see it?"

"I called Maude over to look. Wonderin' if my eyes was playin' tricks on me."

"What did she say?"

"She erased it. Took the camera right outta my hands and clicked that little red trash button." He snapped his fingers. "Gone."

"Why would she do that?"

"On account of the other kids, I guess. She didn't want to get them all riled."

"Ivy was in the picture, but she definitely wasn't there that day? She'd already vanished?"

"Sure, yeah. Labor Day happened"—Dewey squinted—"two, three weeks after she'd gone missin'."

"What did you make of it?"

"A few of us wondered if Ivy might have come out to the inn that weekend and went in the water, ended up drowned."

"Odd that she wouldn't have left something behind, though, right? Her car wasn't found at the inn."

"Them Drakes didn't want us sayin' Ivy's name around there. Maude and I whispered a bit, wondered if maybe they knew Ivy died and didn't want to get blamed, lose their business and all. Maybe they covered it all up."

"They would have gone to great lengths to move her car, hide her body. Do you believe they'd do all that?"

Dewey rocked his chair back and forth. "Rich people are strange folks. They'll do all sorts of funny things to stay out of trouble."

"The weekend that Ivy went missing, were you working at the inn?"

Dewey shook his head. "They closed it right up that weekend. Said they was doing maintenance, but never asked me to do nothin'."

"Had they ever done that before?"

"Couple of times, but I'd still work. Go out and tinker around, cut the grass and whatnot. That weekend Mr. Drake asked me to steer clear. Some kind of rodent guy and bug guy were gassin' the place."

"Did you notice anything unusual when you returned the next Monday?"

Dewey paused the chair in mid-rock. "Seems I did, though I don't remember thinkin' much on it then. Course we didn't know yet the girl had gone missin'."

"What was that?"

"The Drakes had this big wedding photo in the office there. Hung right on the wall behind the desk. It was gone that next week. I ended up finding it in the shed, glass all cracked."

"Could it just have fallen?"

Dewey nodded. "Could have, but then Mrs. Drake would have set it out for me with a note to take into Black Pine and get a new frame and glass. Instead, somebody tucked it into the shed behind a big stack of lawn chairs, almost like they wanted to hide it."

～

DAN ALMOST WENT BACK into town to speak with Maude a second time, but his eyes ached and he needed to shut off his brain.

He drove back to Bennie's cabin and made a sloppy tuna fish sandwich, eating it in four large bites as he stared out the window at the river. Dusk had come and soon the river and the woods beyond would recede into darkness. He sat on the stool and put his eyes to the telescope, searching for movement on the opposite shore. There was none.

He moved to the kitchen table and wrote down everything he could remember from his conversations with Maude, Heather and Dewey. Once he'd gotten it all out, he lumbered to the couch, his feet aching. He picked up a Grisham paperback but he couldn't concentrate.

He dropped the paperback on the couch and put on his boots. He grabbed his flashlight and, as an afterthought, Bennie's camera, which was slung from a hook by the telescope. He moved quickly through the woods to the Dark River Inn. No lights shone in the windows, but he shuddered as he looked up at the cupola.

He found the shed on the back corner of the property. Bushes had grown up around it. A large tree branch likely blown down by a storm at some point lay diagonal across the roof.

There was a padlock on the door, but when Dan shook it, he saw it hadn't been secured. It simply hung from the lock. He slid it off and opened the door, shining his light inside.

Dewey had said the wedding photo was tucked behind a stack of lawn chairs. Dan spotted chairs stacked nearly to the ceiling in the back right corner. He wiggled through the piles of stuff, shoving two kayaks aside. When he reached the chairs, he shone his light behind them, but saw no evidence of a picture.

"Damn," he muttered.

He squatted down and reached into the darkness behind the chairs. Something sharp jabbed into his index finger.

"Shit," he whispered, pulling his hand out. A drop of crimson bubbled on the tip of his finger. He wiped it on his sweatshirt and shined the light into the opening. The beam refracted against the splintered glass. Dan found the frame and shimmied the picture free. He shook it, allowing the glass to fall onto the floor of the shed.

The wedding picture depicted a young James and Regina Drake flanked by their wedding party—the guys in dark suits, the girls in lilac taffeta dresses. Regina beamed, her veil thrown back, the train of her bridal gown trailing across the grass and out of the photo.

Dan lifted Bennie's camera and snapped a photo of the picture, wincing as the flash filled the shed and then blinked out. He stuffed the picture back behind the chairs and stood, slipped from the shed, and returned to Bennie's cabin.

28

The next day Dan found Maude much the same as the first time he'd met her. She stood behind the counter at Burnside Insurance speaking with an elderly man who leaned heavily on a cane. "Mr. Humphrey, you know I can't talk policies with you. I'm a lowly old secretary. Mr. Burnside will be in from one to five today. Can I make you an appointment?"

"You can tell Mr. Burnside I'm taking my business elsewhere," the man grumbled. As he hobbled past Dan, he shook his head angrily. "Best if you find insurance up the street, sonny," he told him.

Dan smiled at him and approached Maude, who looked mildly distressed.

"Sorry about that," she told him. "Mr. Humphrey is harder to please than Ebenezer Scrooge and they share a similar temperament."

"Seems like it," Dan said. "I don't envy your having to deal with him."

Maude reached beneath the counter. "Nothing a molasses cookie can't solve." She brought out a plate of cookies and offered one to Dan.

He picked one up and took a bite. "Mmm... these are really good."

"My grandma's recipe. These cookies are Black Pine's best cookie three years running at the summer festival."

"Easy to taste why," he told her. He set his cookie on a napkin she handed him. "Maude, I chatted with Heather yesterday and Dewey Longfellow."

Maude finished her cookie, wiping her fingers on her own napkin.

"They mentioned some strange occurrences that happened at the Dark River Inn after Ivy vanished."

"Did they now? Another cookie?"

He shook his head, and Maude returned the plate beneath the counter.

"I'd like to hear your version of those events."

"Since when is a detective interested in people's spooky stories?"

"Since they occurred within weeks of a woman who worked there disappearing."

She sighed and walked to the water cooler, picking up a little paper cup decorated in daisies. "Would you like some water?"

"No, thank you."

She filled her little cup and took a slow sip, staring at the blank wall above the cooler. After a moment, she returned to the counter. "There were some peculiar incidents that summer and fall."

"I'd like to hear all of them."

She finished the water and crumpled the cup, dropping it in the wastebasket. "Doors slamming, a woman's scream. I heard those myself a few times. Then there was Dewey's photo. Obviously, he told you about that." Her voice was disapproving, but not angry.

"Did you see the photo?"

Maude nodded.

"And it appeared that Ivy was in it?"

"Yes and no. She was there, but it was like a silhouette of her. Not that she was see-through or anything, just not full, not Ivy. She had a presence, that girl, but in the photo it was if she were in sepia and the other kids were in color."

Dan nodded. "Go on."

"A few guests mentioned things. One family checked in for a weekend stay and when their daughter opened the door to their room, a girl was inside. The mother came down to the front desk quite upset, thought we'd double-booked the room and her daughter had walked in on another guest. Of course, we hadn't done that, but the daughter described a girl who sounded an awful lot like Ivy Trent—dark curls, big blue eyes."

"What was she wearing?"

"A swimsuit, but it was October here, so that was odd."

"Could it have been another staff member? Could it have been Ivy?"

Maude picked at the corner of her eye. "No, I don't know. There's one key for each room and then one master key ring that I carry all the time. I had it that day. I checked it right away. Room seventeen was on there."

"Any significance to that room? Any reason Ivy would break in there?"

"For starters, I can't imagine anyone breaking in anywhere in a bathing suit. I also don't believe Ivy would do that. Dewey and I searched that place top to bottom, didn't find any evidence of a dark-haired girl."

"What other things happened?"

"A man filed a complaint that same October. He said his lights and all the faucets in his room turned on three times in the middle of the night. Lights, fan, faucets. Finally, at four in the morning he stormed down, screamed at Chloe, the overnight girl, and tore out of the inn. It was my job to call him and make amends, offer him a free night's stay for his trouble, and that's when he described what had happened. We'd had a couple other guests say similar things. Lights turning on by themselves, televisions, faucets."

"And all of this started in the fall of 2000?"

"Yes. I'd never heard anything like it before that year."

"Did other staff experience things?"

"Yes. Most of the people there during that time saw or heard something."

"How about the Drakes?"

"Them too. Regina started to seem downright disturbed by it all. She'd sort of jump if you walked into the room with her."

"Did she ever mention what she thought was going on?"

"Oh, no, we didn't talk about it. Only once did she address it with us and she made it very clear if word got out, she'd punish all of us for ruining the reputation of the inn."

"And you didn't feel obligated to report it for the sake of Ivy?"

"To report what? Flickering lights? Slamming doors?" She laughed. "I'd like to see you, a detective, report that and get taken seriously. The only thing my reporting would have done is gotten me laughed out of Black Pine and ensured I'd never get a job in town again."

DAN SPENT the afternoon putting everything he'd learned about Ivy's disappearance on a white board. He put Ivy's name in the middle and started drawing lines out, adding 'Dark River Inn,' 'Black Pine Bus Station,' 'Ohio River Beach,' 'Family,' 'Friends,' 'Bearded Man,' 'Affair.' From these words he added more lines putting in everything he knew and adding additional lines from there. He'd learned the technique from his first partner after he'd made detective. A seasoned detective who'd been just two years away from retirement when he and Dan were partnered up, Phil had been a big fan of mind-mapping, and eventually Dan had picked it up as well.

After he'd completed his spider-web of information he stepped back and considered the places he had the least information on. The affair was the primary one. Older man, married with kids, but no name beside it. He'd put 'J.D.?' but he still couldn't substantiate the man had been having an affair with Ivy. He'd drawn a dotted line between JD's name and the bearded man.

On the table he put Ivy's missing person's poster in the center and arranged James's photos around her.

After an hour of free-writing theories about what had happened to Ivy that night, his stomach grumbled. He left the cabin and headed for town, listening to his messages on the way. Cass had left a message that she'd found some interesting things. He called her and she agreed to meet him for dinner at an Italian place outside of town.

CASS WORE a pair of dark-rimmed spectacles. Her dark hair was secured back from her face with a hair clip. She looked serious, professional, and the image somewhat unnerved him. He could see a shadow of the attorney she'd been, likely a formidable one.

"The bottom line is that in 2000, James Drake was upside down financially. He tried to sell the Dark River Inn, but his siblings balked. He'd gotten tangled up in some bad investments, and gambling appeared to be an issue as well. He was taking trips to Vegas two to three times a year and coming home fifty thousand short of when he'd left. Regina's money bailed them out."

"But Regina was a stay-at-home mom, right? I mean, he mentioned she helped run the Dark River, but—"

"Regina Drake, formerly Regina Beatty. Her father's a big real estate investor. Bought up a lot of prime real estate here in West Virginia, down in Florida, North Carolina and even in California. He made a fortune, part of which belongs to Regina Beatty, his only child, whom he and his wife have doted on since birth."

Dan leaned back, folding his hands across his stomach. "She's rich."

"Yep."

"So there's no way he would have been leaving her for a poor twenty-year-old."

"Are there any men who do?"

Dan shrugged. "Not any with rich wives."

"Exactly."

"So an affair would not only have ruined his marriage—"

"It would have destroyed him financially."

Dan had the motive he'd been looking for. Sometimes silencing the mistress was enough, but it didn't feel enough with a guy like James Drake. He was too slippery, too smart to throw it all away—after all, he could have said Ivy was lying, she'd become obsessed with him—but if money was at stake, if his business and livelihood were on the line, that changed the game.

"But you still don't have evidence that she was sleeping with him," Cass reminded him as if reading his mind.

"But it exists. James might be slippery, but Ivy was an idealistic twenty-year-old in love with an older man. She kept something. I know it. I just have to find it."

"You said you already searched their trailer?"

Dan nodded.

Cassidy bit her lip. "When I was a girl, I kept my diary in a shoe box in the closet."

"Checked those."

"Girls know how to hide stuff. She didn't want Annabelle finding out about the guy. There's something somewhere. I'd search the trailer again."

Dan sighed. "Annabelle looked rough the last time I did that. I hate to put her through it again."

"Then don't. Annabelle Trent is shut up in the trailer twenty-four seven. Give her a break. Here, let me do you another favor." Cass took out her cell phone and punched in a number. "Herb? Hey, put Sadie on the phone, will you? Thanks."

Dan watched Cass, unsure what she was planning.

"Sadie, this is Cass. I'm good, yeah, thanks. Listen, I'm sitting here with Dan Webb. Yep, one and the same. He needs to search Annabelle's trailer again, but we think she needs a spa day. Dan's treat." Cass winked at him. "Would you be willing to take her over to Morgantown tomorrow? There's that great spa in the Marriott . Maybe get a manicure, a facial, go to lunch."

Dan heard Sadie agreeing enthusiastically through the phone.

"Great. I'll make the appointments," Cass told her. "How's noon? Perfect." She hung up the phone and called information, asking for the number to the Marriot.

"Shouldn't we check with Annabelle Trent?" Dan asked.

Cass shook her head as she spoke with the front desk person at the Marriott, scheduling the women's manicures, facials, and adding a hair treatment when the host told Cass they were offering a special.

Cass ended the call. "If you ask Annabelle, she'll say no. You have to tell her, and no one's as good at that as Sadie Dwiggins."

29

"Mr. Drake?" Dan asked the man seated in one of the two club chairs by the fireplace.

James Drake stood and smiled, revealing two rows of sparkling white teeth. Dan saw the image Cassidy had described. James had the coloring of a spray tan, hair free of gray, which implied a dye job, and a perfectly pressed black button-down shirt. His gold Rolex watch gleamed from his wrist.

"Call me James. My secretary mentioned you were interested in the Drake family history. My sister set up a website a few years back, but I'm afraid she let the domain lapse."

"I didn't look online," Dan lied. "When I heard there was a Drake right here in town, I figured I'd go straight to the source. I am curious why your family name is on the Ohio side of the river, but most of the businesses here in Black Pine are Drake as well."

James returned to his seat, crossing his legs. "There wasn't much in Drake to put the family name to, so my father adopted Black Pine. The library, the high school, the hospital, all of it funded at least in part thanks to Richard Drake."

"And you have three siblings?"

James nodded, hands folded on his knees, not a tremor in his smile. "Richard Junior, my eldest brother, Allison, Seymour and myself."

"You're the youngest, then?"

"Apple of my mother's eye."

"And you guys grew up in the Dark River Inn?"

James held up a hand and tilted it from side to side. "We did and we didn't. We lived summers at the Dark River Inn, but my father's law offices are in Columbus, so our primary residence was there, our private schools, et cetera."

"Who turned the Dark River Inn into an inn?"

He smiled. "That was my mother's doing, Ellen Drake. She'd grown up on a big plantation down south. She loved the hubbub, people always coming and going. My father finally gave in to her dream in the late 70s. We kids had started to go off on our own. Rich and Allison had both gone away to college, Seymour was a senior, I'd be coming a year later. We'd all be off to school. She was protecting against that nasty empty-nester syndrome so many of her lady friends suffered from."

"How did it go? The Dark River Inn?"

"Great. They had a lot of connections. Every high-society lady in Columbus booked family vacations at the inn. They'd come down and play croquette, eat croissants on the wide porch. My father hosted Friday night poker games in the cupola. They'd basically transferred their entire social life to their summer house." He chuckled.

"Why did you take it over?"

"Oh, the usual reasons. It lost its shine after a decade or so. My parents had started vacationing in the Caribbean more and more. They wanted to buy a house somewhere south and retire. Rich was running the law firm by then and Seymour had joined him, so they had that place under control for my dad. Allison was a big-shot PR woman in Chicago, so she wasn't going to take the reins on that old place. I was the only option."

"You didn't become an attorney like your brothers?"

He made a face. "Lord, no. Have you ever seen the books you have to study in law school? They weigh more than a small car. None of that for me. I got a degree in marketing and started a company online, a digital marketing agency."

"It seems difficult to run a digital marketing agency out there. I don't even get cell service."

He nodded. "Oh, you're spot on there, but I hired half the guys I went to school with. The agency operated on autopilot."

"When you started the company, were you married?"

"Not quite, courting, but I hadn't popped the question. I met Regina at Ohio State."

"And she didn't mind moving to Drake? Running the inn?"

"Not at all. She loved it. She wanted the country life for the kids. A few areas in Columbus had gotten rough, rising crime, you know the drill. She was more than happy to move down here, especially once she found out she was expecting Hannah. I wasn't married to a place seeing as my business was online. We couldn't live at the inn though, thanks to those pesky internet problems, and we both felt a separation between home and business was for the best. So we bought a house in Black Pine and settled in there."

"Who ran the inn? You or Regina?"

"Well, both of us ran aspects of the inn, but then I hired staff—a manager to oversee it, a chef, a cleaning crew, a groundsman. Regina saw to the guests mostly. Made sure they knew about the sights, kept the place in flowers and chocolate mints. Lady stuff."

"And what did you do?"

"Well, I wrote the checks." He winked at Dan. "And I hosted a poker game just like my dad. I mostly gave final approvals."

"Did you hire the staff?"

"Mostly, yes, though Regina handled some of that."

"Can you tell me who hired Ivy Trent?"

The man's smile faltered, but he quickly replaced it. "Ivy Trent?"

"Yes, I believe she worked for the Dark River for one summer as a lifeguard." Dan kept his tone casual, curious, not giving away any of his suspicions about the man before him.

"Oh, yeah, okay. I remember. She's the girl who ran away, right?"

"That's one theory, her running away, but those closest to her believe there may have been foul play."

"I'm sorry, what did you say your name was?"

"Dan Webb, Detective Dan Webb, though I'm not technically here in a professional capacity. I'm on a vacation of sorts and stumbled across an old missing poster. Piqued my interest and when something catches my eye, I'm like a dog after a bone."

The word 'detective' had the desired effect. The smile on James's face disappeared for a second time. This time it didn't return. "If this is a police interview, I'm quite sure you have to inform me of my rights."

"As I said, I'm not here in a professional capacity. I saw Ivy's poster and decided to do some digging. It's a cop thing."

James stood. "I'm afraid you're barking up the wrong tree, Detective."

"Am I?"

"If you have any further questions, I can connect you with my attorney."

"Really? That's an extreme leap from asking about a girl who used to work for you. I've spoken with half a dozen people in Ivy's life, and you're the first to mention a lawyer."

James smiled coolly. "Not everyone in this community is as well informed as me, Detective. Not to mention most don't have the means to hire a lawyer even when accused of a crime, let alone questioned. I'm not saying you're one of those cops who decides someone is your guy and pursues him blindly, but I've heard of a few in my day. Lawyers help to even the playing field, in my humble opinion. Good day to you."

Dan watched him, noting the stiffness in his posture, the effort to appear casual when inside his guts were likely churning.

James turned and walked toward the door, paused and looked back at Dan. "Webb, you said? Any relation to Bennie Webb?"

Dan bristled. "He's my brother."

James frowned and then an odd little smile played on his lips. "How ironic." He said nothing else, but turned away and continued out the door.

30

*D*an knocked on Annabelle Trent's door. She pulled it open cautiously, opening it all the way when she recognized Dan.

"Annabelle, I need to search your trailer again. A thorough search."

Annabelle frowned, bracing her hands on the doorframe as if holding herself up had suddenly become infinitely harder. "What for? I mean... she's not in here, Dan."

He smiled. "I know that. I'm trying to find a link. The older guy. I need something that connects them. Ivy was a young woman. She had to have kept some memento, some proof. I intend to find it."

A small white pickup truck pulled into the dirt driveway.

"Who's that?" Annabelle asked.

"It's Sadie Dwiggins. She's come to take you for lunch and a day out. My treat."

Annabelle blinked at him and then reached a hand to her tangled hair. "I look a mess. I..."

Sadie got out of the car and waved. "Annabelle, my dear, we are going for a spa day. Hair appointments, nails and even facials. My goodness, could I use it. Come on, girl, get your bag."

Sadie bustled up the steps and passed Dan. Five minutes later she'd ushered Annabelle into a pair of jeans and a blouse and hustled her out to the truck.

"Take your time," Dan told them.

Annabelle paused on the steps, looking back at Dan fearfully.

"There's some, um… medicine in the cabinet. Painkillers. I don't have a prescription."

"Annabelle, I'm not here for that. This is about Ivy and only Ivy. Anything else doesn't exist as far I'm concerned." He winked at her, and she attempted a smile, allowing Sadie to steer her to the passenger side of the truck.

Dan slipped on latex gloves and walked into the trailer. He'd start in Ivy's room and fan out, going room by room.

Dan had already searched through her drawers, but he started again, going one by one, removing every article of clothing and placing it carefully on the bed. When the drawer was empty, he swept a hand along the bottom and sides on the chance she'd taped something inside. He went through every dresser drawer, followed by her vanity. He took the covers and sheets off of her bed before lifting the mattress from the box springs and then lifting the box springs from the frame. He went through her closet, pulling out all the clothes and then replacing them item by item, checking pockets and patting them down.

After he'd searched the room, Dan moved into the bathroom. Shampoos and conditioners, hairbrushes, combs, elastic bands, towels. He removed every item before putting it back. He found a makeup bag he thought had likely been Ivy's based on the sparkly eyeshadows and colored lipsticks. He searched the living room and the kitchen, but avoided Annabelle's bedroom.

It took nearly three hours to search the trailer and when he finished, Dan sat heavily in the floral chair he'd occupied when he'd first visited Annabelle. Nothing. Not an ounce of proof.

He thought of the psychic who'd mentioned the crawl space. He went back through searching the floor for a crawl space but found no evidence of one.

"Where else?" he murmured, staring at the floor. He paused and allowed his eyes to shift up. The ceiling in the trailer was a series of panels supported by wood slats. He reached up and pushed. The panel lifted easily. He returned to Ivy's room, starting at the door. He pushed panels, reaching up and sliding his fingers across the top of the panels beside it. Near Ivy's bed, he pushed a panel up and felt something move. It slid across the panel, lodging on the opposite side. He pushed it up further, angling the panel so that whatever sat on it slid off.

A shoe box tumbled from the ceiling with a puff of dust and bits of insulation. It landed on the bed and fell sideways, spilling its contents onto the floor. A journal, two nighties—both silk, one red and the other black—and a scattering of jewelry lay on Ivy's carpet.

"Bingo," he murmured, allowing the panel above him to remain skewed so he'd know exactly where he found it.

The journal was white with a brightly colored dreamcatcher decorating the cover. He flipped it open to find an inscription.

'To Capture Your Dreams. All my love, J.D.'

"James Drake," Dan said, feeling the euphoria of a big break stealing over him.

He hadn't felt the sensation in months. He'd almost forgotten what it felt like.

He slid the journal into a plastic Ziploc bag and then closed Ivy's door. He scrawled a note to Annabelle.

'I found something. Avoid Ivy's room for a couple of days. I'll fill you in soon. I hope you enjoyed the spa. -Dan'

He drove back to the cabin, wanting privacy to thumb through Ivy's journal. He struggled through the twenty-five-minute drive, his eyes flicking to the journal, tempted to pull over and start reading on the side of the road.

At the cabin, he brewed a pot of coffee and took the journal to the table. He opened a notebook beside it and grabbed a pen.

The first entry was dated on May ninth, 2000, just two months before Ivy vanished. The first entry confirmed what Dan already believed.

'James bought me this journal. Curious considering I'd already been writing about him in my other notebook for months, but he doesn't know that, he can't know about that. I'm afraid of what's begun between us. This wasn't supposed to happen, but now it has and I'd be lying if I didn't say I loved him. I do. I love him, but I won't let that distract me from my true purpose. I can love him and find out the truth. I can.'

DAN FROWNED. He hadn't seen another notebook in Ivy's room. He flipped further through the diary.

She wasn't a daily writer. Usually several days passed between entries, some of which were simple notes about her day.

'A SCARY THING HAPPENED TONIGHT. I closed up the ice cream shop and the weird bearded guy who asked me out a few times followed me home in his truck. I've only just now settled down enough to write about. Bennie is his name, and he gives me the creeps. I thought he was going to hit me. Fitting, I guess. That's how my dad died and on that very same road. My hand is shaking as I write this. I kept waiting for the bumper of his truck to hit the back tire of my bike. No one would have known. My mom would have come home from work and maybe she would have found my body or, worse, maybe he would have taken me with him.

'I want to tell James, but he's been distant lately. Plus, Bennie does odd jobs for him at the inn. They might be friends. I called Marnie, and she said I should call the police. I won't though. The sheriff is Elizabeth Dowker's dad, and she hates me. I can just imagine how he'd look at me, like I'm making it all up, like maybe I deserved it. I hate this town.'

DAN FROWNED and read the entry a second time. Bennie had never mentioned working for James Drake. Dan hadn't asked him, but it bugged him just the same. He skipped to the last entry dated August 15, 2000, four days before she vanished.

'I'M SO angry I don't want to write in this book. I want to take it outside, throw it in our firepit and burn it black. He's not separated. They were never separated. Regina Drake has been in Toledo taking care of her mother who broke her leg. James has been lying from that very first day, lying about every-

thing. If Maude hadn't told me, I'd never have known at all. I feel like someone has stomped on my chest, like my heart is has been broken. No one knows about us, no one can know, and yet I want to tell everyone. And that's not all. He was there that night. I'm sure of it now.'

"SHE WAS GOING TO TELL," Dan said aloud.

"Sheriff. Got someone here to see you," the woman said after she poked her head into the office at the end of the room.

A moment later, the sheriff stepped out, eyeing Dan for a long minute until he seemed to remember him. He said nothing, just offered Dan a gesture that Dan assumed meant 'come in.'

Dan walked through the office, glancing at desks piled with paperwork, overhearing the telephone conversation of a deputy who seemed to be trying to track down a stolen car.

Sheriff Dowker's office was uninspired, with four empty white walls and an enormous metal desk in the center of the room. The shades on his single window were open to reveal the parking lot. Two framed photographs sat on the desk, facing away from Dan.

"Back again?" the sheriff asked and he didn't sound pleased.

"Yes. I apologize again for my previous... mix-up. But whatever I saw that day got me interested in a cold case here in Black Pine."

"Which case is that?"

"Ivy Trent."

The sheriff didn't look surprised, and Dan knew word had gotten back to him that the outsider had been sniffing around. "I see. And?"

"Well, I've found some things that I believe are linked to Ivy's disappearance."

"Enlighten me."

Dan watched the sheriff's face, but he'd plastered on a mask of impassivity. He intended to give nothing away.

"Okay," Dan started. "I believe Ivy Trent was having an affair with a married man here in Black Pine. An affluent member of the community. I believe that person is connected to her disappearance."

"Which means what exactly? That he paid her or that he killed her?"

"I'm leaning towards the latter."

"And why is that?"

"Because there has been no proof of life for Ivy Trent since August 19th, 2000. No activity on her bank accounts or her email. She's never contacted a single family member or friend, written a letter. She's never been sighted—"

"Whoa, hold up there." The sheriff shifted forward in his chair. "We had half a dozen sightings called in for Ivy Trent. A few people said they seen her all the way up in Chicago, Illinois."

"There are always sightings, Sheriff. In every missing person's case people call in to say they saw the girl, but confirmed sightings, have there been any of those?"

"We didn't exactly have the resources to run up to Chicago, Mr. Webb. It is Mr., right? I spoke the assistant chief up there in Novi and they informed me you're on suspension."

Dan felt as if the man had kicked him in the gut. He sat back, glaring at him. "You called my department?"

"It's the natural thing to do when someone is running roughshod all over a peaceful little town, stirring people up."

Dan felt the color rise into his neck, but refused to back down. "It doesn't matter. I'm looking into Ivy's disappearance as a concerned citizen of the United States and on behalf of Annabelle Trent, who deserves answers, not to mention her daughter, who deserves justice."

The sheriff offered him a cold smile and leaned back in his chair. "Mr. Webb, did you have some evidence of wrongdoing you intended to present? If not, I've got a full day and need to get back to it."

Dan thought of the diary, the sightings. None of it proved that Ivy had been murdered. Dan stood and strode from the office, ignoring the sheriff, who let out a little chuckle.

In his car, Dan slammed his hands against the wheel, furious at himself for going to the sheriff in the first place. He should have known after their first encounter on the beach the man wouldn't take him seriously.

"But he took me seriously enough to call Novi," he murmured.

Clearly the sheriff saw him as a threat on some level or he wouldn't have put the effort into calling up to Novi.

Dan dialed Louie as he drove away from the sheriff's office.

"Whatcha got?" Louie asked.

"My foot in my mouth after trying to talk to the asshat sheriff down here. Basically, laughed me out of his office."

"You figured on that, though, so what's your next step?"

"Fuck if I know. Even if I can prove James was sleeping with Ivy, that doesn't mean he killed her."

"Yeah, so how do we crack a case when we've got a hunch but can't prove it?"

Dan considered. "Sweat the guy?"

"Hell, yeah. Turn up the heat on that SOB. See if he talks once the water starts boiling."

Bennie had always kept a camera at the cabin for rare bird sightings. It was equipped with a long lens attachment and would be perfect for what Dan wanted.

Dan parked outside of James Drake's office and got out of his car. He leaned on the hood of his car and waited. When James emerged from the building with two other men in suits, Dan lifted the camera to his eye and took a picture. He took another and another, not attempting to conceal his camera. On the contrary, he wanted James to see it.

James's eyes darted toward them and his walk grew visibly stiffer. He broke away from the men as they headed toward the parking lot and walked across the street to Dan. He looked furious.

"What the hell do you think you're doing?"

"Taking pictures, collecting evidence."

James sneered. "The way I hear it, you're just a regular joe schmoe. Detective nobody."

"Sure, sure. But that hardly matters. Proof of a crime often comes from everyday citizens. No badge necessary to get the ball rolling."

"You'll be hearing from my attorney," James snarled, turning on his heel and stalking toward his car.

~

DAN HADN'T INTENDED to develop the film in the camera—after all, he'd only taken the shots to unnerve James Drake—but when the roll was full, he decided to go ahead and drop it off at the photo shop in downtown Black Pine.

"One-hour printing on these?" the girl behind the counter asked.

"Yeah. That'd be great, thanks."

Dan left the store and walked down the block. He'd riled James up, that had been easy to see, but there was another way, a better way, to get under James Drake's skin and that was by speaking to his wife. Dan wouldn't give up information about the affair, not yet, but he wanted to meet the woman and find out whether she knew her husband had been sleeping around.

When he returned to get the photos, he held out an article he'd printed off with Regina's photo and a headline reading 'Regina Drake raises more than fifty thousand dollars to save Miss Mable's Stables.' "Do you happen to know this woman?" he asked the girl as she handed him his change.

"Mrs. Drake? Of course. Everyone knows the Drakes."

"I figured as much. Any idea where I could find her? I'd love to interview her about some of the good work she's done here in Black Pine."

The girl bit her lip. "Hold on," she told him. She picked up the phone on the counter and dialed a number. "Mom? Yeah, it's me. Do you know Mrs. Drake's phone number? There's a man here who wants to interview her about her work in Black Pine." The girl grabbed a piece of scrap paper and wrote down a phone number. "Sure, macaroni sounds good. I'll be home by five. Love you too. Bye." She hung up the phone and handed the paper to Dan.

"Thanks. I appreciate it."

"Not a problem. As our motto says, 'Customers come first!' She pointed to the sign hanging on the wall behind her.

"Thanks again," Dan said, taking the envelope of photographs and walking to his car.

He called Regina Drake, half expecting a brush-off. She seemed unsurprised by his call and agreed to meet with him the following day. Clearly, James had alerted his wife to Dan's poking around. The question was what had James told her?

BACK AT BENNIE'S CABIN, he brewed a pot of coffee and sat at the table, clearing a space.

He pulled the glossy images from the paper sleeve. The first shot revealed James Drake walking from his building with two other men flanking him. They all looked about the same age, late forties to early fifties, and wore nearly matching dark suits and shiny black shoes. It took four photographs before James's expression changed and he started to look nervously toward the camera.

Dan flipped through photos of birds perched high in trees—cardinals, sparrows, crows and a few shots of a horned owl. Another angle of the forest appeared in the photos, these ones pointing toward the river. The shots grew closer to the water. Dan started to see the curve of dune and beach.

Dan slid a picture aside and froze. The next shot revealed a large swath of beach and in the center a woman reclined on a chair. Only the back of her dark curls and her tan legs showed in the image. He couldn't see her face, but he knew whose photograph he stared at. Ivy Trent's.

3 2

*D*an's breath caught shakily. He flipped to the next image. Again, Ivy on the beach. Again and again. Five more photos of her. In one she'd leaned forward and picked up a water bottle.

He studied that one for a long time. Something in the photo niggled at him. Then he remembered.

Dan stood and strode from the cabin out to the shed. He yanked so hard on the door that the stick securing the lock snapped.

The gloomy shed was as unremarkable as it had been on Dan's first day back at the cabin. Except for one thing. He strode to the plastic shelves tucked in the back corner. They were piled with miscellaneous junk, extra lawnmower blades, WD-40, and a coffee can filled with nuts and bolts.

But there, on the top shelf, stood the water bottle. It was purple with a silver band at the top and another at the bottom.

Dan didn't touch it. Instead, he held the photograph next to it. They were identical.

His brain started offering excuses. There were probably a million just like it. Maybe it had belonged to their mother. Perhaps Bennie had found the water bottle on the beach.

Each felt as implausible as the last.

BENNIE ANSWERED on the second ring. He sounded tired and agitated.

"Hey, how's it going?" Dan asked, holding back his initial stream of demands about the photos and the water bottle.

"It's going. What's up? I just pulled into work. My shift starts soon."

"Bennie..." He considered making small talk, driving up to Michigan and talking face to face. Instead, he forged on. "I developed some film today."

"Yeah, and?"

"It's old, ten years old, and it shows Ivy Trent sitting on a beach."

Bennie didn't respond, and after a moment Dan wondered if he'd hung up. He pulled the phone away but saw Bennie's name still lighting up the screen, seconds ticking by.

"Bennie?"

"Dan, I can't get into all this right now. I'll call you tomorrow."

"Bennie. Did you kill Ivy Trent?"

"God, no. Jesus, Dan. Don't you know me at all? I'll explain everything. I'll call you tomorrow."

"You took the pictures though? Of Ivy?"

"Yeah, I took 'em. Listen, I've got to go. I swear I'll explain everything."

Dan started to ask more, but Bennie ended the call.

Dan set the phone on his passenger seat and drove back to the cabin.

DAN TOOK the Scotch down from the cupboard and filled a coffee mug. He drank it slowly, staring at Ivy's picture in the center of his table. His eyes drifted to the image of James that Dan had scribbled on, adding a beard and sunglasses, but now he saw a different man's face staring out —Bennie's face. And this one wasn't hard to imagine because Bennie had grown his beard long a handful of times in their life and Dan knew now the man who'd snatched Ivy from the beach was not wearing a fake beard. It was real and it belonged to his brother.

When he finally crawled into bed, his dreams were fitful. He dreamed of Bennie standing in the garage staring into the blood-spattered window of their mother's car, but it wasn't their mom behind the wheel. It was Ivy. Blood ran from her nose and ears, twisted to the black mottled skin that started at her neck and slithered down to her legs.

~

Dan woke, startled, and sat up in bed, hand reaching automatically for the gun that sat in the nightstand drawer. He slid the drawer open and closed his fingers around it before his eyes had even registered the dark room.

Silence.

Something had woken him. He felt sure of it, and yet nothing at all stirred in the room.

The temperature had dropped. Not unusual for autumn, but colder than he'd have expected, made more bitter when he'd cast off his blanket and exposed his naked chest to the room.

He pulled on a t-shirt and sweatshirt, walked into the front room of the cabin and gazed around. After sliding into his boots, Dan grabbed his flashlight and stepped out the door into the night.

The night was quiet except for Dan's footfalls as he crushed leaves and snapped twigs in the forest. He trained his light on the trees ahead of him, spotting the glowing eyes of a raccoon pausing mid-climb on a pine tree.

Dan sighed and turned back toward the cabin.

The ghostly apparition of Ivy Trent stood in the forest. Before he could even suck in a ragged breath she faded and vanished.

The chill enveloped him and his breath gusted out in a halo of white.

He walked tentatively forward until he was standing in nearly the exact place she had stood. The air didn't feel any different. There was no vaporous remnant of the woman, but she had been there. He'd seen her.

He shone his light ahead of him, half expecting to see her a few yards away, playing some disturbing game of ghost hide-and-seek, but the forest stretched dark and empty. Only the thick black trunks obscured his view. He shined the light down on the forest floor. Leaves and branches littered the ground, but also… a sharp metallic edge.

Dan squinted at it. He kicked at the metal with his boot. It was mostly buried, only a corner poking from the earth. He reached down and grabbed it, yanking it back and forth. Clumps of thick soil fell from the thing as he pulled it free. It was coated in dirt and it took him a moment to make sense of the object he held. It was a chair. A folding beach chair. He propped his light on the ground and pointed the beam at the chair, wiping at the fabric, his stomach sinking as he made sense of the faded and dirtied colors. It was striped, and it had once been green and white.

"Shit," he muttered, pulling his hands back.

He'd found the chair Ivy had been lying in on the beach the day she was abducted.

THE FOLLOWING MORNING, Dan tried to call Bennie, but his brother didn't answer. He wanted to drive to Michigan, to confront him, but he'd already set the appointment with Regina Drake. He'd deal with that first.

He arrived at the Black Pine Country Club and found Regina Drake seated in a plush room that opened off the lobby.

"Regina Drake?" he asked.

The woman sat primly in a high-backed cream-colored chair. She wore billowy white pants and a black silk shirt. Her hair, also black, was cut in a severe line that framed her face in two sharp sweeps. She looked more like a businesswoman than a stay-at-home mom.

"Mr. Webb, I presume?" She didn't stand, but narrowed her eyes, allowing them to travel the length of his body, appraising his outfit. Her mouth turned down slightly when she reached his boots, which were still flecked in mud from his foray into the woods the previous night.

"Yes, Detective Webb." He walked to her and held out his hand.

She paused, but then, reluctantly he thought, put her own hand in his. It was thin, her fingers long with nails painted a dark red. "Is it Detective when you're on unofficial business? You're not working in a detective capacity currently. Isn't that right?"

"Right it is. Let's go with Dan." In his pocket, his cell phone shrilled. He quickly silenced it, not bothering to look at the screen.

He sat in the chair opposite her. A coffee table divided them, but he was off to her right rather than facing her head on. He stood and dragged the chair so that he could look at her while he spoke.

She lifted a single, narrow eyebrow. "As I mentioned on the phone, I have a brunch engagement, so you'll have to be brief."

"I wanted to ask you about Ivy Trent."

She said nothing, both of them waiting through an overlong pause. "I'm sorry, was that a question?"

Dan smiled, gritting his teeth behind his lips. His phone started to vibrate a second time in his pocket. "Do you remember Ivy Trent?"

"I do, yes."

"Can you tell me about her?"

Regina frowned. "I suspect this method of inquiry is a waste of both our time, Dan." She spoke his name as if it left a sour taste in her mouth. "If you want to know about Ivy Trent, her mother would be a more satisfactory source."

"I've already spoken to Annabelle Trent. I'd like to know your impression of Ivy Trent."

"My impression? Ivy Trent was punctual and friendly."

"That's it?"

"She worked as a part-time staff for one summer, most of which I was gone for. You may not be aware, but a place like the Dark River Inn takes a great deal of focus to run. I didn't make a habit of analyzing the staff. Ivy showed up and did her job. That's what I can tell you."

"Did you like her?"

Regina gazed at him steadily. "It's funny. I always imagined the work of a detective must be so exhilarating. Chasing the bad guys. But now I see it's really quite mundane. You just rush blindly into a dark room and flail about, hoping to grab hold of someone."

"Is that how it seems?"

She shrugged. "Ivy was fine. I didn't form an opinion one way or another about her."

"Really? Maude Ferndale mentioned you once spoke quite emotionally to her and she left crying."

"Did she? I can't recall. You must remember, Dan, we had a rotating staff all summer long. Occasionally I had to reprimand them."

"Did many of them cry?"

She cocked her head. "Have you spent much time with teenage girls? Crying comes only second to gossiping."

"What was your husband's relationship with Ivy Trent?" He watched her carefully as he spoke the question, but she remained expressionless.

"I'd imagine he had even less contact with her than myself. But you'd have to ask him."

"I'm interested in your impression of their relationship."

"I didn't have one."

Dan sighed. He could drill deeper with Regina Drake, but it'd be useless. He might as well be using a screwdriver to poke holes in a steel wall.

"Thanks for your time," he said, standing and offering his hand.

She dismissed him with a nod.

DAN HAD WALKED out of the club to find Louie had been the one who'd called him four times during his meeting with Regina. He climbed into his car and pulled onto the street, hitting send on his cell to call Louie back.

"Dan?" Louie demanded. "Did the hospital call you?" Louie's voice was strained.

"What hospital?" Dan flicked his blinker on to turn toward the road that would lead him to the bridge across the Ohio River.

"The hospital in Kalamazoo."

Dan let off the gas. A truck coming up fast behind him blared its horn and swerved around, sped off down the road. "Bennie? What happened to him? Is he okay?"

"Shit, man. I'm sorry. I don't have all the details. I'm headed up that way now, but I got the call this morning from one of his buddies named Wayne. I guess they took him in last night, pumped his stomach. He chewed up a bottle of painkillers."

Dan's car had come to a full stop now. He stared at the road ahead of him, his heart picking up pace as the words registered. "He tried to kill himself?"

"Like I said, I don't have all the information. Wayne said they'd tried to call you a bunch of times, next of kin and all. Only reason he found out was because the guy who lives across the hall from Bennie is also friends with Wayne. Gave him a call when the paramedics hauled him out."

"Fuck." Dan leaned back in his seat, squeezing his eyes closed.

"Like I said, I'm driving there now. Probably be there in thirty minutes, but you should—"

"Yeah. I'm on my way. It's a six-hour drive from here. I'll be there by three."

"Okay, good. If he wakes up, I'll tell him you're coming."

"Best not, Louie."

His friend said nothing.

"I'll explain when I get there."

33

There'd been a time in Dan's life when he'd loved long drives. Time to ruminate on the latest case, listen to classic rock too loud and just zone out for a few hundred miles. This drive, as many had in the previous months, served not to relax him, but to wind him tighter and tighter. When he crossed from Ohio into Michigan he felt as if he might explode through the windshield.

To a detective, Bennie's suicide attempt revealed one very ominous truth. He was guilty. Bennie had abducted and murdered Ivy Trent and when Dan had started to put pressure on him, he'd done what more than a few perps had done in Dan's time—try to check out rather than foot the bill.

Dan thought of their conversation from the previous day. Bennie's insistence that it wasn't what it looked like, he'd explain everything. Yes, he'd taken the photos of Ivy on the beach, but... he had good reasons. Of course he hadn't killed her. 'God, don't you know me at all?' he'd said. And Dan had ended the call feeling guilty for accusing his brother, putting the blame on the only family he had left in the world. He'd also gone to bed flooded with relief that his brother had not been the one who harmed Ivy.

But his dreams had been plagued by a different voice, the one that tallied it all up. Bennie following Ivy from the ice cream shop, scaring her. Bennie taking photos of her on the beach. Bennie having the water bottle in his shed.

"And let's not forget Ivy herself," Dan muttered. Ivy seemed to be desperately trying to tell Dan what happened to her. Why would she choose Dan? Unless...

"Stop," he commanded his own restless brain. "Just fucking stop."

But of course, the thoughts didn't stop. They churned until he pulled into the parking lot of the hospital and stepped from his car. At that moment, words failed him. What would he say to Bennie? He couldn't walk in and interrogate his own brother while he lay clinging to life in a hospital bed.

For the hours to come, Dan would be a brother, not a cop. He'd set Ivy aside and be Danny, the older brother to Bennie, who'd excitedly shown Dan his bird drawings as a kid and called 'Wait up, wait for me, guys,' when Dan and Louie would hop on their bikes and pedal like mad to get to the ice cream truck before it turned out of their neighborhood.

What came after Dan couldn't know, but for the next several hours, he owed it to Bennie to be his brother.

~

Louie met him in the hallway with an awkward hug. They'd never been huggers and it felt strange to start now.

"Has he woken up?"

"In and out. No coherent words yet, but there's brain activity, so that's good. The doc said he's out of the woods for the most part except for an erratic heart rate."

Dan walked into the room. Bennie lay pale and thin against his pillow. Dan's stomach lurched and for a second it was their mother lying in that bed, her own recent suicide attempt failed, her thin wrists secured to the metal bars on either side of the bed.

Above Bennie, a machine started a steady beeping. It continued and Dan studied the screen, half expecting to see the squiggly green ridges of Bennie's heart rate suddenly flatten into a single straight line.

He peeked into the hallway and gestured at the nurses' station, where two women stood. "Something's going off in here."

He walked with Louie to the cafeteria. His friend bought them each a coffee and a slice of blueberry pie, but Dan wasn't hungry.

"I thought he was doing better," Louie admitted when they settled into a corner booth in the dim cafeteria. "The new job and all, plus him calling me to check on you. He's never done anything like that before. I figured he'd gotten straightened out, you know?"

Dan nodded. He did know and yet his own problems from the previous year had shifted Bennie to the backburner in his mind. Bennie had always struggled in life. Failed jobs, relationships, businesses. He'd moved at least a dozen times, always thinking a new town would equal a new start, only to realize the same old Bennie showed up wherever he went.

"He tried this once before," Dan admitted. He'd never told Louie, never told anyone. It had been years ago and like the silence surrounding their mother's suicide, Dan's father had insisted on a similar secrecy when Bennie, at seventeen, had tried to hang himself in the basement of their house in Holt. The rope had snapped but when Bennie had hit the floor, head smacking against concrete, he'd lost consciousness. Dan's father had found him that way after work.

By then Dan had already gone off to the police academy. Dan had gone home for two days to visit Bennie in the hospital, but they'd never talked about it again.

"When?" Louie asked.

"He was still in high school. You and I were at the academy. He tried to hang himself but the rope broke."

Louie paled. "That weekend around Halloween when you took off out of nowhere?"

Dan nodded.

"You said your dad fell and hurt his back."

"He didn't want anyone to know."

"Just like your mom."

"Pretty much."

"Which means Bennie probably never got any help, right? Like a psychiatrist or anything?"

"They appointed him someone in the hospital. He probably met with the guy twice before they released him."

"What a joke," Louie muttered.

Dan sipped his coffee and thought of everything he'd discovered in the previous days. "I think it was Bennie," he whispered.

"What?" Louie asked.

Dan opened his eyes and stared at his friend. "I think Bennie murdered Ivy Trent."

Louie's mouth fell open. "No. What? Are you serious?"

"I've found things, unexplainable things. Bennie took pictures of her that day on the beach. I found her water bottle in his shed. Last night I dug the beach chair she'd been sitting on out of the weeds not ten yards from Bennie's cabin."

"Holy fuck."

"I didn't want to believe it. I called him yesterday. He swore it wasn't true, said he'd call me today and explain everything."

"You think that's why he tried to end it? Because he was caught?"

"If he weren't Bennie and this was just another case what would you think?"

Louie rubbed at his forehead. "Not Bennie," he said sadly. "Not little Bennie. Fuck…"

AFTER LOUIE LEFT, Dan wandered in and out of Bennie's room. His brother continued to sleep, wires and tubes hanging from his limp form.

A nurse shuffled him out as they replaced Bennie's IV bags, so Dan walked to the cafeteria and bought a bottle of water, which he drank in three enormous gulps standing at a picture window that faced a small airfield. He watched three planes take off and land before he figured enough time had elapsed for the nurses to do their thing.

Dan turned down the hall to Bennie's room and froze. Walking towards him from the opposite direction, a plush cardinal clutched in her hands, was Mel. She registered him and stopped, her face momentarily expressionless, and then a smile slowly spread across her features.

She passed Bennie's room and met him in the hall. "Dan." Her mouth turned down sympathetically. "I'm so sorry." She shifted the bird to one hand and wrapped both arms around him.

Her familiar scent, a lotion she made from the orange and peppermint essential oils, invaded his nostrils and made his head swim. He hugged her back, hard, and buried his face in her soft dark hair. "Oh, God, Mel. You're here."

She allowed him to hold her extra-long, pulling away slowly, to put distance between them.

Dan wanted to cry. He could feel the emotion surging into his throat. He'd never cried in front of Mel, but now he wanted to. He wanted to lay his head in her lap and feel her fingers stroking his temples and forehead and sob into her lap like a child. He closed his eyes and released a shaky breath.

"Dan." She put a hand on his forearm. "Are you okay? Do you need to sit down?"

He swallowed and blinked his eyes open. "There's a waiting room back there. Can we talk before you head in?"

"Of course."

She released his arm and the sensation sent another wave of grief through him. He felt his eyes grow full and he swiped at them, Mel at his back, trying to erase their evidence before they sat face to face.

The visitors' area was empty except for an old man who dozed in a chair by the television. Dan took a chair in the corner and Mel sat across from him. "You went white as a ghost out there," Mel murmured. "I was afraid you were going to faint."

"I didn't expect you is all. I guess seeing you... sort of rocked me."

She smiled. "I didn't know if you'd be here. I mean, I knew you would be at some point. I just didn't know it would be today, now, but here you are. It's good to see you, Dan, though I wish it were under different circumstances."

"My mom killed herself," Dan blurted.

A puzzled expression appeared on Mel's face. "I thought she died of a brain aneurism."

"That's the lie my father asked us to tell everyone. He was trying to protect her and us, but..." Dan wove his fingers together in his lap. "I should have been honest with you, at least with you about what had really happened."

"And you think that's why Bennie...?"

"No. Maybe in some twisted, buried way that even he doesn't understand. I just needed to tell you. I know that now. I lied. I sowed seeds of deception in our marriage before we were even married."

"Oh, Dan. Don't beat yourself up for all that. You had your reasons—"

"They weren't good enough and I'm sorry."

She sighed. "Thank you."

"You cut your hair. It looks nice."

She reached a hand to touch her hair, once long, now framing her pale face. "It seemed like time. I'm..."

She didn't finish the statements, but Dan knew what she'd been about to say and for an instant the breath vanished from his lungs as if someone had stuffed a vacuum cleaner in his trachea and sucked it out. Pregnant. Mel was pregnant.

He let his eyelids drift closed and then forced his lips into a smile. "That's great, Mel. Congratulations."

"I'm sorry to tell you now, here. Everything with Jared happened so fast. I didn't expect it too, but—"

"No, it's okay," he interrupted her. "I'm happy for you. You deserve it all, Mel."

Her eyes had begun to well up. Dan stood and held out his hand. "Time to check on Bennie?"

"Yeah," she murmured, taking his hand and following him out of the waiting room.

They went into Bennie's room together. As Mel took Bennie's pale hand in her own, his eyelids fluttered.

Dan stepped quickly away, moving into the hallway. She emerged from his room several minutes later, lines of worry drawing her mouth down. "Didn't you want to be with him when he woke up?" she asked, concern in her eyes.

Dan shook his head. "I wanted you to have a few minutes. You always had a good thing, hated to spoil it."

"You wouldn't have spoiled it, Dan," she told him, kissing his cheek. "I have to go though. Jared's hosting a dinner tonight for some work friends. Bennie's waiting for you."

He started to step away.

"Dan," Mel said before he entered the room. "I want you to know I don't regret it. Us. Okay? Even though we didn't make it, I've never regretted that we tried."

"I'll always love you, Mel. I hope you know that."

"I do." She smiled at him sadly. "Go take care of Bennie."

She turned and walked away.

34

ennie's eyes widened when Dan walked into the room. He'd sat up in bed and held his cup of water in his hand, the straw trapped between his pale lips. After a moment, he tore his eyes from Dan's and stared at the white sheet covering his body.

"A bottle of painkillers, Bennie?"

His brother looked gaunt against the white pillowcase. His hand shook as he lowered his Styrofoam cup of water back to his bedside tray. "I'm sorry, Dan."

Dan gazed at him, surprised. He hadn't expected the words, believing instead that Bennie would be defensive or, worse, angry that he'd woken up, that his suicide attempt had failed. "Why'd you do it?"

"I don't know." Bennie sighed. "Panicked, maybe. I just... after we talked, I felt..." He shook his head. "The next six months, year, played out in my head and I just didn't think I could go through it. And I didn't want you to go through it either."

"Because you killed Ivy?"

Bennie shook his head, pushing both hands into the hollows of his eyes. "I didn't, Dan. I swear on Mom that I didn't."

Dan hadn't heard the promise in years. It had been something they'd said as kids, in the years after their mom was gone. Somehow her death had made her the symbol on which they based unbreakable vows.

"I was into James Drake for twenty K. He used to host these poker games at the Dark River Inn. Up in that tower on the top. Exclusive games with big money. He and Carter Trent were always upping the stakes, trying to show who had the biggest balls. One night he'd had a few and they were short a guy. I was installing some shelves in the linen closet on the second floor. He invited me into the game. Offered to advance me a month's pay to play. I won a few, lost a few, but I was hooked."

Dan sat with his feet planted wide, hands braced on his thighs.

"One night he showed up at the cabin. He told me, 'I've come to even up.' Course I didn't have a dime and I was in the hole and digging deeper. He talked to me about his family of attorneys—two brothers and a dad, an expert at real estate law, getting liens on properties, forcing the sale of the cabin. He needed that money, you see. He didn't, of course. But I didn't know that at the time. I was scrambling, losing my shirt.

"He put it all on me, the weight of this debt, how quickly he'd strip me of everything, and then he started for the door, opened it and paused. He turned and walked back in. 'Maybe,' he said, 'maybe we can make a deal.'

"'A payment plan?' I asked him, and he laughed.

"'No, much better than that. You see,' he said, 'I've been involved in something rather untoward with a young woman. You know her, I think.'

"When he said Ivy's name, I felt half sick. Like I told you, I'd followed her home that night. Scared her good. Anyway, he said she was threatening him, threatening to tell his wife and kids, threatening to hurt them even. He needed to send her a message. He pointed out the window at the opposite bank on the river.

"'She's meeting me there tomorrow. An afternoon at the beach. I need you to grab her. Sneak up, kidnap her, bag over her head, arms and legs bound. Bring her to the inn. I'm going to scare her into silence, make sure she doesn't expose me.' He swore he wasn't going to hurt her. He just needed her to understand that she was treading on dangerous ground."

"And you agreed to that?" Dan asked, incredulous, leaning forward.

Bennie looked at the ceiling. "I never thought he'd hurt her."

"What did he do, Bennie?"

Bennie's eyes filled with tears. "I swear I don't know. I snatched her from the beach, cuffed her wrists and ankles."

"With handcuffs?"

Color rose into Bennie's face and he nodded. "James gave them to me. I cuffed her and took her to the inn. It was closed for maintenance that weekend. There wasn't a soul around. I carried her into the lobby. James was waiting. He had a chair sitting there. I sat her in the chair. He said, 'We're even. Get out of here.' And I did. I never saw a thing."

Dan put his face in his hands, furious at his brother, terrified for him at the same time. "And then what?"

"And then she never went home. Her mom sounded the alarm. I heard she was missing the following weekend. A few guys were talking about it at the bar. Annabelle Trent was telling everyone in town that Ivy had never come home, something had happened to her."

"And you didn't go to the police?"

"I confronted James. He told me he paid her, gave her a wad of cash, and made her agree she'd leave early for the college she was going to. He left her at her car, he said."

"And you believed him?"

"What choice did I have?"

"You had a choice," Dan muttered. "Why did you take the pictures, Bennie?"

Bennie frowned. "It seemed smart at the time, covering my ass. My camera was in my truck. I took it out there, snapped a couple photos, and then threw it back in the glove box before I went down to grab her. Honestly, I forgot all about them, but I realize now they didn't exonerate me. They made me look more guilty. Things got so crazy after I took her. She was screaming and crying." Bennie shuddered. "I dream about it sometimes."

"And as the years went by and Annabelle Trent's mother grew more hysterical, and the police started a real search, it never crossed your mind to come forward with what really happened?"

"They would have pinned it on me, Dan. I followed her home that night. James implied that he had… proof that I'd taken her."

"Proof?"

Bennie nodded. "I don't know what, but later I wondered if he staged the whole thing."

"You idiot," Dan muttered. "You set yourself up to be the fall guy."

"But… I mean there's no proof that anything bad happened to her. For all I know Ivy Trent is alive and well in New York City."

"If you believe that you really are a fool."

"I am, always have been. Don't you know by now?"

Dan frowned. "That's not true. I shouldn't have said that."

"Nothing wrong with speaking the truth," Bennie whispered.

Dan studied his brother. He could see so much of their mother in Bennie's face. They had the same champagne-colored eyes and small thin-lipped mouths. Bennie even smiled like their mother, a sorrowful smile that never quite looked happy. "Bennie, all those years ago, when you were seventeen, why—"

"Why did I try to kill myself then?"

Dan nodded.

"I didn't. I mean, I did, but I knew the rope would break. If the rope didn't break, the beam that I hung it on would have broken. I just wanted to know if I had the nerve. It takes a lot of courage. I'd been thinking about it for a while. Why did she do it? How did she muster the… the strength to go through with it?"

Dan wanted to argue, say, 'She wasn't strong, she was fucking weak. That's why she did it,' but he didn't really believe that.

"So I found a way to kind of do it. To be faced with the choice and see if I had the nerve to step off the chair." Bennie shrugged. "Thing is, I knew I wouldn't die, so it was just bullshit. She went all the way. She put that gun to her head and pulled the trigger."

Dan sagged back in his chair. He didn't want to see his mother in that car, what was left of her head splattered on the window, but the vision came anyway.

"We should have been in therapy," Dan whispered. "I thought Dad was right, but he wasn't. Hiding it, burying it was a mistake."

Bennie offered a wan smile. "Can't change the past, brother."

"No, we can't. But we can change the future."

AFTER BENNIE FELL ASLEEP, Dan took his brother's keys and drove to his apartment. It was a dreary little place, basement floor with a single grimy window set high in the wall. The kitchen and sitting area occupied a single square room. Cinder block walls, painted white, gave the apartment little to no charm.

Moose greeted him at the door, planting both paws on Dan's chest and trying to lick his face.

"Whoa there, Moose, back down. Down, boy. I know. I'm happy to see you too." He fished Moose's leash from under the ratty couch where Bennie said he'd discarded it after their last walk. He tried not to look at the orange prescription bottle turned over on the coffee table, nearly lost in the scattering of takeout containers, bullets and a Glock 19 Bennie had taken apart and likely been cleaning.

Dan walked Moose outside, directing him down the sidewalk. His cell phone rang and he saw Louie's number. "Hey, what's up?"

"Dude, some crazy shit has just gone down on the Mia Knox case over in Novi. You better call over there."

35

*D*an finished walking Moose before he returned to the hospital to let Bennie know he had to drive to Novi. He'd be back in the evening.

When Dan walked into the police department he'd considered a second home for nearly twenty years, he expected to feel the same emotions he'd felt the day he turned in his badge—shame, sadness, a bit of anger—but oddly he felt nothing, just numbness.

Desk Sergeant Thorpe gave him a hesitant smile. "Dan?" he said, surprised. "How are you?"

"I'm all right. I heard there's been movement on the Knox case. Is the chief here?"

"He's here."

Dan started toward the double doors and the guy spoke again.

"Bushman and Crout are interviewing the Knox girl's mother right now. Room three," he told him.

Dan took the long route to interrogation room three. He didn't want to walk by the chief's office if he didn't have to. He knocked gently on the door that led to the viewing room. Detective Crout cracked the door. He sighed and opened the door all the way, so Dan could slip in.

"Chief know you're here?" Crout asked.

"Not yet. What's the break?"

"Full confession. Happening right now. Forensics found Mia's body.

Her mother stuffed her into a crawl space underneath the house. Nothing but bones left of her."

Dan closed his eyes. He felt as if someone had socked him in the gut.

Detective Crout stepped closer to the glass that looked in on Detective Bushman and Erin Knox. Dan followed, though his legs and feet felt heavy as he crossed the room.

Erin had grown gaunt in the months since he'd last seen her. Deep grooves hollowed out her cheeks and gray tinged the skin beneath her eyes. Her collarbones poked starkly above the neckline of her pink wide-neck shirt. Her dirty blonde hair was unwashed and she'd cut it short. It hung limp below her ears.

Dan felt sick looking at her, sick at the knowledge of what was coming, unable to step from the room.

"You said you were home that day. Mia came home from school and then what happened?" Bushman asked. She had a motherly voice, a 'you can trust me' voice, and she'd gotten more than a few confessions because of it.

"I gave her sleeping pills. Ten of them in a strawberry milkshake. It was her favorite. After she fell asleep, I..." Erin's eyes flicked past the detective to the mirror. Dan wondered if she suspected that he stood behind it. "I... took a pillow into her room. I put it over her face."

"Did she wake up?"

Erin gave a little jerk of her head.

"I need you to answer 'yes' or 'no.'"

"No. Her body kind of spasmed once, her legs kicked out and then she was still." Tears rolled down her face and she didn't bother wiping them away. She looked like a corpse, as gray and dull as the bones they'd pulled from the hole in her basement.

Dan's hands were clenched at his side. There should have been relief. Finally closure after nearly two years, after countless days and nights conducting interviews, studying the case, obsessing, obsessing. But he too had gotten it wrong. They had all gotten it wrong.

"I'd like to talk about why, Erin. Can we do that?"

Erin shifted her eyes to the table. They continued to leak, her shoulders dragging forward, her head hanging like overripe fruit on her spindly neck.

"Erin?"

After a moment, she lifted her gaze slowly as if it took all the energy she had left. "I... Greg McMahon. He was getting transferred to Key West. He wanted me to go..."

"Greg McMahon was...?"

"The general manager at the grocery store where I worked. We'd been seeing each other for six months, but he was moving and he asked me to join him."

"Why not just take Mia with you?"

"He..." She hiccupped and a new flood of tears rolled down her cheeks. "He didn't want children."

"You killed your daughter because Greg McMahon didn't want children?" The detective's voice was gentle, but she was unable to completely hide her disgust for the woman before her.

Erin nodded.

"I need you to answer 'yes' or 'no.'"

"Yes."

"But then you didn't go to Key West?"

"He left... he left without me."

Dan's anger swelled in his chest. He wanted to slam his fist against the glass. He wanted to run into the room and choke the woman he'd once lain in bed with, rubbing her back as she sobbed for her missing daughter.

"Were you angry that he left without you?"

She blinked at the woman, her eyes large and watery. "It didn't really matter anymore. I'd... I'd destroyed the only thing that mattered in my life. I didn't know it before... I was so blinded by my... I'd been alone for so long. When I thought of him moving away, I... I just kind of snapped. Something in me broke and I couldn't see any way with Mia."

"Why didn't you leave her with someone? Your mother or her friends? More than one of them said they would have happily taken Mia in. They loved her. She was an amazing kid." The detective was seeking to hurt Erin with her words and it worked.

Erin began to rock back and forth in the chair. More tears. Her face was splotched and wet and seemed to be falling toward her chin. "I would like the death penalty," she murmured. "I would like someone to kill me."

The detective didn't speak for a moment. "I'm afraid that's not how it works. Did you contemplate suicide, Erin?"

Erin flopped her arms on the table, peeled back the sleeve covering one wrist to reveal several red, lumpy slashes. They'd healed somewhat but the raised skin told Dan the attempt had been within the month. "I'm so weak, I couldn't push hard enough. I took all the pills in the house. There weren't enough."

She didn't ask about Dan. He didn't know if he expected her to. He couldn't have sat in a room with her. Even in her dejected state he wanted to hurt her.

He stepped out and walked from the building.

~

AFTER A WHILE HIS former partner found him sitting on the cement steps staring at the traffic.

"You were right," Arnold said, sitting down beside him. It took him a moment to maneuver his large, blocky body onto the steps. "Mia was dead all along."

"I wasn't right," Dan whispered, thinking of how he'd ruined his own marriage comforting the grieving mother, climbing into bed with her, stroking her limp blonde hair. It was humiliating and more, an ache that went so deep he couldn't isolate where it lived in his body, but lived it did.

"You comin' back?"

"I'm still on suspension."

"Not if you don't want to be. The chief just wants to make sure you're right upstairs, that's all. You give him the word and you'll be back."

Dan didn't look at Arnold. He couldn't.

"She staged it," Arnold went on. "The money stolen from her purse, Mia's I.D. card at the bus stop, even packed a bag with some of Mia's clothes and then drove it out to the woods and buried it. All for some guy who left her and dry. A bleedin' waste."

Dan saw Mia's face then. The metallic glint of her braces. He imagined the vision board the fourteen-year-old had made and hung on her wall. It had been decorated with magazine cutouts of her dreams. Pictures of girls riding horses on the beach, images of veterinarians.

That had been her big dream, to become a vet. Pictures of children, the family she'd one day have. All of it smothered and discarded in the crawlspace beneath the little tract house she shared with her mother.

Dan released a strangled breath and stood abruptly. "I've got to go. Bennie is…" He didn't finish his statement, but strode away from the building and climbed into his car.

~

HE CHECKED in briefly with Bennie, who was eating jello and watching reruns of *Frasier*. He then drove to Bennie's dingy little apartment, walked Moose and filled his bowl with dog food. He added a few slices of deli turkey from the sub he'd picked up on the way back from the hospital.

He flipped off the lights and fell onto Bennie's bed in his jeans and t-shirt.

Dan woke at midnight to Moose's barks and the haunting sounds of piano music already fading as he snapped his eyes open. He sat up and fumbled for the lamp. Except there wasn't a lamp. Bennie had a mattress on a box spring and a pile of laundry on a chair. Otherwise, the room was empty.

Dan stood and stepped out of the bedroom into the main room. Moose's bark had subsided to a low growl.

Dan flipped on the light.

Moose stood, eyes fixed on a corner of the room near the tiny window. It was empty. But Moose continued snarling as if an intruder stood in the space.

"What is it, Moose?" Dan grumbled, smoothing down the raised fur on Moose's neck.

The dog jumped as if Dan had surprised him. Moose turned and whimpered, jumping up to lick Dan's face.

"All right, come on to bed with me, buddy." Dan led the dog back into the room and closed the door. He lay down, and Moose curled up on the opposite side of the mattress.

Sleep didn't come. He lay awake until dawn thinking of Mia Knox and Ivy Trent.

~

"WHAT NOW?" Bennie asked when Dan arrived at the hospital just after 8am.

"I've got to go back to Drake, wrap things up."

Bennie frowned and pushed both hands through his greasy dark hair. It had gotten long since the last time Dan saw him and brushed the tops of Bennie's shoulders.

"You need a haircut, man."

Bennie smiled. "The ladies like it."

"Yeah, I bet."

"I'm going to be in trouble, Dan. You finger James Drake and he's going to shift the blame right onto me."

Dan paced to the window, shoving his hands in his pockets. "I'm not calling him on it yet. Maybe I never will. I don't know, but... I have to go back. I'll take Moose with me."

"Moose would like that. The doc said this morning I probably have a few more days in here and knowing these jokers they'll be calling community mental health and getting me shipped off to the nuthouse."

"Let 'em," Dan said. "Use the resources, Bennie. That's what they're there for. Plus, if something did come up down the road, some mental health stuff could work to your advantage."

"The insanity plea? That's what I have to look forward to? Probably should have taken a few dozen more pills."

Dan stared hard at his brother.

Bennie's dour face turned into a smile. "I'm kidding, brother. Go do what you need to. I swear I won't hold it against you."

DAN DROVE BACK to Bennie's cabin with Moose sitting on the passenger seat, occasionally jumping toward the windshield if a bird flew across their path. After a couple of hours, the excitement wore off and Moose curled up on the passenger seat and fell asleep.

At the cabin, Dan dragged a fifty-five-gallon drum from the shed and threw the box with Mia's files into the bin. He poured charcoal lighter fluid onto the pages, watching them darken as they grew wet. Then he lit a match and dropped it in, watching the papers blacken and curl.

As he watched the black smoke billow into the sky, he thought of the psychic. *Crawl space*, she'd said, and that was where they'd found Mia Knox, stuffed into a star-patterned sleeping bag in the crawl space.

When Mia's file had turned to smoldering dust, he returned to the cabin and picked up the bent photo of Mel. He held it above the bin, gazed at her a final time and then dropped it into the flames.

36

The following day, Dan left Moose at the cabin and drove into Black Pine. He called Louie on the way and told him everything Bennie had confessed to the day before.

"So this James guy set him up and then murdered her?"

"Appears that way."

Louie said nothing for a long moment.

"What? What are you thinking?" Dan asked.

"Well… here's the thing and I'm not saying Bennie is lying, but… everything you've found is proof positive that Bennie grabbed her that day. Right? The photos, the water bottle, the chair by his cabin. Is there anything that supports Bennie's story? That he took her to James?"

"No," Dan admitted, and he'd had the same questions himself, but hadn't wanted to say it out loud.

"Do you believe him, Dan?"

"I want to."

"Yeah, me too. If you stopped digging right now—"

"Then Bennie would just go on living his life. No one would be the wiser."

"Fuck."

"Yeah. I don't think I can, Louie. Annabelle Trent deserves answers and…" He thought of all that had occurred since he arrived in Drake. Ivy had chosen him. How could he turn away from that?

"What are you going to do?"

"I'm going to sweat James. I need to get a sense about Bennie's story, whether it really happened the way he said it did."

Dan drove to Drake Digital Media and parked outside. He spent the day watching James's car, but the man never emerged from the building.

He called Cass from his cell phone.

"Hi, Dan," she answered.

"Hey, there. I just wanted to see if we were still on for the fish fry tonight?"

"You bet we are."

"Great. I've got to jet back to Bennie's cabin and let his dog out and then I'll meet you there."

"It's a date. You've got your brother's dog?"

"Yeah. I had to drive up to Michigan. I'll tell you about it at dinner. See you soon."

THAT EVENING, Dan met Cass at the River Bar. The attorney had vanished again, replaced by the woman with loose dark hair tumbling over her shoulders. She wore a green t-shirt that said 'Born to Fly' with a silhouette of a person casting a fly line beneath it. She'd gotten the table they sat at previously, and stood and waved when he walked into the crowded restaurant. He wove his way through other patrons, many standing around, talking and sipping from their beers, rather than sitting at the tables.

"This place is jumpin'," he said, leaning in to kiss her cheek.

She took a beer from the table and handed it to him. "Sure is. We've got the Moonshine Trio playing tonight." Cass gestured to the corner where three musicians sat on stools in the corner.

A man strummed on a banjo; a young woman played an odd-looking string instrument that rested lengthwise on her lap. A second man sang, bobbing his head, as he crooned about the mountains at dawn.

"What's she got there?" Dan asked, nodding towards the woman's instrument.

"An Appalachian dulcimer. My paw-paw had one. I tried to take it up as a girl, but I couldn't carry a tune."

"We have that in common."

They slid into the booth and Dan took a long drink from the Guinness Cass had ordered him.

"You said on the phone you had to go back to Michigan. Is everything okay?"

Dan puffed his cheeks and blew the air out slowly between his teeth. "I don't know. Bennie…" He shook his head. "He ended up in the hospital. While I was visiting him, Erin Knox confessed to murdering her daughter."

Cass was mid-drink and paused, lowering the glass. "The girl whose case you'd been investigating?"

Dan nodded.

"Her mother did it?" Cass looked as horrified as Dan had felt watching Erin through the glass.

"Yeah. I didn't have a clue. What a fucking idiot."

Cass shook her head and slid her hand across the table to his. She squeezed his fingers. "Don't do that to yourself."

He grinned and took another long swig of his beer. "Easier said than done."

They ate their fish, and Cass talked about a tour group she'd led that morning. One of the women in the group had stepped into a sink-hole in the river and disappeared beneath the water. Cass had to dive down and cut the woman's waders off as they'd filled up and pulled her nearly six feet beneath the surface.

"That sounds like a heck of a morning," Dan admitted after she finished the tale.

"It was. I'd like to end this day on a more positive note. What do you say we head back to my place?" she asked.

"I say yes."

CASS'S LOG cabin sat perched on a high piece of land above the river. Slabs of rock had been made into a staircase that led down to the water where Dan could see a dock and small rowboat.

Cass led him inside. A single light burned in a tall lamp. She pulled her t-shirt off and stepped closer to him. She pushed Dan's own shirt up over his head, kissing his face and neck, before moving her fingers to his belt and pulling it loose. She took a stack of blankets from a wooden chest and laid them in front of the stone fireplace before sitting and pulling him down on top of her.

After they made love, Dan lay and gazed into the fire. Cass stood and walked into the kitchen that was open to the living area. "Water?" she asked. "Or wine?"

"Water. Thanks." He sat up and drank the water in two gulps, looking around at the cabin. Most of the furnishings appeared home-made, carved from the wood in the forest around them. "Did your granddad make all this stuff?" Dan asked, touching the leg of a coffee table carved from driftwood.

"Yes, he did. Quite the craftsman, my paw-paw. In my twenties, when I was still in pursuit of the almighty dollar, I tried to get him to open a shop, sell it to the tourists that came through Black Pine. He looked at me like I was off my rocker." Cass smiled. "Turns out I was."

Above the fireplace Dan saw a large photograph in a rough wood frame. In the photo Cass sat next to a woman, likely her mother, on a small outcropping of rock. A dark gash cut into the stone beneath them.

"Was that taken here?" Dan asked.

"Yep. Me and my mom. My paw-paw took it in the woods behind the cabin. We used to hike out there a lot when I was a kid."

Dan studied the rock, thinking suddenly of a similar formation that lay on the opposite side of the river behind Bennie's cabin. It had been the perfect hiding spot when they were kids.

He thought then of the apparition of Ivy Trent and where he'd found her beach chair. It wasn't five yards from those slabs of rock.

Something twisted in Dan's belly and he stood, pulling on his jeans.

"You can stay," Cass told him. "I have a fishing tour in the morning, but you're welcome to lounge around here. Take the rowboat out."

Dan shook his head. "I can't. Bennie's dog is at my place, Moose. I need to let him out." He didn't add the sudden urge to trek into the woods and peer between those slabs of rock.

He kissed her goodbye and drove back to the cabin.

~

WHILE HE DROVE, Dan dialed the number for the hospital in Kalamazoo. "Can I have Benjamin Webb's room?" he asked the woman who answered the phone.

"Hold, please."

Dan listened to a recording about the hospital's new cancer unit. A moment later the woman came back on. "Benjamin Webb was discharged this afternoon."

"No. That can't be right. He said the doctor told him he had two to three more days."

"I'm sorry. That's all the information I have."

Dan dialed Bennie's cell phone. It went straight to voicemail.

"Fuck!" He pressed the gas pedal to the floor, shooting across the bridge that took him from West Virginia back into Ohio.

As he bumped along the rutted drive that led to Bennie's cabin, he held his breath, expecting to see Bennie's blue pick-up truck parked outside. It wasn't.

Dan let Moose out and waited for the dog to pee. After he'd done his business, Dan put the dog back in the cabin and grabbed his flashlight.

The slabs of rock were mostly overgrown, buried by the forest, mossy. But Dan knew where the crevice was located. As kids they'd wriggled into it, the perfect hideout for hide-and-seek. The perfect place to hide something else…

Dan dropped to his knees. His breath ragged, not from the walk through the woods, but from the sudden certainty of what he would find there.

He snatched at the vines and weeds that had grown up perfectly to obscure what lay behind them.

37

*D*an could not see her face or what was left of it. Only the tangle of Ivy's dark hair, shoved deep into the crack between the rocks, met his gaze.

Dan's breath rushed from his lungs and he closed his eyes, willing the body to disappear. He'd imagined her, imagined it all from the moment he put his eye to the telescope. It had all been a terrible dream. Except it hadn't.

Beneath the hair, he could see the bones of her skeleton, yellowed, and the tatters of her once-peach bathing suit and some other fabric. A robe perhaps.

No one but Bennie would have known about the rocks, about the perfect place to conceal a body.

Beneath Ivy's corpse, another spot of color glowed in the beam of his light. Leaves partially concealed it, but Dan spotted a spiral glint of metal and a blue cardboard cover. It was a notebook. He used a stick to fish it from the crack and pulled it free, sliding the stick into the spiral, so he could carry it back to the cabin without touching it.

He dropped it on Bennie's table and found a pair of rubber gloves beneath the sink. The pages were matted, but he managed to peel it open to the first page.

Several yellowed newspaper clippings lay inside. He saw the first one was the half-page spread covering the hit-and-run homicide of Johnny Trent. Beneath that were names and beneath each name were lists with words like 'motive' and 'alibi.' Many of the names had been crossed off, but two remained: Carter Trent and James Drake.

The pages that followed were filled with cramped writing that Dan struggled to discern. He turned to the last page. None of the entries were dated.

A single scrawled note in the margin of the last page caught his eye.

"'Wedding photo at the inn—Bronco,'" he read out loud.

Dan frowned and read the words a second time. He grabbed the envelope of photos he'd developed and flipped through until he found the single picture he'd taken of the wedding photo hidden in the shed at the Dark River Inn.

It was as it had been before. Regina and James grinning amongst their friends. He recognized Carter Trent among the groomsmen, but that wasn't all. Behind the smiling bridal party stood an olive-green Ford Bronco decorated with cans and white paper flowers. Someone had draped a banner across the hood that read 'Just Married.'

Dan closed his eyes and put his head in his hands. He didn't understand. Ivy had discovered what? That James had hit Johnny Trent? He stood and walked to the fridge. He'd drink a beer. He'd wait until morning to call the police, but as his hand closed on the handle, he saw the note stuck to the center of the refrigerator beneath the cardinal magnet.

'Meet me at the Dark River Inn.'

The words had been cut from a magazine and pasted to a lined sheet of notebook paper.

Had Bennie left him the note? Or James?

Dan didn't know, couldn't know.

His stomach twisted as he walked through the forest to the inn. A muted light glowed in the cupola. It danced and flickered. Candlelight.

Dan tried to imagine who awaited him. And if it were his brother, what then? Arrest him? Or did Bennie have something else in mind? Did he intend to silence Dan to ensure his freedom?

In the hall that led to the inner staircase, Dan paused. He'd tucked his gun into the waistband of his pants. Now would be the time to pull it, to train it in front of him as he ascended the steps. He envisioned Bennie staring down the barrel of his gun and a horrifying thought followed that image—suicide by cop. Leaving his gun in place, he walked up the stairs.

He pushed open the door, eyes adjusting from the dark halls to the room lit by three candles on the poker table.

Regina Drake sat in a wooden chair, legs crossed, a single lit match rising to the cigarette in her mouth. She watched him from dark, cold eyes. She drew on the cigarette and released the puff of smoke into the room.

"Men are so predictable. Here you are."

Dan blinked at her, a part of him wanting to search the room for Bennie. Were she and his brother in on it together? But even as the thought slid by, he understood he'd gotten it all wrong. "I don't understand."

She took the cigarette from her mouth and looked at it. "I haven't smoked one of these in ten years. Not since that night. And that night was the first time I'd smoked since the pregnancy of my first child." She took another drag and ashed the cigarette on the arm of her chair. "I'd never wanted a cigarette so much in my life."

"The night Ivy died. The night you... murdered her."

3 8

"You're disappointing me, Detective Webb. I thought you had it all figured out and here you stand looking like the dumb kid who just got called on in class." She smiled. "Sometimes I wonder if women actually commit more crimes, it's just the men who always get caught. Women are so much cleverer."

"And yet you're sitting there, which tells me you know I was getting close."

She cocked an eyebrow. "Do you think so? Let me clarify things for you. I've found waiting for a man to see the bigger picture can take eons, and still, they only see what they want to see. I came here tonight because I suspected you would be searching for Ivy and you just might find her. Now would you have pointed the finger at me? Not likely. The night she disappeared I had an airtight alibi. I was in Ohio with my children and mother."

"But you weren't."

She looked wistfully towards the dark window. They could not see the world beyond her reflection. "He thought I had no idea what he intended to do."

"James? What did he intend to do?"

She wrinkled her brow. "Scare her, pay her. God only knows. Of course, he fucked her again first. He cried and begged her to forgive him for sending Bennie, for scaring her. Then he gave her money, ten grand, and promised to go visit her at school. He was leaving me, he told her. That hadn't been his plan, but his dick started doing the talking and…" She laughed, a dry, mirthless sound. "He was ready to destroy everything. Our life, our marriage, our family. Men are such sickening creatures, weak and fair-weathered. He intended to end things with Ivy that night, but I knew he wouldn't." She put a hand on her heart. "Because women know the minds of men better than they do themselves."

"So you killed her?"

"I heard you cheated on your wife, Detective Webb. It's true, isn't it? At least she hadn't borne you any children. What an insult. Do you have any idea what it's like to be a wife and a mother? To feel your body get warped and ripped apart? To grow older and uglier beneath the weight of that huge responsibility? A responsibility that men share none of the burden of. None!" She shouted the last word and now when she raised the cigarette to her lips, her hand trembled.

"When did you find out about their affair?" Dan asked. His mind reeled. His gun was tucked into the back waistband of his pants. But he wasn't the only one with a gun.

After Regina had lit her cigarette, her free hand had returned to the armrest of the chair where her gun sat. "If I'd have been home, I'd have known much sooner. As it was, my own mother had been injured that spring. She fell from her horse and broke her leg. My father was in the midst of a lucrative real-estate deal in Texas and had to be gone frequently. I and the children moved in with my mother. My first clue was the credit-card statements. Again, the small minds of men. They can't even be bothered to get cash from the bank before they buy gifts for their whores."

Her eyes narrowed and focused as she spoke. They grew darker, as dark as the sky beyond the windows.

"Frederick's of Hollywood. Disgusting. Have you seen their lingerie? Strippers have more class. I started paying attention. I also started coming home, secret little trips. I told my mother I was having spa days, visiting friends. I'd drive home and watch and wait. On my first trip I saw them. So arrogant he was. He didn't take her to our home. Oh, no. Hotels up in Morgantown. They'd go out for expensive dinners. He bought her dresses, perfume. All of it on our credit card." She leaned her head back and looked at the ceiling. Dan half expected to see tears when she righted her gaze but saw only fury in her eyes.

"Why did he break it off?"

"Because I came home. Because I made it abundantly clear that I was very suspicious. I also reminded him about our financial standing and who stood to lose if our marriage dissolved."

"He knew that you discovered the affair?"

"Oh, let's not give him that much credit. He'd lost the freedom of my absence. He knew that. But they carried on still."

"She thought you were separated. That's what James told Ivy."

Regina glared at him. "And is that good enough, Detective Webb? Does that make it all okay? Would that have made our children feel better? Does that justify destroying a family?"

He shook his head and thought sadly of Mel. "No."

"No. But even as you say that to me, you yourself have acted on your primal impulses. Pants are the only proof that men have evolved beyond Neanderthals. Sad, so very sad your internal lives must be. No loyalty, no integrity."

"What about Bennie? What if he'd gone to the police?"

Regina shrugged. "It was apparent to me that very night that I would not be implicated. The blame would fall either to my husband or your brother. Both of whom deserved whatever came to them. A part of me hoped for that, but I also knew they'd likely never find Ivy's body and prosecutors don't like to try bodiless cases. It's the oldest story in the book. They play to win. If they can't win, they don't play."

"Will you tell me what happened that night?"

"Confess? Reveal my secrets?" She took a final drag on her cigarette and put it out on the chair. Her eyes lingered on the dark mark. She tapped a fingernail against it. "Even this, ashing my cigarette, I think about. There isn't a chair in the Dark River Inn that anyone would have dared to treat in this manner. Except in this room. My husband's little playboy room where they gambled and got stupid drunk. Nothing was safe from them in here. We had a beautiful Tiffany chandelier in here when we first took over the inn. It was cracked that very first summer." She grimaced, revealing her straight teeth, which had a small animal-like quality.

She picked up the gun. It was a 9mm and she'd already disengaged the safety. She trained it on him.

"I'll tell you. Why not? I've had it all bottled up for so long it's almost as if it doesn't exist anymore. Sometimes I feel as if it's the most extraordinary thing I've ever done. The planning, the act, the pulling it off. My husband struts around town as if he is so very cunning." She smirked. "That trait belongs to me. I wonder if this deep, dark secret has kept our marriage alive. I always have this in the back of my mind, this truth about what I am capable of regardless of what I see reflected in his eyes. Just a typical housewife. That's what he thinks."

She gazed at Dan as if the mere thought astounded her. "I have a bachelor's degree in finance. I graduated top in my class in high school. I ran track, played volleyball, even in college. I've birthed three children, naturally!" She spit the last word and her hand twitched on the gun.

Dan's instinct was to lunge back even if it meant falling down the stairs, but he stood his ground.

"My parents are multi-millionaires. Do you know how many men courted me? Begged for me to consider them?" She pursed her lips and yanked one hand suddenly through her dark hair. The gesture left it standing like a strange wave up from the side of her head. "None more than James. He picked me up for our first date in a stretch limousine." She touched a shaky hand to the hollow of her throat. "A limo that took us to a burger joint where girls on roller-skates came right up to the window." A blush rose into her neck and her eyes were a confusion of joy and fury.

Dan said nothing. He'd been in this scenario before, many times. *The faucet's on*, he and his partner used to call it when a suspect started talking, not just talking, but talking as Regina was now with that faraway gleam in her eye, with one foot in another time. When the faucet was turned on, the detective shut the hell up and let the well run dry.

"After that we drove up Miner's Mountain to the overlook there. He'd planned it all. A picnic basket with a bottle of wine, chocolates. By the time he dropped me home, I'd lost myself. That's what it's like, the total loss of autonomy to this relentless need to see them, talk to them, to know what they're doing. Waiting by the phone, driving by their house, calling and hanging up."

She let out a strangled laugh. "It's a sickness, a disease. I almost lost him to Misty Jackson." Regina's lips pursed into a flat angry line. "With her big ratty curls and her grotesque mouth. She was a cheerleader at Ohio State. What a degrading position. And yet it epitomizes our role in this society, don't you think? Put on a tiny little sequined skirt and jump and scream while the big, brawny Neanderthals knock their heads together on the field. We're all eyes on them and they barely register our existence."

She shifted the gun and gazed at it. "Amazing the power in this. We have the Chinese to thank for these." She tapped the gun on the arm of the chair. "The damage of just one single shot." She lifted the gun and focused it on Dan's belly.

His muscles tightened in his stomach, but he slowed his breath and said nothing.

"I saw them one night, James and Misty, at a drive-in movie at the southern end of Columbus. He took her there because he didn't want to run into me. I'd bet my life on it. But my girlfriends dragged me out —no sitting by the phone on a Saturday night—and who do I see except James with his hand up Misty's shirt, pawing at her like an adolescent boy.

"But I took care of that. Though I was much less focused in those days, much less prepared. Ivy was my masterpiece. I don't remember quite when I started to imagine her death, but I do know when it shifted from a dream to a plan. James had bought her these beautiful sandals, sandals that I had pointed out to him in Morgantown. He took her to dinner and got a room at Town's Inn in Harper's Ferry."

She shifted her eyes from the void to Dan's face, to his own eyes. "He'd done that exact thing with me fifteen years earlier. All of it, every detail. Men and their unoriginality. 'If it isn't broke, don't fix it,' he loves to say. It was raining in Harper's Ferry that night and I stood there in the rain, my hair and makeup ruined, and I knew that he was marching Ivy Trent down the path of our future, our life. It would only have been a matter of time before he knocked her up. That's what they do, these men with their whores. His eye would have wandered, and Ivy would have done the one thing that would bind him to her for life, create a child."

Regina tap-tapped the gun on the arm of the chair. The sound grated on Dan's brain, but he stayed motionless though his feet had begun to ache and grow tingly.

"That's when I knew I had to stop them both. I scared him first. I contacted my lawyer. James was plainly told that a rumor of an affair was circulating. James was nearly in financial ruin." Regina released a cruel laugh. "I majored in finance but he insisted on running his own books. Wouldn't let me touch them. Of course, I kept control of my own money. 'A fool and his money are soon parted,' that's what my dad liked to say, and he said it more than once in reference to James, and like most things he was right. That little birdie in his ear scared James. He knew he had to end things with Ivy before I got wise to their tryst. But I knew that wouldn't be enough. I'd seen the look in her eyes. She wouldn't let him go so easily. But I had to be careful. I had to plan everything perfectly so that it couldn't be traced to me."

Regina pointed at the ceiling. Dan glanced up at a small white fire detector.

"My girlfriend Sloane gave me the idea. She'd been using nanny cams on the au pair she'd hired to watch her girls. She showed me one day. This perfect little camera tucked inside a stuffed bear." Regina's eyes glittered. "I did one better and bought ten of them. I bugged every room James spent time in. This room was always the most revealing. His little bachelor pad. I watched on video while he planned her abduction with Bennie. That plan was his gift to me, the perfect opportunity for me to remove Ivy without anyone being the wiser. I must admit their little plot disturbed me. For both of those men it fulfilled some sick sexual fantasy. I saw the erection in James's pants when Bennie brought her in, sobbing, struggling in his arms."

Dan studied Regina's face. Her words implied some sympathy for Ivy's experience that night, but it was not reflected in her expression. Rather, she seemed to be reveling in her own perverse memory of the occurrence. "Why did he ask Bennie to kidnap her?"

Regina scowled. "Because men are dogs. It wasn't enough to break it off, tell her to keep her mouth shut. He wanted to scare her, hurt her. You think he's innocent, but he's not. He might not have pulled the trigger, but he murdered her the first time he put her on her back. She forgave him. Not twenty minutes into her arrival and they were on the floor, crying and kissing and screwing." Her hand had tightened on the gun. It continued its tap-tap but harder now.

"He had a plan, he told her. He'd give her money to go to school early, even some extra for Annabelle, the whore mother. He needed to secure his finances and ensure he'd come out of the divorce in good standing." Her eyes widened as she spoke and she swiveled her gaze up to Dan. "Can you imagine? What he intended was to swindle as much of my money as he could before he took off to be with his whore. That's when Ivy dropped the bombshell on him. She knew what he and Carter Trent had done."

"What do you mean?"

She narrowed her eyes at him. "Am I meant to believe you have no idea what I'm referring to? No wonder they got rid of you in Novi."

Dan's jaw tightened. "The Bronco. Carter and James hit and killed Johnny Trent?"

egina's mouth turned down. "Bingo. Carter was behind the wheel, some grand plan to go stir things up at Annabelle's trailer while Johnny was at work. They were three sheets to the wind, of course. You know what James told me later? Carter did it on purpose. He saw Johnny in the road and he never even tapped the brake. Hit him going fifty miles an hour. Amazing there was even a body left to find."

"Why would he do that?"

Regina shrugged. "Money, most likely. Rumor had it that Johnny's mother and brothers were suppressing his father's will to ensure Johnny didn't get his share. Johnny might have hired a lawyer, but who really knows."

"And Ivy found out?"

"She thought she did anyway. James didn't know that. He never suspected his little whore had ulterior motives when she climbed into bed with him, thought it was all his good lucks and charm." Regina snorted. "The look on his face when she confronted him was priceless. Then the little bitch walked into our office and snatched our wedding photo off the wall, shoved it in his face. The nerve of her."

Dan shifted from foot to foot, trying to bring some feeling back to his numb legs. He felt the pressure of the gun against his lower back. He'd begun to sweat and the rivulets of perspiration rolled beneath his shirt.

"Police told the media they were looking for a green Bronco. How is it possible they didn't find it if your husband owned one?"

"He didn't own one. It belonged to one of the other groomsmen, Larry Schmidt. He lived in Columbus. The weekend Johnny was murdered, a bunch of the guys were doing a boys' weekend at the inn. Most of the guys from our wedding were there. James and Carter went to town on a beer run in Larry's bronco. They decided to drive out to Annabelle and Johnny's trailer. By the time news of the Bronco was released Larry and his vehicle were long gone. I doubt Larry ever heard about the hit and run. Black Pine doesn't exactly make the national news."

"Why did James cover up for Carter Trent?"

She smirked. "Because James worshiped the ground Carter walked on, that's why. You think James's business would have taken off if not for Carter's pull? Not a chance. James owed Carter and then conveniently, after Johnny was dead, Carter owed James."

"If you hated your husband so much why not let Ivy just take him and Carter down?"

"Is that what you think? I hated my husband? I didn't hate James. I loved James. I still love him, even if he doesn't deserve it. But Ivy was trouble. Long before I had an inkling that she was onto Carter and James, I knew she was trouble. That's why I did what I did that night.

"I put my children to bed in Columbus. I kissed my mother good-night and I climbed into my mother's car and made the two-hour journey back. I drove to the skeleton tree where she'd left her car, unlocked—little fool. Of course, I'd planned for that too and brought a tool kit to open the door if need be. I slipped on my gloves and climbed into the backseat. I'd bought a blanket that matched the car's interior. I lay on the floor in the back, gun in my hand, and waited."

"How did you know he'd take her back to her car? That he wouldn't just spend the night here at the inn?"

"Because I'm capable of planning ahead, of seeing how things will unfold and ensuring every detail goes my way. I had called James that morning and told him we had a friend coming to our house in Black Pine very early in the morning to pick up a painting I'd donated for a fundraiser. He would never have risked not going home, having it get back to me that the house was empty when my friend showed up. I added that I had a friend coming to the inn to pick up some paperwork I'd left in the check-in booth."

"Were either of those things true?"

"It was all true. I planned every last detail. I sat in Ivy's car for an hour, maybe a little more, and that was a long hour, let me tell you. My back started to hurt. I didn't get tired. Oh, no. I drank three pots of coffee to ensure I'd stay awake. That turned out to be a problem. I had to use the bathroom, but I held it. Women learn to endure all sorts of physical discomforts."

Dan imagined the woman before him lying in wait in the backseat of Ivy's car. In all the scenarios he'd envisioned in the previous weeks, this had not been one of them.

"Ivy slid behind the wheel after a very long goodbye with my husband. He drove away and she sat there for a few minutes crying. That big wad of cash was on the passenger seat beside her. I waited until she'd started the car and pulled onto the road. I didn't want to risk her jumping out and running away. After all, I'd been in the backseat for an hour. I could barely feel my toes." She chuckled. "I sat up and watched her for a moment in the rearview. Her eyes were all puffy and then her eyes flickered up to the mirror and back to the road and I saw everything in her tense. She looked again and her mouth fell open like one of the nutcracker dolls, bottom teeth hanging down to their chest. I put the gun to the back of her head. 'Drive to the inn,' I told her."

Regina took a deep breath in and studied Dan. "Planning. That's something I'm very good at, Dan. In fact, by standing here all this time, I think you must feel a bit like I felt that night. I bet if you tried to run right now, you'd trip over your clunky feet. Am I right?"

"Pretty much."

"And I know too that you're working out your own plan, but remember I was here when you arrived. I was already one step ahead of you and I'm still one step ahead of you, regardless of what you might think."

Dan thought of his gun in the waistband of his pants. It was loaded, he'd checked before he left. He tried to imagine what kind of trap Regina had set for him, but beyond the gun in her own hand, he simply didn't know. "Did she listen to you? Just drive right back to the inn?"

Regina smiled. "She had the barrel of a gun to the back of her head.

What do you think? You more than most know the power of one of these—not just what they do to the physical, but, well... the mental. This is compliance. This little beauty can make anyone do anything. I don't think I saw how powerful it was until that night. She drove straight back and I marched her through the inn and all the way up to this room." Regina waved at the room. "It was fitting. It was the place they'd begun their little affair."

"How so?"

"He asked her to bartend at one of their little card games. Paid her cash. That was how they started, that very night. Fitting for it to end here. I'd covered this room in plastic. It was easy. It's small, contained. Plastic on every surface."

"What if he'd brought her up here?"

She smiled. "I was fumigating, I told him the week before. I'd seen a cockroach. Keep the door closed, whatever you do. He didn't want to bring his little whore into a room stinking of bug bombs. The plastic was worth the look on her face. She dropped to her knees when she walked in here, started crying, begging for her life, apologizing. The things people do when they get caught, never a moment before. That's how you know if there's truly remorse, regret. If it only comes when there's a gun to their head, you can rest assured it's false."

"And then you shot her?" He didn't want to force the story or feed her words, but his knees had begun a slight quaking. He needed to move, to take a few steps but didn't dare with the gun aimed at his stomach.

"Eventually. I'll spare you the hours leading up to that moment. They were ugly to be sure. I had to shut her up. In the end the bullet into the top of her head was the easiest way to do that."

"And then what did you do with her body?"

"Well, that's the one true secret, isn't it? The thing you want most of all. No body, no crime."

"I've seen plenty of cases prosecuted without a body." Dan tried to keep his voice even.

"Not without evidence you haven't. Not winning ones. There's not a shred of me in that girl's car. I brushed my entire body before I climbed in. I put on brand-new clothes I'd never worn. I brushed my hair and covered it with a shower cap with a knit hat on top. I wore a pair of my husband's shoes." She laughed and put a hand to her mouth as if amazed at her own audacity.

"You wanted to frame him?"

"Not at all, but if it was going to come back on someone, it wasn't going to be me. And I did rather enjoy watching him and Bennie scramble in the following days. There were more than a few harried phone calls between them. They both thought the other had done it, but neither could speak out for fear of implicating themselves. My God, it was like watching a rerun of *The Three Stooges*. In the end, they didn't look too deeply. They didn't want to know. That's the bottom line. They did not want to know.

"You know what the worst part of the night was? Not cleaning up the blood, not disposing of all the... stuff. It was planting the car at the bus station and then walking the four miles back to my own car. I had to row across the river too. I couldn't risk walking that bridge at night. The adrenaline had worn off by then. I'd changed into my own shoes on account of the distance, but I had to travel in the woods just in case someone drove by. By the time I reached my car, I was tuckered out. I had blisters on my feet the next day. I drove back to Columbus, climbed into bed and slept like a baby. I woke promptly at eight even though I'd just gone to bed three hours before. I took my mother and children shopping. I rented a DVD of *Home Alone*. It was just another ordinary day."

"I found her diary, Regina. She discloses her affair."

"And?"

"And it's going to put police on the scent of your husband."

Regina shrugged. "Where is the diary, Detective? In your cabin, I presume?"

"Do you think you can get that lucky twice? Make me disappear and everything that connects you and James to Ivy's disappearance?"

"I don't need luck, Dan. Your brother is clearly the person who murdered Ivy Trent. And when you got wind of it, he took care of you too."

Dan thought of Ivy with her huge dreams. She had considered ending things with James multiple times. If only she'd followed through, walked away before Regina Drake had discovered the affair. "Ivy intended to end things with James. She felt terrible about the affair. She was going to break it off."

Regina smiled coolly. "That's your own conscience speaking, Detective Webb. You've fought for this girl and need her to be redeemable to justify your effort. That's fine. But it doesn't change what went on, what was coming. Ivy was going to ruin us. Either by stealing my husband or by exposing what he and Carter Trent did."

Dan studied Regina's thin frame. He had eighty pounds on her. But as he'd watched her with the gun, he understood how comfortable she was with it, how easily she handled it. She'd learned how to use her gun, she'd carried it, gotten good at shooting it. There was no fear about the thing that she clutched in her hand and that gave him a strong disadvantage because his gun was in the back of his pants and long before he could yank it out she would have put a bullet in his head.

He blinked and realized that the sound he'd heard when he walked in was plastic beneath his feet. Clear plastic stretched tightly from wall to wall and went halfway up to the window. It wasn't the same plastic she'd used with Ivy, the kind you noticed. This plastic was so clear he genuinely hadn't noticed it until that moment.

Regina had every intention of killing him that night.

"While you've been investigating us, Detective, I have been investigating you. What a mess you've made of your life. Goodness. And let me tell you, lips are not sealed at your old precinct. Your ex-wife just got married, thanks to you and your adulterous betrayal." The line of Regina's jaw hardened as if she'd clamped her teeth together. "If that wasn't a blatant case of abuse of power, I don't know what is. Sleeping with a woman whose only child has disappeared." She stared at him with such open disgust that the shame of those earlier days rushed back.

Some of his resolve seeped out. A thought flickered through his mind. *What do I have to live for?*

It had been the refrain for so long that it almost comforted him, but then he saw the plastic gleaming beneath him and he thought of Ivy with her half-packed bags, and the bright future the bitter woman before him had stolen.

He flexed and unflexed his feet, before tensing his calves and then quads. Slowly, a bit painfully, he worked some blood back into his aching feet and legs. "I'm a lot heavier than Ivy, Regina. How do you plan to get me out of here?"

She didn't answer, but he saw a flicker of something in her eyes and knew she likely hadn't thought that all the way through. "Ever moved one of those big rugs, Dan? The Oriental kind that are twelve feet long and weigh two hundred pounds? I have. And we're on the top floor. Gravity will assist me."

"To the ground floor, but are you sure you can haul me down two flights of stairs and not leave a trace of blood? I'm assuming you'll shoot me in the head. There's going to be a lot of blood."

"Dan, you're forgetting the most critical aspect to our situation. You are a shamed detective who took off on a bender to an isolated cabin in the middle of nowhere. Do you think anyone will come looking for you here?" Her smile widened. "That's good old-fashioned ego right there. From what I heard, the only person in the world who gives a damn about you just tried to off himself."

"He did something else too. He confessed to abducting Ivy for your husband, to bringing her to the Dark River Inn. They might not come here looking for me, but they sure as hell are coming for her."

"My husband's family are some of the most ruthless attorneys in this country. If you think one single investigator will set a foot in this house, you are sorely mistaken. But"—she laughed at this part—"I did have a contingency plan that's been... undecided. You see, when you started digging around, I started thinking about the best way to really destroy evidence. Bleach is lovely, but it's not exactly foolproof."

"And?"

Her eyes lit up and she reached for the box of matches in her lap. "It's so very simple."

"Is it? Arson isn't as easy as you might think."

"Oh, it will never look like arson. I've been coming out here, loosening a hose here and there, leaving some things around that are highly flammable. It takes thirty minutes for fire responders to get here and that's if they leave the moment the call comes in, which they won't for a few reasons. One, they're slow and lazy. I've met the boys at the fire station in Drake. Let's say I wouldn't hold my breath. Two, this place has been vacant for a decade and they are well aware of it. They won't be in a hurry, I promise you."

"And you think that's going to conceal two bodies? Burning this place down."

She smiled. "I never said anything about concealing bodies. We're merely talking about destroying evidence, Dan. Blood, fingerprints, those tiny little hairs you see expert witnesses talk about on court TV shows. They make it sound very dramatic, but I bet in real life, half the juries are snoozing in their little box."

Dan shifted from foot to foot, wincing at the tingling in his toes.

Regina smirked. "I rather enjoy watching you trying to piece it together. Maybe I'll move Ivy's body after all..." Regina murmured as if having an epiphany. "Maybe I'll move her a little closer to Bennie's place. Stick her in the shed." Regina grinned. "Though if anybody decides to come looking for you, they'll find Ivy eventually. And who do you think they'll blame? James? Me? Oh, no. Bennie is the clear choice. The body is on his property after all. Bennie showed that spot to my daughter, Hannah. He gave me the perfect area to conceal Ivy's body. It couldn't have been more perfect."

"Where was Bennie that night? What if he'd taken a walk? Found you hiding her body?"

"Your brother's a drunk, Dan. I got Ivy into a wheelbarrow, covered her up, and took a quick walk to your brother's cabin. Just as I figured, he was passed out on the couch, bottle of Jack Daniels on the floor." Her eyes glittered in the candlelight. "Tell me the truth, Dan. You thought it was him, didn't you? Even his own brother believed he murdered her."

From the dark stairway the distant sounds of music floated up.

Regina froze, the muscles in her jaw tightening.

The haunting refrain of *Mad World* drifted into the room as if someone sat in the lobby below, fingers floating over the keys. Dan recalled the lyrics and murmured them out loud, watching Regina's stony face drain of color.

'And I find it kind of funny
I find it kind of sad
The dreams in which I'm dying
Are the best I've ever had.'

"Shut up," she hissed, hand twitching on the gun.

"It's her, Regina. Even if you kill me tonight, it won't be over for you. You can't murder someone twice."

Her eyes had left him. They were locked on the stairs, bulging, her head pitched slightly forward as if she expected Ivy to rush from the darkness.

Dan seized his chance. He threw himself backward and sideways, tucking in his legs as he hit the stairs. The breath surged from his lungs, but he didn't stop. He rolled down the last of the stairs and scrambled sideways as the first shot rang out above him.

The bullet tore past him, but all other sound vanished beneath the blood pumping in his ears. His feet throbbed and he took two steps and dove into the first room, plastered himself against the wall. He reached for his gun in the waistband of his pants. It was gone, likely fallen out when he tumbled down the stairs. He crept into the bathroom to the window.

He couldn't hear Regina and didn't know if she'd already entered the room behind him. Gritting his teeth, he pushed the window up and climbed on the edge of the tub, bracing both hands on the ledge.

"Stop," she snarled behind him.

Dan didn't. He shoved himself forward with all his might, Superman-diving through the window. His hips and legs bashed against the ledge and he scrambled forward.

Regina pulled the trigger and the slug caught him in the lower right side of his back. The intense pressure soon gave way to burning and when his legs thudded against the roof, Dan felt sure he'd been paralyzed. Relief flooded through him when he managed to bend his knees and, pushing up onto his hands, he crawled sideways out of the line of the window. The warmth of his blood trickled beneath his shirt and down his side.

An eave jutted from one corner of the house and Dan crouched beneath it, confident that Regina couldn't see him from any of the windows. He reached a tentative hand to his back and felt his saturated shirt and top of his jeans. He swallowed, noticing the first pinpricks of dazzling black spots in his vision.

After a moment Dan heard her, not in the house, but outside. Grimacing, he forced his body flat on his stomach and shimmied closer to the roof edge so he could see her below.

He heard her, the erratic sound of her breath and something else, liquid splashing. After a moment, he smelled it. Gasoline.

Regina moved into the overgrown yard, dropping a gas can. She hunched over as she fumbled things from a dark bag. She looked nothing like the woman he'd met just days before at the country club in Black Pine. Her dark hair was plastered to her forehead with sweat and her eyes were peeled wide, unnaturally so. She curled her lips back from her teeth as she focused on whatever she held. He could hear words spilling from her mouth, disjointed mutterings.

"All wanted me, all of them. Could have anyone. Whore, whore with her simpering stupid face."

After a moment, he saw the orange flame as she held a lighter towards a bottle stuffed with a rag.

Blood loss and pure fascination held Dan rooted to the patch of roof, watching as Regina prepared to burn the house beneath him.

The rag lit, plumed orange and bright, and as Dan stared mesmerized at Regina's twisted face, a shadow slid from the forest behind her. Pale, ghostly, it did not walk so much as flow across the gap between them.

As Regina lifted the flaming bottle above her head, the pale thing took shape. For an instant Ivy Trent became as solid as stone. She reached her arms high and thrust her hands into the flames. The fire shot down, catching Regina's hair.

Regina shrieked, still managing to let the bottle fly. It shattered on the wooden porch, and the accelerant, burning, raced across the deck to the house.

Regina thrashed and screamed, running towards the river as the fire engulfed her. She splashed into the water, howling, clawing at her face.

Dan blinked out for a moment, the world swimming beneath him. His head shot back up when he heard the crackling of the wood as the fire took hold of the house. He tried to sit up but his arms had grown weak, legs too. He had to get off the roof.

Gritting his teeth, he rolled sideways, clenching his eyes shut when the roof disappeared and the air opened beneath him.

Dan landed in the tall grass, his head snapping back. Pain coursed through him, but his awareness shifted quickly to the sensation of heat. He'd landed too close to the house. The left side of his body was blistering and then something, someone, was near him.

He saw a wisp of her dark hair, her strange white eyes, but not only Ivy stood near him. Around her, within her, as if they were one and yet not, were others. He saw his mother for an instant, the cool touch of her palm on his forehead. Faces undulated and merged above him and then he heard the whisper of voices. The most beautiful voices. Something soft and vaporous enveloped him.

He thought that this was death and it was not so bad, not bad at all.

"*He's* waking up."

Someone touched Dan's wrist, squeezing. He opened his eyes, the lids heavy and dry. Louie stood next to his bed, Bennie beside him. "This is not what I expected heaven to look like," Dan croaked.

Louie grinned, but Bennie's mouth stayed pressed tightly closed. Dan realized his brother's chin trembled as if he were about to cry.

"It's okay, Bennie. I'm okay," Dan told him, though he didn't really know if that were true. "Aren't I?" He looked at Louie.

Louie nodded. "You're okay, Danny boy. The bullet caught your hip, shaved off some bone and took a hunk of flesh, but no organ damage. You're a bit singed, but you managed to get far enough from the house before the whole thing went up in flames, so you're pretty lucky there."

"Lucky," Dan whispered, remembering the apparition that had appeared beside him. It had been Ivy, but not only Ivy, his mother and dozens of others, maybe more. He hadn't moved himself away from the house.

He reached a hand to the left side of his face. A bandage covered it from midway across his scalp to his chin.

"It's a burn bandage," Bennie told him, putting a hand to his mouth. "That's what the nurse called it."

"Drake police are here. They've got questions," Louie told him, glancing toward the closed door.

"I bet," Dan murmured. "Regina?"

"She was admitted too. I passed her room earlier and she was screaming all kinds of crazy shit. I think they sedated her."

"Did she confess?" Dan asked.

"Confess to what?" Bennie gazed at Dan.

"She murdered Ivy Trent. It was Regina, James's wife."

"No frickin' way," Bennie breathed. "Regina Drake?"

Dan nodded, grimacing as pain coursed through his left ear. "How'd you guys get here?"

"Drake P.D. called us," Louie explained. "They found your cell. You had me listed as emergency contact. I'd picked up Bennie when they discharged him from Kalamazoo and took him back to our place in Farmington Hills. He was going to crash with me and Sherry for a few days while he recouped. We got the call just after midnight. Jumped in the car and got here lickety-split."

"Bennie was with you," Dan whispered, thinking back to the night before, and how he'd been sure after getting discharged Bennie had made the trek to the Dark River Inn.

A knock sounded on the door. A nurse pushed it open and stepped inside. "My turn, guys," she told Bennie and Louie.

"Want anything from the cafeteria?" Louie asked as he and Bennie trudged toward the door.

"No, thanks, man." Dan directed his attention at the nurse. "I could use something for the pain though."

She smiled and stepped next to his bed, looking at the IV bag. "We've got something ready, but the police would like to speak with you first if you're up for that?"

"Sure, send them in."

EPILOGUE

*D*an held Annabelle's hand as they waited at the Drake Police Department.

The detective pushed open the door and walked to Annabelle. "How are you, Annabelle?"

Annabelle nodded weakly, but said nothing.

"The medical examiner confirmed what Regina Drake confessed to. Ivy was shot twice in the head. Although he can't give us an exact time of death, she's been deceased for years. In all likelihood she passed the night she went missing."

Annabelle bowed forward, placing her head in her hands. After a moment soft sobs shook her shoulders.

DAN WALKED with a cane to the Jetta, allowing Annabelle to open the driver's door for him. Once they'd both settled into their seats, he turned to look at her. "Annabelle, there's something else."

Annabelle blinked at him through bleary eyes.

"I have reason to believe Carter Trent and James Drake are the men who hit and killed Johnny."

Annabelle's eyes widened and she sagged against the seat, putting a hand to the hollow of her throat. "Why? Are you sure?"

"Ivy was looking into it. I believe it's part of the reason she started

231

seeing James Drake. She suspected he knew what had happened. The FBI is involved now. Ivy was abducted and taken across state lines. If we're lucky, they'll uncover the video footage from the Dark River Inn. Regina had bugged the place. Everything is likely to be in those videos. The kidnapping plot, Ivy confronting James about the hit-and-run—"

"Her murder..." Annabelle whispered, closing her eyes.

"That I don't know. Regina covered her tracks. She may have shut the cameras off before that. She may have destroyed all the footage, but I doubt it. I think she would have kept James and Bennie plotting Ivy's abduction and the abduction itself because it pointed to them as the perpetrators."

"It's all so much. What should I do?"

"Nothing. Cass is going to connect you with a good civil lawyer. If you're up for it, you're going to take James and Carter to court for wrongful death in Johnny's case, but let the FBI do the legwork first. They'll compile their evidence. A criminal prosecution might happen if they can prove it. If they can't, you can and you should sue them in civil court, Annabelle."

"What's the point? Ivy's gone. Johnny's gone."

"You're the point. Ivy wanted a better life for you. Johnny wanted that. Get out of Black Pine. There's nothing left for you there."

"No, I guess there's not." She wiped her hands across her wet cheeks. "Will there be a trial?"

"Most likely, yeah. Though things don't look good for Regina. She confessed in the hospital, but now she's recanted and hired an attorney. She won't be pleading guilty to anything. One challenge is that James and Bennie are plausible scapegoats. Regina's attorney will try to pin this on one or both of them, most likely Bennie."

"Will he be okay?"

"Yeah, he will. I'll make sure he is. And I'll be back and forth until it's all said and done. Okay? You need anything, you call me."

CASSIDY AND SADIE DWIGGINS sat outside the trailer when Dan arrived with Annabelle. Sadie stood and wrapped her arms around Annabelle, who'd begun to cry again.

Dan walked to Cass where she stood beside her Subaru.

"What now?" Cass asked.

Dan gazed at the gnarled apple trees in front of Annabelle's trailer. As he watched, a cardinal flew onto one of the branches.

"Back to Michigan," he said, still watching the scarlet bird. "Bennie needs the help, and I'm ready for a change of scenery. My parents used to take us north. We vacationed once a year in a place called Gaylord. My cousin lives nearby. Thought I'd look into getting transferred, maybe sharing a house with Bennie, seeing if we can't work together to get him back on his feet."

"That's generous of you."

"It's partially selfish. I'm not exactly solid on my own feet."

Cass smiled. "Sometimes we need to reevaluate what it means to be on our feet."

"I'll be back. Bennie and I will both be called to testify. He's likely facing criminal prosecution of his own for grabbing Ivy off the beach. My hope is he can turn state's evidence and get a deal, but only time will tell on that. I'd love to see you when I'm in town. Maybe you could come visit us up north. We've got a lot of good fishing lakes in Michigan."

She looked at him and then leaned in to kiss him on the mouth. "I think I'd like that."

Dan watched Sadie and Annabelle walk up the porch steps to the trailer. Annabelle paused and dug something out of her purse. She dropped her pack of cigarettes into a trash can before she opened the door and disappeared inside.

DON'T MISS HELME HOUSE

Want more of the Troubled Spirits Series?

Check out Helme House.

Or dive into the completed eight-book stand-alone series:

The Northern Michigan Asylum Series.

Do you believe in ghosts?

THE STORY THAT INSPIRED DARK RIVER INN

On August twenty-sixth, 1995, a twenty-three-year-old woman was sunbathing alone on the beach of the Ohio River in Kentucky. A man on the opposite side of the river noticed the sunbather as he was gazing through a telescope. As he watched, a bearded man crept from the woods behind the woman and grabbed her by the hair, dragging her into the woods.

She was never seen again.

Authorities searched the beach for the abducted woman, and a decades-long investigation into her disappearance produced several persons of interest; however, her case remains unsolved.

Dark River Inn was inspired in part by this woman's story. That being said, *Dark River Inn* is a work of fiction. The characters, locations, and circumstances are entirely fictional.

If you'd like to know the details of the true story, you can learn more here.

ACKNOWLEDGMENTS

Many thanks to the people who made this book possible. Thank you to Team Miblart for the beautiful cover. Thank you to RJ Locksley for copy editing Dark River Inn. Many thanks to Will St. John for beta reading the original manuscript, and to Travis Poole And Emily Haynes for finding those final pesky typos that slip in. Thank you to my amazing Advanced Reader Team. Lastly, and most of all, thank you to my family and friends for always supporting and encouraging me on this journey.

ABOUT THE AUTHOR

J.R. Erickson, also known as Jacki Riegle, is an indie author who writes ghost stories. She is the author of the Troubled Spirits Series, which blends true crime with paranormal murder mysteries. Her Northern Michigan Asylum Series are stand-alone paranormal novels inspired by a real former asylum in Traverse City.

These days, Jacki passes the time in the Traverse City area with her excavator husband, her wild little boy, and her three kitties: Floki, Beast, and Mamoo.

To find out more about J.R. Erickson, visit her website at www.jrericksonauthor.com.

Printed in the USA
CPSIA information can be obtained
at www.ICGtesting.com
LVHW051042270124
769863LV00002BA/243